Royal 1

ALSO BY RUTH CARDELLO

WESTERLY BILLIONAIRE SERIES

Up for Heir

In the Heir

LONE STAR BURN

Taken, Not Spurred

Tycoon Takedown

Taken Home

Taking Charge

THE LEGACY COLLECTION

Maid for the Billionaire

For Love or Legacy

Bedding the Billionaire

Saving the Sheikh

Rise of the Billionaire

Breaching the Billionaire: Alethea's Redemption

Recipe for Love (Holiday Novella)

A Corisi Christmas (Holiday Novella)

THE ANDRADES

Come Away with Me

Home to Me

Maximum Risk

Somewhere Along the Way

Loving Gigi

THE BARRINGTONS

Always Mine

Stolen Kisses

Trade It All

A Billionaire for Lexi

Let It Burn

More Than Love

TRILLIONAIRES

Taken by a Trillionaire

Virgin for the Trillionaire

TEMPTATION SERIES

Twelve Days of Temptation

Be My Temptation

Royal Heir

RUTH CARDELLO

Montlake
Romance

Published by Montlake Romance, Seattle

www.apub.com

Amazon, the Amazon logo, and Montlake Romance are trademarks of Amazon.com, Inc., or its affiliates.

ISBN-13: 9781503901742
ISBN-10: 1503901742

Cover design by Eileen Carey

Printed in the United States of America

To my sister Judy, who left this planet too early. She is never far from my thoughts, therefore never far from me.

Don't Miss a Thing!

www.ruthcardello.com

Sign Up for Ruth's Newsletter:
https://forms.aweber.com/form/00/819443400.htm

Join Ruth's Private Fan Group:
www.facebook.com/groups/ruthiesroadies

Follow Ruth on Goodreads:
www.goodreads.com/author/show/4820876.
Ruth_Cardello

Westerly

Family Tree

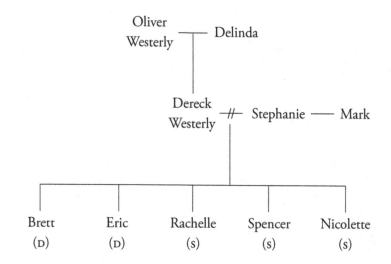

Oliver Westerly — Delinda

Dereck Westerly —‖— Stephanie — Mark

Brett (D) Eric (D) Rachelle (S) Spencer (S) Nicolette (S)

(D): stays with Dereck after the divorce

(S): stays with Stephanie after the divorce

A note to my readers

What is a water bear?

Water bear bugs (a.k.a. tardigrades) are microscopic eight-legged creatures that live in water and are said to be able to survive even an extinction-level event. They could survive not only without water for thirty years but also in the vacuum of space. They are popular enough in some circles that people sell plush-toy replicas of them.

I may have to give one to my children this holiday season, just to see their expressions when I do. Water bears—so ugly they're cute.

Chapter One

Rachelle Westerly stopped halfway down a long corridor lined with closed doors. When her brother Eric had said his London home was large enough for her to stay as long as she wanted without it bothering him, she'd thought he was being kind. No, he'd been serious. In the week since Rachelle had arrived, she'd seen him once. His house staff, large and efficient as it was, could never quite tell her his location.

Having grown up in a modest suburban home outside Boston, Rachelle didn't know what to think of the majestic seventy-plus-bedroom English estate. *Is this what I'd be used to if I had gone with Dad?* When her parents divorced, the three youngest children had remained with their mother, who had raised them on a frugal nurse's salary and taught them the importance of clipping coupons. They'd never been hungry, but they'd all worked and contributed to the family's budget because their mother considered money the root of all evil. It was— according to her mother—what had torn the family apart.

If this is hell, it has a remarkable number of antiques.

And staff.

Years of teaching first grade had honed Rachelle's ability to link faces with names. Not much crushed a child more than forgetting his or her name. Still, Eric had such a large staff that she wondered if any- one knew all of them. Some cleaned, some cooked, some tended to the gardens, while others maintained the vehicles or the buildings. There were several pool cleaners, a security team, and Reggie, the full-time electrician who had given Rachelle a tour of which parts of the estate were not currently safe.

Who has a house so large parts of it are unsafe to venture into?
Movie stars.

When Rachelle had asked Eric about those areas, he'd said renovations were the norm for any estate from the 1800s. Homes that were once built and owned by royalty were now often sold off to "commoners" because the cost of maintaining them was staggering.

"Then why own one?" Rachelle had asked.

Eric had shrugged and said, "It seemed a shame to let nature reclaim it. Besides, it's not like I can't afford it. You could as well if you asked Dad for your inheritance."

"Don't you mean our grandmother?"

Eric had shuddered. "There's not enough money in the world to make asking Delinda for anything worth it. You don't have to go through her to get to your inheritance. Just ask Dad for a loan. There's nothing he likes more than writing a check. It's what he does best."

"Is that how you pay for all this?" Rachelle had asked. Getting to know her brother was why she'd come.

"I wish. No, I pay for it with my privacy and my dignity."

The pain she'd seen in his eyes had validated what she'd sensed as she'd spoken to him at their brother Brett's wedding when she'd found Eric standing off to one side—alone. He might have always been able to afford anything he wanted, but it hadn't made him happy. It saddened Rachelle to realize that the fame Eric had found on the big screen hadn't, either.

Her family teased her for always wanting to mother-hen them, but she couldn't help it. She worried about people. Every child who had ever occupied a chair in her classroom had left with a piece of her heart. She remembered a veteran teacher once telling her she'd need to toughen up or she'd never make it as a teacher. She hadn't even tried. If caring too much was wrong, she'd never be right.

Unfortunately, that pretty much described how her life had been going lately. She was having difficulty reconciling how she'd always seen herself with how she'd behaved lately. She used to describe herself as caring, honest, confident.

Recently, if she was honest with herself, the woman in the mirror looked scared and clingy. When her brother Spencer had found out his biological father was their mother's second husband from an affair she'd had while still married to her first husband, all hell had broken loose in her family. She'd tried to contain the damage, but her efforts had only made it worse, and she'd ended up hurting the very people she loved. Although apologies had been made and forgiveness had been granted, the experience had left Rachelle shaken.

Every time her mother had stumbled, Rachelle had been there to help pick her up. After the divorce, Rachelle had cared for her youngest sister, Nicolette, and Spencer. When Mark, her mother's second husband, had gotten ill, Rachelle had helped care for him as well. She'd picked up the parenting slack as much as she could, and she'd never resented the added responsibility. She thought that's what people did when they loved their family.

Somehow it had been too much. *Like coming here?*

But how could I pretend I didn't see the yearning in Eric? He wants to find his way back to us.

Right now I'd be happy to find my way back to my room.

Or the main foyer.

The corridor dead-ended at a large double door. Rachelle tried to open it, but it was locked. She jostled it again, more out of frustration than because she thought it might suddenly open.

"Are you lost again?" Reggie asked from behind her.

Rachelle spun around. He reminded her of Lurch from *The Addams Family*, but younger. Tall. Pale. Jet-black hair. She guessed he was not much older than she was—in his early thirties, perhaps. He was American, so Rachelle felt somewhat of an affinity for him, but he was also quite odd. "I thought I saw Eric come this way."

"Unlikely. This wing isn't currently in use, as repairs are scheduled. I'll show you back to your suite."

Rachelle nodded and stepped away from the door. "Do you know where Eric is? I tried to call him, but he never answers his phone."

"He's a busy man. As am I." He turned and began walking away.

Rachelle quickened her pace to keep up. His title might be electrician, but there seemed to be more to his role. "The thing is—his premiere is tonight, and I wanted to wish him luck."

"You won't be attending?"

"I wasn't invited." Rachelle groaned at how pathetic that sounded. She hadn't meant for it to.

Reggie paused and scanned her face. "Would you like to go?"

Rachelle could have lied. Her pride would have preferred that option, but of all the staff, Reggie was the only one who seemed willing to talk to her. The rest scuttled away as if speaking with her put their jobs at risk. "I would, but if Eric wanted me there, he would have asked me to go."

"You're here without an invitation, and he seems okay with that. You should go to the premiere."

Her pride bruised a bit. Falling into step beside him, Rachelle said, "Eric invited me. He said I could stay as long as I want."

"And how long will you be staying?"

"I haven't decided." She frowned. *I don't have to explain myself. And why would an electrician care?*

Because he knows the truth. He was there when I arrived and saw Eric's initial reaction as clearly as I did. Eric didn't expect me to take him up on his offer. He hurried to assure me I was welcome, but he doesn't really want me here.

Maybe anyone else would go home, but I can't. Not yet.

6

She folded her arms across her chest. "Listen, I love my brother. Maybe I shouldn't have taken a leave of absence from my job to come here. Maybe I should have waited for him to call back before coming. I might be doing this all wrong, but I love him, and I'm not leaving until I know he's okay."

Reggie arched an eyebrow. "So attending his premiere is what would be too much?"

Low blow. "I just want to get to know him."

Reggie stared at her for an awkwardly long moment; then he smiled for the first time since she'd met him. "Family is important."

"Exactly," Rachelle said with relief. *Lurch understands.*

"Go to the premiere."

I've come this far. Maybe I should.

Oh my God, what am I going to wear?

◆　◆　◆

Crown Prince Magnus Gustavus Valentine de Bartelebon looked out the side window of a Rolls-Royce while rubbing his temple in irritation. London had been his stomping ground in his teens, but there was no longer room for foolishness in his life. His father's health was failing, and whether Magnus wanted it or not, the crown would soon be his.

His years of freedom, of personal achievement in the business world, were about to come to a crashing halt. King Tadeas had ruled Vandorra with grace and dignity, but it consumed his life. It wasn't that Magnus didn't admire his father's relationship with their people, but Magnus didn't know if he was capable of taking on that role as well. Few if any of his father's grand ideas for how to modernize a previously agricultural country would have been put into practice if Magnus hadn't fought in the trenches for them. Creating employment opportunities to support their growing population required making deals with surrounding countries. Ensuring those deals remained favorable for his people sometimes meant getting his hands dirty.

At the end of the day, it wasn't his royal lineage that gave Magnus the upper hand in negotiations, it was his reputation for being ruthless. He was neither proud nor ashamed of what he'd done for his people. His father was an eloquent public speaker who advocated peace and harmony. That kind of idealism was only possible when someone was buffered from the harsh realities of the world by someone without those morals.

If Magnus could have vomited up a brother who would wear the crown, prance before the paparazzi, and be the politically correct social media figurehead his father hoped Magnus would become, he would gladly abdicate and continue to work for change behind the scenes. What he wouldn't do, however, was allow his father's brother and his greedy, half-brained, never-worked-a-day-in-his-life son to assume any power. They would defund the universities and training programs that were his father's legacy and reallocate the money to their pockets.

Not while I'm alive.

Respect for his father, despite their differences, ran deep. When his father had asked him to visit a children's hospital in his place, Magnus had gone. On the advisement of his business partner, he'd brought clowns. According to his friend Jules, it was preferable to the idea of Magnus attempting to converse with them.

How was I supposed to know that clowns scare children? I don't have children. I don't even like them.

Once the crying started, Magnus had attempted to stem it by telling the children to stop. They'd cried louder. Magnus had raised his voice above their cries, and only then did silence return.

Magnus would have left at that point, but he didn't believe in retreating.

He'd walked into the room of the nearest child, a young boy who was watching him with enormously rounded eyes. It was then that

Magnus noticed the IV in the boy's arm and the frailness of his frame. It moved Magnus in a way he wasn't used to. He took a nearby chair and sat next to the boy. His voice was still harsh when he asked, "If you don't like clowns, what do you like?"

The boy had visibly swallowed and raised his chin. He was only about ten years old, but he was braver than many of the men Magnus knew. "Water Bear Man."

"Who?"

"You don't know Water Bear Man? WBM? He's only the greatest superhero in the world. Nothing can kill him. Nothing scares him. When I grow up, I'm going to be just like him." The boy's face tightened. "If I grow up. I need a new heart. We need to find a donor, and then the doctors say even if I do, I may neglect it."

A woman walked over and took the boy's hand in hers. "Reject it," she corrected softly. "And don't say that, Finn. Stay positive. We'll find a donor. All we have to do is believe, and it will happen."

"Mom, stop. I don't need you to lie to me." For a moment Magnus had found it difficult to breathe as Finn searched his face. "You always say what you think even if it makes people angry with you. Do you think we'll find a donor?"

Magnus looked from the pleading eyes of his mother to the solemn eyes of her son. "I don't know, but I'll do what I can to see that it happens."

"I don't believe you," Finn said.

The doctor at the door had gasped. Finn's mother wiped tears from her cheek. Finn merely held his gaze and waited. Magnus found himself admiring the young boy more.

He's negotiating for something. "What would it take for you to believe me?"

The boy shrugged and looked away. His fragile shoulders slumped.

And Magnus felt a flash of uncertainty. He hadn't come to make any of the children feel worse. His father would have had all of them smiling and hanging on his every word. There had to be something he could say that would bring the boy some comfort.

Finn looked up suddenly and said, "I want to meet Water Bear Man. Bring him instead of a clown, and I'll believe you."

Magnus had nodded once and stood. "Done."

That, of course, had been before he discovered that the actor who played the role didn't take phone calls, not even from royalty. Had he known then that speaking to a narcissistic Hollywood pretty boy would require attending his premiere, he might have negotiated for something less tedious.

Chapter Two

Rachelle slid out of a limo and into a blitz of camera flashes. She was so focused on keeping her knees together and the top of her gown in place that she forgot to smile. Temporarily blinded from one particularly bright flash, she stumbled and grabbed the arm of the driver to steady herself.

"Is anyone else getting out?" one of the photographers asked.

"Doesn't look like it," someone else answered.

The flashes stopped.

"Who is she?"

"Westerly's sister? I forget her name. Trust me, she's nobody."

Ouch.

Rachelle thanked the driver and started down the red carpet with her head held high. They were right. She didn't belong on the red carpet, but her request to go in early had been denied. Had she spoken with Eric before attending, he might have resolved the issue with ease. But even if she had been able to find him, what would she have said? "I know you didn't invite me, but I weaseled a way in through your publicist. I don't mean to go all high maintenance on you, but could you also make sure I arrive in the fashion I'm used to—beneath the cloak of invisibility?"

What matters is that when he does realize I was here, he understands it was because I'm proud of him.

Becoming famous as a cape-and-tights-wearing hero who had gained his superstrength and powers by being bitten by thousands of radioactive water bears (a.k.a. hardy microscopic tardigrades) might not have been Eric's dream, but his fans adored him. At least one child in every first-grade class she'd ever taught had found out Rachelle was related to Eric Westerly, Water Bear Man. She'd even made the mistake once of saying she was. The children had wanted to write to him, FaceTime with him, connect with him in some way that one would expect to be able to when their teacher was his sister.

The dynamics of her family weren't something she could explain to a room full of six-year-olds, or even their parents when they'd become equally excited. Eventually Rachelle had added a qualifying word out of necessity. Whenever she'd been asked about Eric, she'd said he was her estranged brother, and for those who required more clarification, she'd added, "We don't talk."

I'm here to change that.

Brett says family is what we make it. Nicolette believes our family defines us. Mom says love doesn't just happen—it takes work. And as Grandmother likes to say, "We are what we do. If you want something but do nothing to attain it, you are no better than someone who isn't intelligent enough to know what they want."

I can't believe I'm taking advice from any of them.

Her oldest brother, Brett, hadn't been part of her life until he'd gotten engaged to her best friend. Her mother was still recovering from being exposed as a liar. Rachelle had defended her out of love, but she still struggled with how her mother could have cheated on their father, let everyone assume the divorce had been his fault, then married Mark, the man she'd had an affair with—without ever telling anyone he was Spencer's biological father.

Nicolette was still struggling with not knowing for sure who her father was. She'd recently decided to table the conversation and spend time away from the family instead.

And Delinda? It wasn't so much a choice to take her advice as much as Rachelle being unable to not hear her voice in her head. Rachelle only visited her grandmother on days she was feeling unusually confident. Delinda was gifted in knowing exactly what to say to demolish a person's self-esteem. Unlike Nicolette, who didn't hide her disdain for the matriarch of their family, Rachelle usually defended Delinda. She was, after all, their only living grandparent.

Spencer, who used to avoid their grandmother, too, now said she had a nicer side. Rachelle had yet to see it, and that *he* did was confusing. He was now the one jumping to Delinda's defense. The very fabric of her family was changing, and that was another reason Rachelle had needed to leave.

Yes, she'd come to London for Eric, but also for herself. Rachelle had lost her footing. She was no longer sure where she fit into her family.

Luckily, I have this experience to put it all back into perspective. Comparatively, I was doing well back home. This is how it actually feels to not belong.

She walked by more photographers, who didn't raise their cameras as she passed. Putting on a brave face, she flashed a smile anyway. Three hundred feet had never felt so far.

There was a sudden change in the energy in the crowd. A palpable excitement swept over them. They surged forward as security came down the aisle, ensuring they stayed behind the ropes.

Unable to resist, Rachelle stopped and turned. The crowd behind the photographers came to life, screaming with excitement. "Prince Magnus!" started as a call out of recognition and then was repeated by enough to sound like a chant.

A tall, muscular man in a light-gray suit stepped out of a Rolls-Royce, his dark-brown hair conservative and short. The way he filled out his tuxedo instantly made Rachelle wonder what he'd look like without it, and she shook her head. Her reaction to him surprised her, since he definitely wasn't her taste. She preferred someone less dynamic, someone softer. His features were so ruggedly perfect that she would have thought they were airbrushed if she'd seen him in a photo rather than in person.

He started down the red carpet, disregarding the photographers as if they were of no more importance than anything on the bottom of his shoes.

A woman in the crowd yelled out, "I love you, Prince Magnus."

He didn't acknowledge her. Was he that accustomed to public adoration?

Rachelle realized she was holding her breath. She didn't want to find that level of arrogance attractive, but it was hot. What kind of woman would turn such a man's head?

One of the photographers yelled out, "How sick is the king? Do you think it will be days? Weeks?"

Another called out, "Is it true you're about to ask Princess Isabella to marry you? What are you more excited about? Becoming king or tapping that?"

The prince froze and turned on his heel toward the photographer who'd asked the last question. A hush fell over the crowd. The prince's lips twisted. It was the kind of smile a predator indulges in just before it goes in for a kill. He took a step toward the photographer who had raised his camera to take advantage of the opportunity.

"Ask me that question one more time," the prince commanded in a low tone.

The photographer continued to snap photos.

The prince stepped closer. "Look me in the eye and ask me. But before you do, consider that right now you are no one to me. Do you

14

want me to know you? Do you want me to remember you when I leave here? Be sure you do before you utter another word."

The photographer lowered his camera.

"He's threatening you," the man beside the silent photographer said. "Are you going to let him get away with that?"

"I meant no disrespect," the photographer said.

"What a pussy," the other man jeered.

The prince's attention turned to the second man, and the smile returned. "Do you have something you'd like to say to me?"

That man squared his shoulders and looked like he might spit on the prince. "You think you're above us because you have a title? You're lucky we want to photograph you at all. Without us, no one would care about you. The whole idea of a ruling class is outdated and pathetic. I can say whatever I want. What are you going to do, throw a jewel at me?"

The prince's smile widened, revealing perfectly white teeth. "You think he's afraid of me because of my title? That's so cute. I'll remember that. And you. Thank you for giving me something to do after the premiere."

"What does that even mean? Can you believe him?" the man snarked, looking around for support. He found none. The people on either side of him had retreated.

With a nod, the prince turned away from him and started down the red carpet again. One could have heard a pin drop. Rachelle understood what held them enthralled—she had never seen someone with such presence. He felt *dangerous*.

Legally, Rachelle didn't think there was much a prince could do while outside his country. The paparazzi were notorious for antagonizing to create a story. Royalty, even more than regular people, couldn't go around threatening anyone in public without facing consequences for it—could they?

Not a single camera raised as he walked by, but for an entirely different reason than why they hadn't for Rachelle.

Rachelle couldn't tear her eyes from him as he approached. Her stomach quivered with a sexual anticipation that was new to her. She'd never been one to idolize celebrities or plaster her walls with images of half-clothed men, but she could now understand why some did. Here was a man worthy of a fantasy or two. Or three.

When his attention settled on her, her jaw went slack. His eyes were not light brown. Not green. They were somewhere between with flecks of yellow—gold. Absolutely stunning. Closer and closer until Rachelle forgot where she was. There was only him and how her body hummed beneath his slow appraisal.

"Waiting for me?" he asked in a low growl.

Only my whole life. She opened her mouth, then snapped it shut and swallowed what would have been a humiliating admission. He towered above her, and she chastised herself for instantly imagining how easily he could lift her if he wanted to. She'd had sex with other men, but none of them had sent her genitals into code-red lust.

She remembered being slightly disgusted when her best friend had used their teenage color-code categories of attraction to explain how she felt about Brett. No one wanted to imagine anyone feeling that way about their brother. Plus, Rachelle had considered it an exaggeration. A code red was romance-novel crap. She'd maintained that that type of mindless attraction didn't happen in reality.

I was wrong.

Holy shit.

He offered her his arm. "A gentleman never refuses a beautiful escort."

Beautiful? Me? Feeling as if she'd stepped into a dream, Rachelle laid her hand on his arm. It flexed beneath her touch, and she swayed against him.

Wow. Just wow.

◆ ◆ ◆

As Prince Magnus escorted the beautiful but apparently mute woman down the rest of the red carpet, he found himself unusually tempted to accept Eric Westerly's token of apology. This woman might not speak English, but he'd find a way to explain his refusal once they were inside. She wasn't the first woman to be offered up to appease him, and she likely wouldn't be the last. It was a practice Magnus found repulsive. He would say as much to Westerly after the idiot visited Finn in the hospital.

His mother had been the heart of his family. Although she'd been gone for more than a decade, she'd ingrained in Magnus a deep respect for women. They were the backbones of civilized society. Which was why men viciously tried to control them or reduce them to nothing more than a gift to another man. Weak men were threatened by the power of change a good woman could wield.

His father's legacy had begun as a tribute to his wife while she was alive, yet had sadly only come together after her death. The high number of women graduating from his country's universities was evidence that his mother continued to make a difference. Women were remarkable when given a chance to be.

He glanced at the woman on his arm. She hadn't come from nowhere. Somewhere she had a mother and a father. Did they worry about her? With a nudge in the right direction, would she return to them? He'd give her name to Jules. He handled the philanthropic side of their business. He'd have connections to agencies that could offer this woman options other than the life she'd somehow fallen into.

For now, he would handle the situation with discretion. Without knowing Westerly's arrangement with her, he had no way of assessing if refusing her services would endanger her.

As soon as they were inside the building, he led her off to one side of the room. "Do you speak English?" he asked.

"Yes," she answered huskily.

"If you wish, you may be my escort for the premiere. I will make it appear that you please me. No one need know what I am about to say to you."

Her eyebrows shot up, but she remained silent.

Magnus took out a business card and wrote his friend's cell phone number on it. He handed it to her. She accepted it as if she'd never seen a business card before. It was hard not to feel sorry for her. "Call that number. Jules Mansfield is a good man. He'll help you leave here if you wish to. He can set you up with a job and whatever else you need to start again. The choice is yours, but you have a choice if you want one."

"I don't understand."

Westerly had good taste when it came to women. Despite the truth of her situation, this woman had an air of innocence that was appealing. Looking into her eyes, Magnus felt a reluctant attraction to her. He reminded himself he was a healthy male responding as any man in his prime would. However, what he felt in that moment didn't matter any more than it mattered in any other part of his life.

One of the photographers had asked if he intended to marry Princess Isabella. Her parents were pushing for the union. So far he hadn't refused that offer, although it was not his first choice. Marrying her would secure relations with her bordering country, but his mother had loved his father, and Magnus was reluctant to settle for less than a woman who adored him. Princess Isabella was quite in love with herself. Thankfully that was not his immediate concern. The confused woman before him was. He chose his words with care, attempting to make his point without insulting her.

"No matter what brought you here, you are not trapped in this lifestyle. Call the number on the card, and you will receive safe passage and assistance."

"I'm sorry? Passage?" Her delicious little mouth rounded, challenging his moral stance.

Could such sweetness be an act, or had Westerly sent him a novice? His heart pounded in his chest, and his cock twitched to attention. For her sake, he needed to put distance between them. "I cannot accept your services this evening. Call the number on the card."

"My services?" Her mouth snapped shut, her chin rose, and her eyes narrowed. "You don't know me. Why would you think I would be offering you anything?"

Fuck, she's hot.

If I'd met her any other way, she'd be mine tonight.

He traced the length of her beautiful neck with the back of his hand. "Don't let your pride stop you from making that call. Trust me, I'm tempted. You're beautiful, but you deserve better than this."

"Don't touch me." She whipped herself back from his touch, and her hands settled on her hips, an act that pushed her breasts forward and nearly out of the slip of a gown she wore. "I don't know who you think I am, but what you're implying is disgusting."

He could have accepted her claim and left her, but he didn't. He had offered such help to women in the past. Some had accepted. Some had not. He'd always been able to walk away with a clear conscience. This was different.

He didn't like the idea that leaving her there might mean she'd end the night with another man. Still, this was a novel attraction better not pandered to. He had no problem filling his nights with less complicated women—women who, like him, sought sex without emotional entanglements. This had the potential of being messy and full of drama.

Yet he couldn't look away. Each angry breath she inhaled outlined her nipples against the thin material of her gown. He imagined picking her up, tossing her over his shoulder, and taking her somewhere where he could spend the night exploring every inch of her sweet body. "Disgusting isn't how I'd describe it—simply ill advised. Take comfort in the knowledge that I would love nothing more than to spend the night with you, but I wouldn't feel right about it."

"What you shouldn't feel right about is talking to anyone the way you do." Her slap took him completely by surprise. His head jerked back, and he instinctively grabbed her by the arm, hauling her closer.

"I'm trying to help you." Mind and body warred—offering his protection even as his cock throbbed with need for her.

"I don't need help." She attempted to pull her arm free from him, but after failing, raised her other hand as if she might slap him again. He caught that hand easily. He gentled his hold on her and told himself that the right thing to do was to take her out of there and ensure she found her way to a better place.

"What's going on?" a male voice asked from beside them.

Still holding on to the woman's arm, Magnus turned and found himself face-to-face with the very man he'd come to meet. Eric Westerly was his height, with an impressive build, but Magnus dismissed him as soft. Everything he'd read about Westerly spoke of a privileged upbringing before fame on the big screen. Magnus had little respect for a man who'd never had to fight for anything. He had even less respect for him now that he knew he was the type to *gift* a woman to someone. "Your friend and I are merely having a conversation."

"Take your hand off her," Westerly said between clenched teeth.

A surge of possessiveness swept through Magnus again. Was she from Westerly's private stock? Had he had her? If so, it was for the last time. There was no way Magnus would hand her back to him. "Too late to change your mind, I've already accepted your offer."

"My offer?" Westerly asked, his expression hardening. "Get your hand off my sister."

Magnus's head whipped around. "You're his sister?" His hold on her went slack, and she pulled herself free then.

"Rachelle Westerly." She smoothed her hands down the sides of her dress as if trying to wipe his touch off. "I would have told you my name, but you were too busy trying to save me from a life of prostitution."

Magnus smiled as he realized what this meant. She was not some unfortunate woman being served up against her will. He didn't have to deny how she made him feel. Spending a few days in London suddenly held more appeal.

"I think you should leave," Westerly said firmly. "Now."

The reason for his visit came back, overshadowing his excitement. There would be time later to enjoy Rachelle, but first he had a promise to fulfill. "Not before we talk. My name is Prince Magnus—"

"I know who you are." Westerly raised a hand and started speaking over him. "I wasn't interested in speaking with you when you called. Now that you've offended my family, I have even less of a desire to. I'm sure my publicist has informed you I don't do appearances. So, the door is that way. Thank you for coming."

Magnus stood his ground as his temper threatened to flare. Finn's doctors had told Magnus that the boy was telling everyone he met that his prince was so powerful that he was going to bring him a superhero.

However, Magnus admitted to himself that by allowing his dick to rob his brain of coherent thought, he had made the situation more complicated.

A man showed up beside Westerly and said something into his ear. Westerly nodded and said, "I have to go. Stay away from my sister." He left without making sure that would happen.

Westerly had been smart enough to not have security attempt to remove Magnus. Talking the cocky actor into visiting his country would not be easy, but few negotiations were. Westerly wanted something, and when Magnus figured it out, he'd have the upper hand.

His attention returned to the woman beside him. Rather than still be angry, she looked hurt. He didn't like the idea he might have put that expression on her face. "Are you okay?"

She clasped her hands in front of her and blinked a few times quickly. "I didn't have a chance to tell him why I'm here."

It was a curious comment. "I'm sure he knows."

She spun on him. "You're sure about a lot of things that are wrong. I'm not a prostitute, and my brother doesn't know how I feel, but he needs to. At least I thought he did. I hoped I could make things better by coming here. Now I'm not so sure." She wiped a tear from the corner of her eye.

He put a hand on her lower back and began to guide her across the room. "Come, I see a chocolate fountain in the corner. It'll make you feel better."

She started huffing again. "That's so sexist I should slap you again. Your arrogance needs a trim." She frowned, and in a calmer voice said, "No, that's wrong. Violence is never the answer. I shouldn't have slapped you."

"I accept your apology."

She stopped in her tracks and turned toward him. "Well?"

She really was a stunning woman. "Well, what?"

"This is where *you* apologize."

He chuckled. Outside of his father, no one spoke to him in that authoritative tone. She was fire and honey. He raised her hand to his mouth and kissed it. "I sincerely apologize for offering to rescue you from a life of illicit hookups. I must admit, however, to never having been more relieved to have been mistaken. Now that I know you could come to the decision of your own free will, I would love to spend the night bringing you pleasure."

She tensed beneath his hand, but he saw passion in her eyes. "You heard what my brother said. He told you to stay away from me."

Magnus shrugged. "Words. He doesn't care. If he did, he wouldn't have left you standing with me."

She gasped and shoved him away. The hurt in her eyes took him by surprise. "Don't say that. Don't you dare say my brother doesn't care about me. In fact, don't say anything else. Just stay the hell away from me."

She strode off, and he let her. He hadn't meant to imply her brother didn't care about her, merely that he didn't care about them being together.

His instincts had been correct about one thing—any involvement with her would be messy and emotionally charged. He'd be better off focusing on his reason for attending the premiere.

He wasn't leaving London until Westerly agreed to visit Finn in the hospital. All things considered, he shouldn't leave without Westerly beside him on the plane. He had told Finn he'd meet Water Bear Man, and that was exactly what was going to happen.

Chapter Three

Rachelle did what any self-respecting, mature woman would do after being mistaken for a prostitute and slugging a prince. She found the nearest exit that didn't lead to where the paparazzi were and stepped out into the night, propping the door open behind her. If she were a smoker, she would have been puffing away. If she were a drinker, she would have grabbed a bottle of something and been well on her way to the bottom of it. *I don't even know any really good swears.*

She took out her phone and called Alisha, her best friend back home. Thankfully, despite Rachelle's initial negative response to Alisha falling in love with Brett right after Spencer found out the truth about his paternity, they'd remained friends. Good friends didn't require perfection. Best friends shook sense into you when you needed it.

I need it now.

Alisha answered in a whisper. "Hey, Rach. I just put Linda down for a nap. Let me go downstairs so she can't hear me."

"Okay."

With a groan of satisfaction, Alisha said, "Ah. Peace. It may have been a mistake to sit down on the couch, because I didn't get any sleep last night. So if I start snoring, yell at me."

Simply hearing Alisha's voice had Rachelle feeling a little better. "If you want to take a nap, we can talk later."

"No. No. I need adult conversation. I'm just warning you that I'm flying with one engine today. So, how is Eric?"

If nearly anyone else had asked, Rachelle would have softened the truth, but that was another wonderful thing about having a best friend who was like a sister—Rachelle had never felt she needed to hide anything from Alisha. "I don't know if I should have come here. What was I thinking?"

"You were thinking you wanted to get to know your brother. Flying over to stay with him was a bold move, but sometimes life requires leaps of faith. Are you still staying with him?"

"Oh, I'm in his house, but it's been a week, and I've spoken to his staff more than I've spoken to him." Deep breath. "I'm actually at his premiere tonight."

"That's fantastic."

"Yes and no. He didn't invite me, but I came anyway. Then I assaulted someone, and now I'm hiding in the side alley."

"This doesn't sound like you."

"I know. I met a code red, and then I may have publicly slapped him across the face."

"May have?"

"Fine. I slapped him, but he thought I was a prostitute or something. I knew this dress was a little tight, but really? Really? A prostitute?"

Alisha laughed. "Okay. Rewind. I need to hear this story from the beginning."

Rachelle laid it all out for Alisha, not prettying up any part of it. She wasn't looking for approval from Alisha as much as the kind of guidance a good friend can give you when she has all the facts. Well, all the facts that mattered. She left off the part where she'd stood there on the red carpet, drooling over a prince.

"So, here I am. Do I go back in? Do I go home? I used to trust my instincts and follow my heart. Mark always said if you made a decision based on love, it couldn't be wrong. I don't know if I'm here for the right reasons. Am I really here for Eric, or is this about me?" She closed her eyes and leaned back against the wall. "When I think about how I treated you last year, I feel guilty calling about this shit."

"Stop, Rachelle. We talked that through. Of course you wanted to protect your mother. Of course you were concerned about Spencer. I look back at that time and see a hundred ways I could have handled the situation better. We can't go back and change what we did, but we made it through. And we're all still here. You can love someone and still need something for yourself. That doesn't mean your intentions aren't good. Brett said if anyone can reach Eric, it's you. I agree. You love with all your heart. You fight for people, and sometimes you make mistakes, but we all do. Don't change. I love you just the way you are."

Rachelle blinked back tears. She didn't want to add looking like a raccoon to how the evening was going. "Thank you. Linda is lucky to have a mom like you. When did you get so wise?"

"Wise? I don't know about that, but I do know you. I know your heart. I've also learned a few things about love lately. It requires trust—and faith. You know why you're in London. Even if Eric isn't responding to you yet, have faith that he will. I've seen you reach students no one else could because you don't give up. So, what do I think? I think you're where you're supposed to be."

Opening her eyes, Rachelle looked around at the trash cans. "Technically, I'm still in an alley."

"Okay, so physically, you're not where you should be—but you know what I mean."

"I do. Thank you, Alisha. You don't know how much I needed this."

"Oh, we're not done. I want to hear every last detail about this code-red guy. I mean everything. You leave something out and I'll fly over there to kick your ass. Got it?"

Rachelle chuckled. "Got it. I'd also like to start by apologizing for doubting that code reds exist. I thought you were exaggerating how you felt about Brett." She described seeing Prince Magnus for the first time and then where their conversation had led.

"It's like I said—when it's the right one, you know. Nothing else compares to it."

"I wouldn't say he's the right one. He is so wrong, so full of himself, you couldn't imagine a person less right for me. I have no plans to talk to him again, but he's gorgeous and a prince, so I suppose imagining us starring in a porn together is natural."

Alisha burst out laughing. "I can see the title now: *The Prince in Me*."

Only Alisha could take Rachelle from near tears to laughing until her sides hurt in the span of a few minutes. "That is so tacky I love it. How about *Royally Screwed*?"

"Or better than that: *The Prince's Virgin Bride*. You could pretend."

"Yes. That's me. A twenty-nine-year-old virgin."

◆ ◆ ◆

There were some words a man could hear no matter how loud the competing noise was, and *virgin* was one of them.

Prince Magnus had been in a foul mood. He'd spoken at length with Westerly's producer and learned that neither promise of money nor threats had ever resulted in convincing Westerly to make a public appearance outside of a premiere. Westerly didn't even attend award ceremonies. He didn't seem to have a goal he was reaching for or an enemy he was fending off. So far, Prince Magnus had learned nothing that would be of use when it came to convincing the actor to visit Vandorra.

When the lights had flickered, announcing it was time for everyone to head into the theater for the viewing of Westerly's latest film, Prince Magnus had scanned the room for the woman he'd told himself he'd be better off avoiding. He'd felt an unsettling amount of disappointment at her absence, so he'd headed in the last direction he'd seen her.

He'd noticed an exit door propped open with a woman's high-heeled shoe. He didn't know any women who would hide out in an alley during a movie premiere, but she was American, and it was often difficult to predict what any of them would do.

Before he even reached the door, he recognized her voice. He listened for a moment to ensure that she was not in distress and then stayed because he had never heard himself described in such detail or with such candor.

His chest puffed with male pride at the knowledge that she found him physically pleasing, until he winced at her description of his personality. She deepened her voice in a mockery of their earlier conversation that was not flattering in the least.

The idea of the two of them starring in a private home video—which he would allow her to call porn if it pleased her—had him sporting a royal erection.

It was that last comment about being a twenty-nine-year-old virgin that confused him. She might have been joking. What he was conflicted about was what he'd prefer the truth to be. On one hand, the idea of being the first man to be with her was captivating. On the other, sex was a whole lot less complicated with an experienced woman who didn't confuse intimacy with emotion.

He was lost in that lusty quagmire when the door opened, and she hopped through it while putting her shoe back on, essentially tumbling into his arms. He helped her back to her feet, still holding her against him, not at all embarrassed by how prominently his excitement pressed against her. After all, she found him wet-panties attractive. Had they not been in public, he would have run a hand up her thigh to her sex to confirm the accuracy of her claim.

"Sorry," she said quickly, referring to how she'd crashed into him.

"My pleasure," he said with a wicked smile.

She stayed there, resting against his throbbing cock for long enough to drive him nearly mad. Her chest rose and fell against his, another excruciatingly erotic tease. He groaned. This wasn't the place for what he wanted, and no matter how good this felt, he had no intention of leaving without speaking to her brother.

She glanced back at the door, then up to him again. "You—you didn't . . . How long have you been standing here?"

"Not long. The movie is about to start, and since neither of us appears to have a date, I hoped you would sit with me." Prince Magnus could have said the truth, but a gentleman never embarrassed a lady. Plus, he now had the upper hand in a game he'd ensure they both enjoyed.

As far as her potential virginity? Since either possibility was acceptable, the fun would be in discovering the truth.

"Sit with you?" The breathless way she asked it rocketed through him.

Eavesdropping might not be a practice he normally condoned, but that day it had paid off in spades. He loved knowing where her naughty little mind took her when she looked at him.

It made the fact that his went the same places that much more exciting.

Royally screwed? *You definitely will be. Later.*

First I must convince your brother that he's not too big of a douche to visit a children's hospital. Then we'll fuck.

Confident that the evening would work out the way he planned, Prince Magnus stepped back and offered Rachelle his arm. *It's time to show her my charming side.* "Yes. We started off on the wrong foot, but perhaps we could start over. My name is Magnus Gustavus Valentine de Bartelebon, crown prince of Vandorra. You may call me Magnus."

She searched his face before answering. "You know my name. Rachelle. I'm a first-grade teacher. Nothing fancy. I'm sorry I snapped at you earlier. The reason I was upset had nothing to do with you. This week has been an emotional roller coaster. I didn't mean to take it out on you." She smiled, and his heart did a funny little flip. "If I actually were a prostitute, what you said to me could have changed my life. Thank you."

"You are most welcome. Shall we?"

She nodded and tucked her arm through his. He stole a sideways glance at her. A teacher? Westerly's sister had a job? The dress she wore looked inexpensive. Her shoes were scuffed from wear. All implied she was on a limited budget. Fascinating.

Just as she'd said about him earlier, Prince Magnus could not imagine a woman who would be more wrong for him, but even the purely innocent way they were touching was enough to keep him interested.

But there was more.

Why was she there? Why didn't she think her brother cared about her? Considering Westerly's level of fame, why was she acting as if this was her first premiere?

He wasn't accustomed to feeling this level of curiosity about someone. Who had she called in the alley to spill her thoughts and desires to? A beautiful puzzle. It was a struggle to join the crowd heading into the theater rather than haul her off somewhere private.

From the other side of the room, surrounded by his entourage, Westerly watched them enter the theater. He didn't look happy.

Good. Anger was easier to redirect than indifference.

An usher led them to seats in an overflow section. He turned and saw that Westerly had entered the theater himself, still watching them from near the doorway. Although the seating was insulting, Magnus cared more about what it said about Westerly than appearances.

What a prick.

This is how you treat your sister?

Finn, I said I would bring you Water Bear Man. Does he have to be alive?

Chapter Four

Prior to that evening, Rachelle would have described her love life as perfectly average. Not bad. Not anything to brag about.

Yet here I am sitting next to a prince.

Right next to him.

A drop-dead-gorgeous hunk of a prince.

If I shifted my arm just a little, we'd be touching. But I don't want to give him the wrong impression. Sitting with him at the premiere is probably no big deal, but that's as far as this can go. I'm here for Eric, not some X-rated royal romp.

Hey, I need to remember that one to tell Alisha. She'd get a kick out of it.

Although she felt a little guilty about not watching the movie, her mind was racing with questions about the man next to her. One was persistent enough that she whispered, "Magnus?"

He bent his face toward hers. "Yes?"

For just a second, she forgot what she'd wanted to say and fantasized about how he might kiss. Would his touch be tender? Or forceful? He wouldn't be a sloppy kisser. No, a man like him would have polished his technique.

Or, even in bed, would he consider himself so important that he wouldn't bother to take the needs of his partner into consideration?

The second man she'd slept with had been like that. Nothing more disappointing than a man who thought his orgasm was the only one that mattered.

Which kind of lover was Magnus?

He bent closer. "You were about to ask me a question."

"I was," she answered automatically, unable to tear her eyes from him long enough to collect her thoughts.

He smiled. "Ask me anything."

I can't. I can't ask you what I'm thinking. But—oh yes. "What did you want to speak to Eric about? It sounded important."

His smile faded somewhat. "It is. Very important, but it's not something you need to concern yourself with. I'll make it happen."

There was a determination in his voice that wasn't a surprise, but then there was something else. Whatever he wanted to ask Eric about mattered to him on a personal level. "Is that a nice way of saying I should mind my own business?"

He brought a hand to her face and gently ran his thumb over her bottom lip. "I'm not that nice."

She shivered, because he was serious. "And you're proud of that?"

He lowered his hand. "No, but I am the man I have to be. I was born with certain responsibilities that must supersede pride or regret. Both are luxuries I cannot afford."

His words reminded her of something Eric had said about paying for his fame with his privacy and dignity. Perhaps her mother had been right about some things. Wealth and power didn't necessarily make people happier. "I should warn you that, although Eric doesn't talk about his family in public, he is far from alone. If whatever you're looking for from him isn't to his benefit, you would be bringing the wrath of some very powerful people to your door."

"Is that a threat?" he asked in a low growl.

Even though she told it not to, her body warmed and tingled at the hint of danger in his tone. *Why? I don't even like scary movies. I'm all about the happily ever after, feel-good stories. This is not good.* "No, but I love my brother, and I thought you should be aware I would never let anyone hurt him."

A smile returned to the prince's face. "You'll be relieved to hear that what I want from your brother would not be detrimental to him. In fact, it would be good for him."

On impulse, Rachelle touched his arm. "Tell me. I might even be able to help."

Magnus looked away. For a long time he seemed lost in the action on the screen. Without turning back to face her, he said, "There's a little boy in a hospital in Pavailler, Vandorra's capital city. His name is Finn, and he's waiting for a heart transplant. He idolizes Water Bear Man. I promised him your brother would visit him at the children's hospital. I'm not leaving London without your brother."

Rachelle's hand tightened on his arm. *I swear to God, if he's lying, I will castrate him, because that is the most beautiful thing I've ever heard.* "Have you spoken to his publicist?"

"Yes. He said your brother doesn't do public appearances."

"Does Eric know the circumstances?"

"I doubt it. So far he has refused my attempts to speak with him." *I know that feeling.*

"So, that's why you're here? To ask him in person?"

"Yes."

Don't ask. Don't ask. You don't want to know. "Is that also why you're sitting with me?"

He met her gaze again. "I sought you out because I want you—in my bed tonight, if you agree. And every night after that until whatever this is between us burns itself out."

That's a little offensive.

He continued, "But that doesn't mean I won't use how your brother feels about us to force his hand."

And dark. "You're admitting that you'd use me to get Eric to do something."

"I don't need to lie or manipulate to get into a woman's bed. I want you. I want to taste every inch of you. I want to hear you calling out my name, begging me not to stop and then crying out in ecstasy when I don't. I can separate that from my reason for being here. You'll end up in my bed soon enough. *Yes* is already in your eyes. But I promised a little boy that your brother would visit him, and I'll do whatever it takes to make that happen."

Feeling like a swimmer who'd just been knocked off her feet by a crashing wave, Rachelle sputtered, "There is no *yes* in my eyes. And there's no room in my bed for you and that gigantic ego of yours."

A corner of his mouth twitched as if her comment amused him. "You can come home with me tonight or make me wait. I'll enjoy it either way. There's something to be said for postponing pleasure. I don't mind if you've been with other men, but I'd also enjoy if you're actually a twenty-nine-year-old virgin. So take your time, but know that you will be mine."

Rachelle turned back to face the screen. *Oh my God. He heard me talking to Alisha.*

I should be outraged.

Or scared.

Or anything but imagining how tonight would end if I said yes. See, I just pictured him naked again. That's not good.

She shivered from a hunger unlike anything she'd felt before. *Code-red men are dangerous.*

Deliciously dangerous.

But still a bad idea.

◆ ◆ ◆

If the gasps and sputtering sounds the woman next to him made were any indication, Magnus had shocked her. Good. He didn't like his women too jaded.

Another man might have withheld the truth about why he was there. Only the weak hid behind lies. What Rachelle thought of his reason for being there or what her brother felt about doing appearances would not change the outcome. *She will be mine.* Success in life didn't come from asking oneself if something was possible, but rather determining how far a person was willing to go to make it happen.

Unfortunately for Westerly, Magnus had royal immunity in most countries and a reputation for not being afraid to test the boundaries of it. Magnus would give Westerly one more chance to agree before he coerced him. Every man should be allowed an opportunity to do things the easy way.

After that, Magnus would change Westerly's mind in a less pleasant way. He'd already isolated two of Westerly's weak points—Rachelle, and an obsession with privacy. People didn't hide unless they had something they didn't want the public to see. Magnus would discover what it was, and he'd use the connection to the woman next to him as leverage to get that information if he needed to. He'd told her as much, and she was free to walk away.

She wouldn't, though. Even before he'd heard her describe him to her friend, he'd known she wanted him. Part of her beauty was how expressive her eyes were. Everything she felt was right there for the world to see—innocently unprotected.

If he were in London to kill her brother, he might have felt some remorse about involving her. However, shaking the shit out of Westerly's life until he agreed to meet with a sick child might actually be considered one of the nicest things Magnus had ever done. In the end, Rachelle would likely thank him. It was obvious she cared more for her brother than he cared for her. When Magnus finally did go head-to-head with Westerly, he'd address that issue as well. Family and duty defined a man. Prancing around in a cape and pretending to have the powers of a microscopic bug was pathetic, even if it was financially lucrative. That man needed to be woken up to what mattered in life.

He glanced at Rachelle and was taken once again by her soft beauty. "I intend to speak to your brother once more before I leave tonight. It's your choice whether you are at my side as I do so."

She expelled a harsh breath. "Of course it's my choice. Do you know how impossibly full of yourself you sound?"

He smiled. He liked her spirit. "Do you know what I love about Americans?"

She shook her head and rolled her eyes.

"Your arrogance."

"I'm arro—*I'm* arrogant? Really?"

Her outrage was so adorable he almost kissed her, but they were still very much in the public eye. "You barely know who I am or my thoughts on retaliation, and yet you've already swung at me out of anger."

"Are you saying you're planning to hit me back?"

He laughed at the horror in her eyes. "I don't hit women."

She looked suddenly irritated with him. "I wouldn't be surprised to hear you did."

He leaned over and tucked her long hair behind her ear, then whispered, "I'd rather have them beg me than fear me."

Even in the darkness of the movie theater, he could see the blush darken her cheeks. "I'm sure that line works with some women, but I'm not impressed."

"There it is—the arrogance that makes me wish we were alone right now. You are deliciously irreverent. I will enjoy teaching you how to speak more respectfully."

"Respect isn't something you teach—it's something you earn."

He leaned closer and whispered, "Then I will earn it one mind-blowing orgasm at a time. Just as I will allow you to do with me."

She licked her bottom lip before saying, "Listen, I don't care what you heard me say to my friend. I'm not interested. Call it arrogant or simply call it intelligent, but I'm not going to have sex with you."

"Then why are you still beside me?" he growled in challenge.

She turned to look him in the eye. "Because I don't trust you. I will be there tonight when you talk to Eric, but I won't be on your side. I'll be on his. If you were honest about—"

"I don't lie—"

"I don't know that. I don't know *you*. But if there really is a little boy named Finn who is hoping to meet Eric . . ."

"There is."

"I'll help you explain the situation to Eric." She gave Magnus a long look. "He'll say yes once he hears the whole story. You don't have to threaten me or pretend you're interested to get me to help you. Eric would have already agreed if it had been presented to him differently."

"I have no doubt about that," Magus said, dismissing her brother before addressing something else she said. "I would normally wait, but for the sake of clarification—" He cupped her chin and guided her forward, claiming her mouth with his.

He'd intended the kiss to be brief and reassuring, but her lips parted for his in an invitation he couldn't refuse. The heat that shot through him nearly made him forget where they were. The taste of her, the feel of her tongue tentatively dancing with his, was driving him wild. He wanted more. Needed more.

He broke off the kiss while he still had the fortitude to keep his hands from sliding beneath the thin material of her dress and exploring those pert breasts of hers, those tight little buds that had been teasing him all night. When he raised his head, her ragged breath matched his. "There is nothing fake about that."

She sat back and turned her face toward the screen again. He could practically see the wheels spinning in her head.

"If you want me to help you, don't kiss me again."

"I don't require your help," he said, more because he wanted to get a rise out of her than because it was true.

She gasped again and glared at him. "You are impossible. Sleep with you? I don't even like you."

"Liar. I'm the man you wish had been your first and every fuck since."

Her chest puffed so much her breasts practically burst out of her dress. He'd have to remember that dress. She would wear it for him again. Her mouth opened and closed a few times—as if she almost said something, then decided against it, chose something else to say, then decided against that as well.

"A man who brags about himself knows that no one else will," she said with authority.

"'It's not bragging if you can back it up'—Muhammad Ali," he answered without missing a step.

She huffed again, but not before he saw her almost smile. She turned away and fumbled with her phone before turning back and saying, "'Don't accept your dog's admiration as conclusive evidence that you are wonderful'—Ann Landers."

Ah, the culture of shared, uploaded searchable knowledge. How would it fare against an impeccable education? "'Be not afraid of greatness'—Shakespeare."

"How appropriate. I do see some Malvolio in you," she snapped back.

"Touché, my little American." Magnus laughed, to the consternation of those around them. Her reference to the man who had been the brunt of a joke that had included the greatness quote revealed she was also well schooled. Yes, here was a woman who would not bore him.

"Stop. We're being rude."

Magnus shrugged. "No, whoever decided your seat was not beside your brother tonight was rude. *We* are merely not entertained by an insect superhero."

"Speak for yourself. I'm enjoying the movie immensely."

"Really? Then tell me where the alien creature went who was attacking the city a moment ago. Was he killed? Did he flee? Do you know what his rationale was for attacking? Amid the gratuitous explosions, I doubt there is a plot to be followed at all."

She folded her arms across her chest. "Now you're just being a jerk."

When several moments passed without her speaking, he relented. It was not his intention to offend her. "Are you honestly enjoying the movie?"

"I'm trying to," she said.

"Which part, outside of that your brother is in it, pleases you?"

"No. I'm not having this conversation. You don't get to mock something I care about and then ask me what I think of it. You want to please me? Stop talking."

Magnus felt like a young child holding in mischief during a ceremony. Part of him acknowledged that he should allow her to view the film without interruption. However, it was not as if a film were a once-in-a-lifetime event. Ridiculous as the plot was, Westerly's movies would have a global tour at the theaters and then likely dominate on television after that. This electricity might have a significantly shorter shelf life and was therefore of more importance. "I don't believe anyone has ever told me to be silent."

"Well, then I'm honored to be the first, and I'll gladly be the next."

He laughed again, and she swatted his arm.

"I'm serious. Stop."

He took her hand in his and brought it to his lips for a kiss. "I like you, Rachelle Westerly. For that reason, and that reason alone, I will be silent." He placed her hand beneath his on his thigh and laced his fingers through hers.

"Thank you," she said tersely, but she didn't pull her hand away.

He turned back to the screen and smiled. He hadn't expected to enjoy any part of his trip to London. He certainly hadn't expected to meet a woman who could excite him as easily as she did.

Would she be in his bed that night?

Not knowing made their exchanges even sweeter. He half hoped she turned him away, because he had not had this much fun with a woman in a very long time.

When a man is offered a fine brandy, he does not gulp it down. He rolls it on his tongue, savoring the burn.

Chapter Five

"What do you mean, he left?" Rachelle asked Eric's publicist as soon as the audience began to file out. "Isn't he going to the after-party?"

"He never does. He even makes sure it's in his contract that he isn't required to. You're welcome to attend it, though."

"Where is he now?" Rachelle asked, looking around, clinging to the hope that he hadn't actually left.

"I have no idea," the publicist said.

"Coward," Magnus said from beside her. She didn't know if he was referring to the publicist or her brother.

She took out her phone and sent Eric a text. Are you still here? I have a question for you.

When no answer came back, a lump of emotion clogged her throat, and her eyes blurred with tears she refused to shed. *I came even though he didn't invite me, and instead of showing him how proud of him I am, I sat with a man who mocked him. He's probably furious with me.*

And he has every right to be.

I have to find him and apologize.

Magnus touched her arm, but she shook his hand off. "Don't." She walked away. Although the area was crowded, people stepped aside for her as she made her way to the main door. She had to get out of there.

A man in a dark suit opened the door before she reached it. She stepped through it and was temporarily blinded by the number of flashes going off. It was only then that she realized Magnus was still at her side. She lengthened her stride and texted her driver to come for her.

Several men in dark suits flanked them as Magnus joined Rachelle near the street. "He's not worth your tears, Rachelle."

"He's my brother," she growled back, wiping away a stray tear with the back of her hand. "He's the reason I'm here. The only reason. And tonight I probably embarrassed him in front of everyone. I don't blame him for not answering me."

"Do not put this on you, Rachelle."

She spun and waved a finger at the man who had her insides tied up in confusing knots. "You're right. It's your fault. You and your big perfect smile I let make me stupid. You don't care about me. You don't care about Eric. Tonight was some kind of game to you, and I went along with it. Well, I'm done. I'm worried about my brother. Maybe it's hard for someone as self-absorbed as you to understand, but my family is more important to me than anything else. So go. Go find some woman who is impressed with your title and your big muscles and all that I'm-so-good-in-bed talk. And just leave me alone."

Her car pulled up to the curb, and the driver rushed around to open the back passenger door for her. "Rachelle, your brother is fine. He's not in danger. He just—"

She slid inside. "You don't know that. Goodbye." With that, she closed the door.

As soon as the driver was behind the wheel, she instructed him to take her home. She refused to look back to see if Magnus was still there. "Where does Eric go after premieres?" she asked the driver.

"I have no idea, ma'am."

"Could you call and ask someone?" Rachelle's radar was up and overheating. Something wasn't right. Eric was in some kind of trouble.

"Who would you suggest I ask?"

"I don't know. Someone has to know where he is. Does he go home? No one just disappears into thin air."

The driver didn't have a response.

Am I overreacting? It wouldn't be my first or even my biggest mistake today. Rachelle sat back and covered her face with her hands. She hated that when she closed her eyes, she could still see Magnus. She felt guilty she'd let how good he made her feel influence how she behaved at the premiere.

I don't even have a good defense. I'm not a silly teenager. I have found men attractive before without making a complete ass out of myself.

In reality, what is a prince except someone who was born into a job rather than having to work for it? No wonder he speaks the way he does. He's probably had everything he's ever wanted handed to him.

She remembered how little he thought of Eric and regretted not standing up right in the middle of that conversation and moving away from him. *Alisha says I'm the loyal one in the family. I sure didn't live up to that tonight.*

A short time later, she was back at Eric's house—alone. The army of staff was absent from the main hall. Rachelle stood at the bottom of the elaborate stairway, hugging herself.

I'm not the woman Magnus thought I was.

Even though it felt good to be her for an evening.

For just a few hours she'd felt young, sexy, and confident. Gone was the daughter who had failed to protect her mother. She wasn't the smothering, overopinionated sister Nicolette accused her of being.

Every moment with Magnus had been one when she wasn't the misguided woman who had traveled halfway across the world to stay in the house of a brother who wouldn't even return her texts.

I traded that feeling for my chance to show Eric how family makes everything better.

God, I really am arrogant.

For all I know, Eric is perfectly happy without us. He couldn't be more clear about not wanting me in his life. Maybe what I should really do is go home and figure myself out instead of thinking I need to fix other people.

"Would you like the cook to make you anything before you retire?" Reggie asked, appearing from seemingly nowhere.

Rachelle muffled her scream with a hand. "Sorry, I thought I was alone."

"Never. Mr. Westerly asked me to look after you. I'm always around, even if you don't see me."

Who is Reggie to Eric? "I shouldn't have gone to the premiere, Reggie. I embarrassed him. Could you arrange for a car to take me to the airport tomorrow? I think it's time for me to go home."

"Wow, you give up easily."

"Excuse me?"

Reggie shrugged. "Earlier you went on and on about how much your family matters to you. You get ditched on television by a prince, and you're running back to your mommy and daddy. I hope my children have more spine than that."

Rachelle waved her hand in the air in clarification. "I did not get ditched by a prince. I walked away from him. And, hang on, you have children?"

In response, Reggie took out his phone and turned it so she could see a GIF on his social media feed. It was of her and Magnus at her car. It looked as if she'd spoken to him, but he turned away from her. She took the phone and played it again. The caption read: "Be a prince, say no to American trash."

"That didn't even happen."

"So that's not you?"

"That's me." She played the video back. "But it's playing backward. Magnus followed me to the car, and I left him standing there."

"It's none of my business. I shouldn't have mentioned it. What time would you like the car?" He reached for his phone.

Rachelle clung to it and played the video clip again. "It's so vicious. Who would do this?" She remembered Magnus saying he would use her to get to her brother. Was this what he meant? Did he think that by hurting her he could hurt Eric? *If so, the joke is on him. My brother would have to care about me to care about this.*

"Let me see it again." Reggie snatched his phone. "You're right, it's playing backward. Can't believe I didn't realize it. It was probably because of the snappy caption."

"You mean cruel."

Reggie repocketed his phone. "You left a prince standing on a curb. Not bad for your first premiere."

Rachelle laughed, because if she didn't she would cry. "How many children do you have?"

"Two."

"You're married?"

"Are you flirting with *me* now?" Before Rachelle had time to answer, Reggie started laughing. "Don't get your panties all in a tangle. I'm happily married. But you need to relax. Unlike our apocalyptic American media implies, not every day is the end of the world."

Reggie certainly wasn't shy when it came to sharing his opinions. What was his real role in the household? *Not that it's my business. My brother won't even answer my texts. That's a pretty clear message.* "I'd welcome an apocalypse tonight. I'm going to bed."

"You want to know what I've learned from the English?"

Rachelle sighed. "Why not?"

"Don't run. Go out in public tomorrow as if nothing happened. Your brother is attacked in the media on a regular basis. What they don't know they make up. You'll lose yourself if you start to care what social media says about you."

Now I feel bad about calling him Lurch in my head earlier. "Thanks, Reggie. That's actually good advice."

"You don't need to sound shocked. I'm a lot smarter than I look." Rachelle opened her mouth to say something, but Reggie continued, "There's no good response to that."

Rachelle laughed because he was right. "Good night, Reggie. Thanks."

"So, no car tomorrow?"

"No, you're right. I've never been one to run away. I can't leave before I talk to Eric one more time. I'll tell him I love him, and then I'll go home. If he doesn't want a relationship with me, I'll respect his decision."

"You're not the complete whack job I thought you were when you first arrived."

Rachelle laughed again and started up the stairs. "See you tomorrow, Reggie."

◆ ◆ ◆

"Keep him there. I'm on my way," Magnus barked into his cell phone before repeating the address to his driver. Magnus dropped his phone back into the pocket of his jacket and flexed his shoulders. Whatever Westerly was doing in a poorer section of London was about to come to an abrupt end, just as Magnus's good mood had.

The sadness in Rachelle's eyes when she'd realized her brother had left without her haunted Magnus. He considered regret a waste of time, but he didn't like that he'd contributed to how badly her night had ended. He understood the practice of serving someone's head up on a platter, because he would gladly have done so with Westerly's if he thought it would bring comfort to Rachelle.

Instead, he'd settle for the bastard apologizing to her. Magnus didn't doubt for a second that Westerly would be willing to by the time he was finished with him.

His car pulled over to the side of the road in front of a run-down building. Magnus double-checked the address against the one he'd been given, half convinced there must be a mistake. Then he saw one of his most trusted men leaning against a tree nearby. He straightened as Magnus exited the car. "What's he doing here?"

Phillip shrugged. "We followed him, as you asked. He stopped once to change cars, then came here. And there's one more thing."

"Yes?"

"His nose was bigger when he got out of the car. At first I thought I imagined it, but I think he wears a disguise."

Magnus looked up at the apartment building. "Interesting."

"Do you want backup, Magnus?" He spoke with the familiarity of someone who knew that Magnus didn't care about titles when in private.

"No. I'm good. Is he alone?"

"It's impossible to say."

Magnus nodded and took the steps of the building two at a time before ringing the doorbell. He knocked loudly, knocked again, then tested if it was locked. It was. Shaking his head, he stepped back, assessed the old door for a weak point, and kicked to the left of the doorknob. It crashed open.

When the sound brought no one to meet him, Magnus entered slowly, scanning each room he passed. The living room was furnished, if cheaply, and it smelled musty. The bedroom next to it was empty. He opened the door to the next room, and his lip curled in response to what he saw. Fully clothed and sprawled across a bed lay Westerly. The needle he'd used to inject himself rested at his side.

"Fuck."

You can't break a man who's already broken.

Chapter Six

Back in the United States.

At nearly eighty-two, Delinda Westerly was forced to accept pain, in some fashion or another, as a constant companion. The clock running down on her life made every moment matter; there was so much she didn't want to leave undone. It also freed her from worrying what people thought of her—not that she'd ever valued the opinion of many. Born into wealth and tested through tragedy, Delinda knew she'd have some explaining to do at the pearly gates, but if she were given her life to do over, she wouldn't do much differently.

The door of her solarium flew open, and Hailey Tiverton, her grandson's fiancée, rushed into the room. "I came as soon as I saw your text. What's wrong?"

Looking worried, Alessandro Andrade, a man Delinda loved like a son, strode in. His mother, a woman who had been one of Delinda's dear friends, would be proud of the patriarch he'd become. "Did you call the doctor? Is he on his way?"

Hailey sank to her knees beside Delinda's chair, searching her face. "Where's Michael?" She laid a hand on Delinda's forehead to check for a fever.

Delinda smacked her hand away. "Michael is making travel arrangements for me. I don't need a doctor."

Hailey took out her phone. "I don't understand. You asked me to come over because you were sick and almost dead."

"What?" Delinda squinted at Hailey's phone screen. She reached for her glasses and made a face at what appeared to be a text from her that said exactly that.

Alessandro sat in a chair next to Delinda. "I received the same message."

"Because I included both of you in one of those group-message things. Spencer assured me that texting was better than calling, but I don't see how, when my phone takes literary license with what I enunciate into it." She pushed the phone away. "I said, 'I'm sickened by what I just read.'"

Hailey rose to her feet and laid a hand over her heart. "I tried to call you back, and when you didn't answer, I almost called 911. If we didn't live so close, I would have."

"I was on my way over or I would have done the same," Alessandro said, shaking his head. "You aged me today, Delinda."

Delinda pursed her lips briefly. Apologies had never come easily to her, but these were two of her friends as well as her family. "It's a new phone, and it kept beeping and binging to the point that I silenced it. They call it a smartphone, but it announces everything like some bumbling idiot." She sighed. "I didn't mean to worry either of you."

"It's fine," Hailey said. "I'm just glad you're okay."

"My health may not be in immediate decline, but I am far from *okay*." She reached for her tablet and woke it with a tap. "I knew Rachelle shouldn't have gone off to London without me. Look at what they're saying about her."

"Come now, it can't be all that bad," Alessandro said in a tone he often used when he thought Delinda was working herself up over nothing. He might be nearly sixty, but she still saw the precocious and carefree boy he'd once been. Delinda handed him the tablet and showed him a video clip of Prince Magnus walking away from Rachelle, followed by a slew of nasty comments.

Hailey gasped. "Oh, that *is* bad. People are horrible. Poor Rachelle."

"It's being translated and shared everywhere. How would you feel if this was about Maddy?" Delinda asked.

Alessandro's hands tightened visibly on the device. Gone was his normally jovial expression. "I have friends in London. They can quash this."

Delinda took the tablet back and scrolled to an article put out by online social pages. "It's too late for that. Unlike the press, you can't control the Internet. Did you see that some second-rate princess agreed? She called Rachelle American trash. My granddaughter? She is a sweet, educated woman who put her career aside because her brother needs her. Who do they think they are? With her inheritance, Rachelle could buy and sell every palace in those ridiculously outdated and minuscule countries."

"It's not good for you to get worked up, Delinda," Alessandro cautioned. "You really could make yourself sick."

Hailey merely sat there with wide eyes and a pained expression.

Delinda put the tablet down and rose to her feet. "When I'm done with them, they'll be sorry they ever came after a Westerly."

"Is she going to war with Europe?" Hailey asked with an uncertain chuckle.

"No. Delinda, calm down." Alessandro stood. "Rachelle is stronger than you think. She'll rise above this."

Delinda smiled and she nodded. "Yes, with my help she will. The prince doesn't think my Rachelle is good enough for him? He'll be singing a different tune when I'm done with him. Hailey, do bring Skye over for dinner tonight. I'd like to see her before I leave for Vandorra, especially considering I'm not certain how long this will take."

Hailey joined them, looking bemused. "How long what will take? I don't understand."

Alessandro tried to pin Delinda with a look, but she refused to meet his eyes. "If I thought Eric would be supportive, I would tell him that I have finally found a role worthy of my consideration."

"Oh boy," Alessandro said.

"I'm still lost." Hailey threw up her hands in confusion.

"Those Europeans like their royalty and their fairy tales," Delinda said. "In the end, that's what this will be. Princess Rachelle de Bartelebon. It has a ring to it, wouldn't you say?"

"No more matchmaking," Alessandro warned.

"I don't care if they actually marry," Delinda bit out, "but Rachelle will receive a proposal from that prince, and it will be a public one. She can turn him down if she wishes."

Hailey chewed her lip nervously. "I haven't known Rachelle as long as you have, but I don't think she would want us to get involved."

"That's why she won't know," Delinda said firmly.

"Oh no." Hailey looked to Alessandro for help.

"Don't do this, Delinda."

"It's done. I fly out tonight."

A heavy silence settled over the solarium until it was broken by the arrival of Michael. "Would anyone like tea?"

"Michael," Delinda said, "if Cinderella were real, could you imagine a better fairy godmother for her than me?"

Michael took his time before answering. "If Cinderella were real, I doubt she'd need a prince anymore."

Delinda smiled smugly. "Exactly the point I will make clear to Prince Magnus de Bartelebon."

Chapter Seven

Magnus paced the library of the Duke of North Cumberland, who had generously offered up his sprawling private estate the night before. The move meant an impromptu holiday for his family, but the duke understood that some relationships were worth such inconvenience.

And there wasn't a part of this that wasn't inconvenient.

The appearance of Dr. Stein, his family's trusted physician, halted Magnus midstep. The doctor was short, bald, and had been old as long as Magnus could remember, but he was also brilliant and discreet. "Is he alive?"

"Yes, and now simply sleeping. But you won't like what I learned."

Magnus waved the doctor in. "I didn't expect to."

"This isn't a case of drug addiction, not in the classic sense. Your friend either injected himself or paid someone to inject him with a powerful anesthetic drug. He wasn't looking for a high. He was looking to check out—maybe for a night, maybe forever. I've seen similar cases in the news, but sadly only after it ends tragically. I don't know Eric Westerly beyond having seen him in movies, so I can't speak to his motivation for sedating himself, but I'd say it's at least partially to combat insomnia. My guess is he has worked his way through less extreme substances without success. If he continues to self-medicate and mixes this anesthesia with anything else, he won't be your problem for long."

Magnus ran his hand through his hair as he digested the news. "Is it addictive? Would there be withdrawal issues?"

Dr. Stein rubbed his chin in thought. "That will depend on the frequency of his use. Most of the data on addiction to this drug comes from studies about, surprisingly enough, people in the medical field who have access to it. It has a short half life and rapid metabolic clearance, so it often doesn't show up in the bloodstream later."

"So, it's a matter of stopping him from taking more?"

The doctor shook his head slowly. "This is a deeply troubled man, Magnus. He needs to be admitted to a rehab center where he can address whatever he's willing to risk his life to escape from. People don't choose this drug—they resort to it out of desperation."

So much for this being easy. "I don't understand. He's at the top of his career. He has enough money to buy himself out of any situation. Why the hell would a man like that be desperate?"

"How long have I known you, Magnus?"

"You delivered me."

"Then may I be frank?"

"Please."

"You were born with the heart of a warrior. You are at your best when there is a battle to be waged, but life is not always about the victory. I heard about your behavior at the children's hospital. You scared the children more than the clowns did."

Magnus pocketed his hands and frowned. There were few, if any, people he would accept speaking to him the way this man was. "Going there at all was my father's idea. He was unable to go himself and believed it would be good for my public image."

"Magnus, your father does not visit the sick for his public image. He goes because he understands they are more than his responsibility— they are his people. He loves them, and that is why they love him. You fight for Vandorra, but do you do it because you think it is the role you were born to? That's not enough, my son. A king, one worth still having in this world, would lay down his life for his people because they have his heart as well as his sword."

Suddenly impatient, Magnus demanded, "What does this have to do with Westerly?"

The doctor held his gaze for a moment before speaking. "You will not be able to help him if you don't first try to understand him. I believe people come into our lives for a reason. Perhaps you need Eric as much as he needs you."

"I don't need anyone."

Dr. Stein grimaced. "Your pride, my son, will stop you from becoming the king Vandorra needs. Don't think that simply taking Eric to Finn will change anything for either of them. Consider Finn the voice of your people. They're asking if you will open your heart to them. What will your answer be?"

I don't know if I can be the king my father was.

Magnus thought about the small Vandorran town where his mother had chosen to raise him. It had been important to her that Magnus had bonds with their people, and he did. Perhaps he did not show his love for his people openly, but it was there. "Send Phillip in. I have a task for him."

The doctor nodded and left the room. A moment later, Phillip, the head of Vandorra's royal guard, entered. "You sent for me?"

"I did," Magnus said. "I want you to dig deeper about Eric Westerly and his family in the United States. If one of them is so much as battling with a cavity, I want to know it. I need you to keep Westerly here until I decide what to do with him and watch him closely. I also want a full background check done on Rachelle Westerly. Everything."

"She's the buzz of London this morning."

"What do you mean?"

"Someone reversed a video clip, so it appears that you turned away from her publicly. They shared it on social media with some unflattering text. I don't imagine she's very happy about it."

Fucking fantastic. His hands clenched at his sides. "Who? Who's responsible for it?"

"I tracked the initial video to a Twitter account belonging to a friend of Princess Isabella. Perhaps this was her way of humiliating the Westerly woman before she became competition? It's no secret the princess would like to be the next queen of Vandorra."

"Can the video be pulled down?"

"I'm afraid it has gone viral. There is already discussion of it on a variety of social pages. The damage is done." He called up the video and showed it to Magnus.

"Get me Rachelle Westerly's phone number."

"It's already added to the contacts on your phone."

Competence was a welcome sight in the middle of what was turning out to be a shitfest. "Thank you, Phillip. That's all for now."

"Of course," Phillip answered, then left.

Magnus pulled up Rachelle's contact information on his phone. He'd never been one to soften the truth, but this was a novel situation, and Dr. Stein's words still rang in his ears. Tempting as it was to tell Finn his movie-star hero was not worth his adoration, and Rachelle that she was right to be worried about her brother, neither one of them had done a thing to deserve the pain that news would bring them.

Magnus had forced foreign leaders to change the terms of their treaties with his father without ever asking for advice on the matter. He was used to quickly determining what needed to be done in a situation and then doing it. Wins required decisive actions.

I won't be able to help Westerly until I understand him. What the fuck am I supposed to understand about a man who has decided his life has no value?

Pacing the office again, Magnus asked himself a question he hadn't in a long time: *What would my father do?*

A short time later, armed with information about the Westerly family and a plan, Magnus called Rachelle. She answered on the third ring. "Hello?"

"It's Magnus."

"Calling to gloat? You'll be disappointed to hear that I'm having lunch at a lovely, very public outdoor café. The sun is shining. The food is delicious. I couldn't be in a better mood."

A lie, but there was no need to call her out for it. If she was indeed sitting in a café at that moment, he was again impressed with her. That kind of grit was the way he would advise anyone to deal with a public scandal. "I have determined the source of the video clip. Would you like her apology to be private or public?"

Her gasp was audible. "It wasn't you?"

"Little Rachelle, why would I want to see you hurt?"

"I thought—you said . . ."

"It was not me, but I assure you the person who was involved will regret the folly."

"No. Please don't. I'm not the vengeful type. But I am confused. Why would anyone want to hurt me? I'm no one."

He could have argued that she was far from being a no one, but that was a conversation for another time. "Jealousy trumps decency in some. I'm afraid it was the attention I showed you that brought this on you."

"I'll be fine. It's not actually as bad as I thought. The more attention the clip gets, the more people comment that obviously it was reversed. In fact, my phone has been ringing all day with people lending their support. I've never received so many invitations from complete strangers. Some of them are prominent enough that Eric must have felt bad about leaving last night and made a few calls. It's the only explanation that makes any sense. Unless you—"

"I did not."

She was quiet, then said, "He never came home last night."

"Rachelle—"

"Yes?"

"What do you know about your brother's private life?"

"Why do you ask? Have you seen him? Do you know where he is?"

Rather than lying, he said, "I'm still gathering information. However, if I could locate your brother, what would you want from him?"

"That's a strange question. Is it because you think I'd somehow stand in the way of your promise to that little boy?"

"Yes," he said, because denying that would have required an assessment of why he really was asking, and he wasn't ready to do that.

"We aren't on opposites sides, Magnus. I love that there's a little boy out there whose life may be changed simply by meeting my brother. But what do I want?" She paused, and let out an audible breath. "Eric moved to London to build a life away from us. I don't know why, but I sense he regrets that. I used to think he was naturally aloof, but lately I've wondered if he feels . . . abandoned. I'm sorry. I'm sure you don't want to know all of that, but I'm worried about him. He shouldn't be alone. I need him to know we're here for him if he needs us. That's all I want to say."

Magnus sat on the arm of the office couch. He was driven by facts and duty. She operated on emotion and instinct. She felt that her brother's welfare was her responsibility. That motivation he understood.

"I know where he is," Magnus said.

"You do?" Her voice rose several octaves. "Where?"

"I'll send a car for you. Be ready in an hour."

"Ready? Like dressed? I'm already dressed."

"I mean packed. You and your brother will accompany me back to Vandorra this evening."

"You've spoken to Eric? He's agreed to go?"

"A car will retrieve you from his home in an hour." Magnus hung up and called for Phillip.

"Yes?" Phillip inquired from the door.

"Get Westerly up, showered, and dressed. Bring him to me when he's presentable. His sister will be here in less than two hours. Have a helicopter ready to take us to the airfield. We return to Vandorra tonight."

"And if Westerly resists?"

"Do your best not to hurt him, but use whatever force is necessary. None of my plan works if he's dead."

◆ ◆ ◆

Rachelle clutched her phone on her lap in the backseat of a Rolls-Royce as it sped beyond the city limits of London. Her stomach was churning nervously, even though she kept assuring herself she'd made the right choice.

She'd almost called home and told her family where she and Eric were headed, but she wanted to tread softer this time. She'd learned that Eric was obsessive when it came to his privacy. Perhaps he didn't want there to be a chance the press would know where he was going. Of course she wished he'd been the one to tell her he'd decided to do the appearance, but what mattered was that he wanted her to go on this trip with him. It was an opportunity she wasn't about to pass up—not for all the stomach butterflies in the world.

A little voice in her head kept whispering that something wasn't right. Perhaps it was the additional man in the front seat. Two drivers?

One to drive and one to make sure I don't run? She laughed nervously, then squashed the thought.

I'm going on a trip with my brother. There's nothing scary about this. The additional man is probably in case I had a lot of luggage.

She remembered Magnus's warning that he would use her if he had to. She shook her head. *I have definitely watched too many movies. Instead of wondering what they'd do if I said no to going, I should be glad they asked me to.*

She was excited to see Magnus again. Oh, she'd deny it to him, but there was no use lying to herself. It was impossible not to wonder if what she'd felt the night before would still be there.

Would his cocky smile send her heart racing?

Would every innocent touch of his hand inspire instant, filthy fantasies of where she wanted his hands to go?

Was it wrong to want to feel sexy and confident again even if she knew it couldn't lead to anything? *I'll be back in my old life soon enough— I just want one more taste of how it feels to want someone that much.*

And hopefully when I go home, I can find a sweet, humble, normal man who makes me feel the same way.

The crowded city streets gave way to winding, tree-lined roads. "How far is it?" she asked the driver.

"Five minutes more, ma'am," the man said.

"Does Prince Magnus own a home there?"

"I believe the home he's staying at belongs to a duke."

"I'm surprised the prince didn't choose to stay in the city. This doesn't seem like a convenient location." *It feels more like where'd you stay if you wanted to do something out of the public eye.*

The car pulled up to an intricate iron gate that swung open, then closed behind them. The sprawling English estate was impressive, although not the size of Eric's. Men in suits occupied stations around the lawn, and a helicopter waited nearby.

They parked at the top of the circular driveway in front of the prominent entryway. As soon as the driver stepped out, the second man turned in his seat and handed Rachelle a black card with nothing more than a phone number printed in white. "You are never alone. If you need something, anything, call that number, but show it to no one."

The side door opened before she had time to ask whose number it was. She tucked it inside her phone case and took her cue from the man who had handed it to her and pretended they had not exchanged anything.

Holy crap, what was that?

"Please follow me," her driver said. "Prince Magnus is in a meeting, but he will meet you in the library shortly."

"Before that, I'd like to see my brother. Where is he?"

"This way, please."

Rachelle followed the driver into the house as the other man brought her one suitcase to the helicopter. She hadn't brought much. She couldn't imagine the trip would be for more than a couple of days.

Once inside, Rachelle hesitated when she didn't see her brother in the library. She sent him a text telling him that she was there.

No response.

The hairs on the back of her neck rose. "I want to speak to my brother."

The man nodded. "It should not be long. Is there anything we could offer while you wait? Are you hungry? Thirsty? There is a washroom down the hall if you would like to freshen up."

Two men in dark suits stationed themselves on either side of the door. Rachelle had never considered herself a paranoid person, but the sight gave her the chills. "I would like to use the washroom, thank you."

If only to prove to myself that I'm suffering from an overactive imagination.

She left the library and made her way down the hallway in the direction the driver had pointed. She glanced over her shoulder, half expecting someone to be right behind her, but no one was. She laughed nervously.

Nicolette is right, I need to get out more. I've lived a too-sheltered life.

The security isn't for me. Magnus is a prince. Of course he has bodyguards. I'm reading meaning into things that mean nothing.

Rachelle relieved herself, washed her hands, then looked in the mirror. Her cheeks were flushed, and she looked more excited than she wanted to. *Last night went badly because I let it be about me and what*

I wanted. Eric needs me. I can't let Mr. You Wish I'd Been Your First and Every Fuck Since distract me from why I came.

She gave herself a stern look, then took a deep breath and opened the door. When she realized the security duo from the library was now standing outside the washroom, she nearly closed the door again. But since she wasn't about to leave before she saw Eric, she didn't have many options. She raised her chin and walked past them to the library.

Once inside, she checked her phone again for a message from Eric. Nothing.

On impulse, she texted Magnus. I want to see my brother now. If you don't bring him to me immediately, I will call the police.

A moment later one of the guards stepped into the library with three bottles of water. "Prince Magnus will be here in a moment," he said, juggling the bottles from hand to hand as he seemed to search for something in his pockets. He stepped closer. "He sent me a message. I'll read it to you." He held the water out. "Could you hold these for a moment?"

Confused, she accepted the bottles he thrust at her and didn't realize until too late that he used the exchange as an opportunity to relieve her of her phone. "Please forgive me, Miss Westerly, but I was instructed to take this."

He left as quickly as he'd arrived, leaving her standing there, mouth open, with three bottles of water. She moved to follow him, but the two men at the doorway stepped inward to form a barricade with their bodies.

Holy shit, is this a kidnapping?

How do I even know Eric is here?

Oh my God, the only one I told where I was going was Reggie.

My survival might depend on Lurch.

Chapter Eight

"Are you finished?" Magnus asked at the end of Eric's litany of threats. He folded his arms across his chest and leaned back against the office desk while Eric paced the office like a caged animal. He couldn't make it out of the room if he tried, but Magnus hoped it didn't come to that. It was unfortunate enough that Rachelle had arrived shortly after her brother had been brought to Magnus. He'd hoped this conversation would be done so he could greet Rachelle himself.

Recently, however, the universe seemed to be working against him. Rachelle had already sent a text that implied she wouldn't wait patiently for their conversation to conclude. Hopefully Phillip had resolved the immediate concern of her phoning the police.

"You're delusional if you think you'll get away with this," Eric spat. "When I get out of here, and I *will* get out of here, I will destroy you."

"Terrifying as that sounds," Magnus said dryly, "I will give you one more chance to agree to come with me of your own free will. All I require is one day of your time. One inspirational visit to a children's hospital. Perhaps a few autographs. After that, if you still want me to, I will return you to where I found you." *Not exactly how it will go, but he needs to start agreeing to part before he'll agree to the whole plan.*

"You're fucking crazy. I'm not going anywhere with you."

With a sigh, Magnus stood and flexed his shoulders. He preferred to do things nicely, but sometimes it wasn't possible. "In two minutes I will open that door and give you a choice to stay or go. However, life is full of what I call natural consequences. I don't want to disappoint a young boy who idolizes you, but perhaps his opinion of you will change once word gets out about your drug use. You think your life is hell now. Imagine how the press will hound you when your double life is exposed. There will be nowhere you can hide. How will Water Bear Man fare in the box office once the truth about you gets out?"

"You don't scare me. Do your worst. I don't fucking care."

"It'd be a career ender."

"You'd be doing me a favor."

Magnus sat back on the corner of his desk again. He almost had Eric where he wanted him and wasn't about to relent, but that didn't mean he was indifferent to the man's pain. "Finn is ten years old. Ten. The doctors don't know if he'll see eleven. He wants to grow up to be as strong and brave as Water Bear Man and wants to meet him. I promised him he would—both meet you and survive. So, regardless of what you think, this is me being nice. If I were you, I'd agree. You really don't want to test how far I'll go to make this happen."

Eric groaned as if trying to wake up. When he looked up again, there was more life in him than Magnus had seen to date. "There's a lot of superheroes out there. Find one who does appearances."

Despite his bravado, it was easy to see that whatever Eric's demons were, they were winning. If Magnus eased off now, he had a feeling the next time he saw Eric might be in an obituary. "This is how it will go down. We'll fly to Vandorra today. You'll act as if all of this is your idea and that you're happy. Reassure Rachelle that everything is fine. Tomorrow you'll visit the children's hospital. We'll stay one night in Vandorra. My father will likely wish to meet you. You will not say a word to him about any of this. The next day you'll discreetly check into a clinic where I've reserved a suite for you."

"What the hell are you talking about?" Eric ran his hand through his hair in frustration. "I'm not going anywhere with you, and I don't need rehab."

Eric took a step toward the door, but Magnus moved to block him. "Yes, you do."

"Excuse me?"

"You might as well agree, since I'm not offering you a choice."

"Buddy, you've let your title go to your head. Now get out of my way."

Magnus took a calming breath. "Listen, I wouldn't normally give a shit about you, but there are two people I don't want to see hurt by your stupidity—one idolizes you and the other loves you. You need help, Westerly. I can't make you take it. But I'm here, right now, offering you a chance to get some without anyone needing to know about it. Your sister believes there's something in you worth saving. It'd be nice if you proved her right. In fact, she's here, so you can tell her your decision now." Magnus nodded for the guard to open the door. "She's in the library."

Eric strode out of the office and into the foyer. Magnus followed.

As soon as she saw him, Rachelle flew to Eric and wrapped her arms around him. "Eric, are you okay?"

He stood awkwardly stiff in her embrace, but studied her face. "Of course. You?"

"Just worried. I'm sorry about last night, Eric. I don't know what I was thinking. I wanted to be there for you, not embarrass you."

Clearly uncomfortable, Eric stepped back and pocketed his hands. "You've never embarrassed me."

Rachelle's voice shook with emotion. "If you don't want me to go to Vandorra with you, I'll understand. I know you didn't expect me to show up at your door or the premiere. Nicolette says I have trouble with boundaries. Sometimes I can't help myself. I had a feeling that you needed me. I just want you to know that even though we were raised apart—you're important to me. I love you. That's all. I can go home now, because that's what I should have said the first day, and it's what I needed to say before I could leave."

Westerly's shoulders hunched slightly. The bold action hero from the big screen wasn't visible in this man who seemed at a loss for what to say. Magnus felt more pity for him than he expected to, but he didn't like that Westerly had yet to say he was going to Vandorra. Short of forcibly hauling the actor onto a helicopter, there wasn't much more Magnus could do.

"I'm not going to Vandorra."

Shit.

Rachelle's eyes filled with confusion. "No? But Eric—"

"I never wanted to be Water Bear Man. He's a ridiculous character with an implausible backstory in a spandex costume. I took the role as a favor for a friend. It was never supposed to be a career. I'm not a role model, I'm a fucking joke," Westerly said.

Rachelle touched her brother's arm. "You're not a joke. You're an inspiration. Do you know how many children I've taught who wanted to grow up to be strong and brave like Water Bear Man? Think about the little boy in Vandorra. Meeting you will give him courage."

Westerly withdrew from her touch and rubbed his hands over his face. "It shouldn't. I'm not a superhero. I'm a fucking mess. I don't want to meet that kid. He'll see right through me."

Rachelle looked to Magnus as if he'd know what to say. Magnus didn't. This was uncharted territory for him as well. Clasping her hands in front of her, Rachelle took a moment to gather her thoughts. "Maybe your career isn't what you hoped it would be. So what? Everyone I know is still a work in progress. We're all doing the best we can—hoping to God we get enough right to make up for everything we get wrong. You can't focus on what you don't have. Go to Vandorra. That little boy needs to know that you care." When Eric didn't immediately answer, she added, "If you go, that's what he'll see."

Eric covered his face with one hand. "One visit. One kid. No press."

Rachelle looked like her heart was breaking for him. "You'll be glad you went, Eric."

Eric raised his eyes to Magnus's and shot him a not-so-subtle silent warning. "Would you like to come, Rachelle?"

With a tentative smile, Rachelle said, "I'd like that." Looking as if she'd lost a battle with herself, she threw her arms around Eric again and hugged him. "I was so worried when you didn't answer my texts last night."

Eric awkwardly patted her back. "Sorry, I misplaced my phone."

Rachelle looked past him and met Magnus's eyes. "That's funny, I lost mine recently as well. Since I know it's here, though, I have high hopes of finding it quickly."

Magnus fought a smile. *She's angry with me.* "Things happen. I'm sure it will turn up."

"I hope so, since I'm not going anywhere without it."

I do like her spirit. "I find that when I am patient and calm, I don't lose things."

She stepped away from her brother, and her chest heaved. She placed her hand on Magnus's arm. "Could I have a moment alone with you?"

"Absolutely," Magnus said, surprised at how much he enjoyed even that brief touch.

Eric looked as if he wanted to say something, but he didn't.

Magnus led the way to the office and closed the door. She had impressed him again. He was also pretty proud of how his plan was coming together. Eric was on board with making the appearance. Rachelle had had her moment with her brother. Finn would meet his hero. If everything else went as well, the trip would end with Eric in a rehab center and Rachelle in his bed.

I should tell her there's no need to thank me now. What I'm imagining for later will be thanks enough.

The finger she poked into his chest took him off guard. "I don't know how things are done in your country, but we need to clarify a few points before I go anywhere with you. First, what's with the goons? They're freaking me out. Are they keeping me safe or keeping me here? Either way, they're too much. I was half convinced you were kidnapping me before I saw Eric."

Magnus smiled, which only made her more angry.

"You think it's funny to scare people? If so, I hope your country has a second option for a king or I feel sorry for them."

His humor and smile faded away. "Be careful, little Rachelle."

Even though she only came up to his shoulders, she stepped closer and put her hands on her hips. "No, you be careful. Don't become so enamored with power that you forget how to treat people with respect. I was raised around people like that. It's not pretty."

"I haven't treated you poorly. In fact, I have gone way out of my way to help you."

"Really? If you're helping me, then why take my phone? That's not helping; that's controlling. Don't confuse the two."

Magnus sighed. "I was in the middle of something when you texted me that you were about to phone the police. You left me with no choice."

"That's where you're wrong, Magnus," she said angrily. "I'm so sick of people blaming others for their own bad behavior. You always have a choice when it comes to how you treat people. I won't be bullied. I want my phone back, and I want an apology." She folded her arms across her chest and glared up at him.

Had anyone else spoken to him in that tone, he would have quickly put an end to such insolence, but it was different coming from her. Perhaps because her motivation was selfless. Her only agenda was the happiness of those she cared about. His mother had been similar and had also taken people to task when they disappointed her. Something his father often said he'd loved about his wife—he was a better husband, father, king, because she had never feared telling him what she thought. Not in public, but in private, as Rachelle had.

Magnus didn't like that he might have scared Rachelle, nor did he like the way she was looking at him. Her eyes flashed, but not with the desire they'd held the night before. He wasn't a man who wasted his time worrying about what others thought of him, but he wasn't comfortable with the opinion she currently had of him.

"Phillip," Magnus called out. His head of security opened the door. "I believe we have something of Miss Westerly's."

"Of course." Phillip handed the phone back to Rachelle.

"That'll be all, Phillip."

Once they were alone again, Magnus took a moment to replay what Rachelle had said. Dr. Stein had said something similar the night before. "It was not my intention to scare you."

"And?"

"And the guards were meant to be my eyes and ears while I was otherwise occupied."

"And?"

He almost smiled again, but he was learning. "And I apologize for taking your phone."

"Thank you." Her eyes narrowed. "Something doesn't add up. You said Eric was going to Vandorra, but he hadn't agreed, had he?"

"No, he had not."

"Then why did you tell me he had?"

"I did not."

"Yes, you did. You said—" She stopped and seemed to be going over his words in her head. "You said you would be taking both of us to Vandorra, not that he had agreed. What was your plan if Eric said no?"

"It's of no consequence now, since he has agreed to go."

She searched his face again. "Is he in some kind of trouble?"

"That's not for me to say."

"Where did you find him?"

"That is another question best answered by your brother."

She raised her chin. "Did you promise him you wouldn't tell me? Feel like you'd be betraying him if you did?"

Magnus couldn't meet her eyes. He had told Eric that this would all go down in a way that no one would find out.

"No matter what you promised, I deserve the truth about Eric. It's no different than what I must do with information my students give me—"

"Your brother is not a child."

"You think you have all the answers, but what if you're wrong?" She moved away to sit in one of the chairs. "What if he needs me and you don't give me the chance to help him?"

Magnus took the seat across from her. Was this how quicksand felt? Every move he made sucked him in deeper.

Rachelle felt she deserved the truth about her brother, but would knowing help or push Westerly even closer to the edge?

He didn't want to see Rachelle hurt, but neither would he lie to her. Although he had essentially promised Eric that he'd keep his secret, she had left her job to travel across the world because she was worried for her brother. She deserved the truth. "Your brother has agreed to receive help for what he is dealing with."

"Is it drugs?" she asked.

There was no point in telling her less than all he knew. Magnus described how he'd found Eric and what Dr. Stein had said. He assured her that the clinic in Vandorra was one of the best in Europe . . . and discreet. He would not be the first, nor sadly the last, they treated for using such sedatives.

She clasped her phone on her lap. "I've heard about people using them. Oh my God, why would he take an anesthetic? Doesn't he know that people sometimes don't wake up?"

Magnus leaned forward, his hands braced on his knees. "He knows."

"But he doesn't care if it kills him? Does he want to die? Has he said he wants to?"

"Not in so many words, but he's in a bad place, Rachelle. He needs to talk to a professional."

She bent over as if she was about to retch. "I knew it. I mean, I had a feeling that he was struggling with something, but I didn't know it was this bad." She covered her mouth with a shaking hand. "Now I don't know what to do. Should I tell my family? Should I tell Eric I know?"

They sat there quietly for several minutes. Tension thickened the air. "Why are you helping Eric? You don't seem to even like him."

If Eric were one of the citizens of Vandorra, Magnus would have answered that it was his duty to serve his people. Eric, though, was not his responsibility. "I promised Finn he would meet him."

"You could fulfill that promise without doing more."

He stood. The realization that what he was willing to do for Eric was tangled up with how he felt about the woman before him was disconcerting. Yes, he was still attracted to her, but there was a quickly developing depth to it that was new to him. She was brave, fiercely loyal, and passionate. He wanted this to work out for her.

Because I care about her.

Rather than attempt to put his feeling into words, he cupped her chin and guided her lips to his. This wasn't a plundering, but rather a tender invitation. She rose to her feet, and her hands came to his chest as if to push him away, but she didn't.

When he lifted his head, she stayed where she was, but confusion warred with passion in her eyes. "Are you helping my brother so I'll sleep with you?"

"What a flattering opinion you have of me." He brushed his lips over hers again. "You will be mine, Rachelle. It's only a matter of time. I also wish to help your brother. You will have to trust that one is not contingent on the other."

"You're wrong. I'm not going to sleep with you. I don't believe in casual sex."

"So, you are still a virgin?"

"No, of course not."

"Divorced?"

"No."

"Left at the altar, then."

She pushed away from him. "I don't need to explain myself to you, but no, I've never made it to the altar. I was, however, in a committed relationship each time."

"Each time?" He arched an eyebrow. "How committed could you have been?"

Her eyes narrowed. "You are a real ass sometimes, you know that?"

He laughed. "Only sometimes? That's an improvement." He tucked a stray lock of hair behind her ear. "Would it help if I told you that I normally avoid complicated, but you're one hot mess I can't get out of my head?"

"No, it wouldn't," she said, but she smiled cautiously. "But I am grateful for what you're doing for Eric."

Progress.

"I'll take that."

"Just not *that* grateful."

He placed his hand on her lower back to guide her out of the room and decided to have a little fun with how easy it was to rile her up. "Of course, true gratitude will come after I've had you."

She stopped, her eyes flew to his, and he loved that the fire was back. "I wish I could tell if you're joking."

"There's only one way to find out. You'll have to get to know me."

Her eyebrows came together in the most adorable frown. "Last night fell apart because I let this—this—whatever this is distract me from why I came to London. I'm here for Eric. Anything else will have to wait until I know he's okay."

She needed time—reasonable, considering the circumstances. He checked his watch. "If we leave now, we'll be in Vandorra before nightfall."

◆ ◆ ◆

A short time later, Rachelle accepted an offer of a drink from a female attendant on Magnus's plane. A glass of wine might calm her nerves. So far, the spontaneous travel had not relaxed her. She was seated beside Eric, who had suddenly become protective of her. His distrust of Magnus radiated from him. Across from them, Magnus worked on his laptop—answering e-mails and occasionally barking scheduling changes to the men seated behind him.

Magnus looked up and said, "Once in Vandorra, while in public you should both refer to me as either Prince Magnus or Your Royal Highness. Anything else is considered an offense punishable by imprisonment."

"Sounds like a fabulous country to visit. Can't imagine why I've never been," Eric said.

"He's joking." Rachelle couldn't imagine such a law could survive in modern society.

"I am not," Magnus added matter-of-factly before returning to his work.

"It's going to be fine," Rachelle assured Eric. "I'm sure Magnus wouldn't let anything happen to us."

"Don't you mean Your Royal Highness, *Prince* Magnus?" Eric asked dryly. "I've never understood the fascination with royalty. I mean, what do they even do? Magnus, tell me, what was the last thing of importance that could actually be attributed to you? You know, outside of redesigning your family's crest or something."

Magnus looked up from his laptop and met Eric's gaze. "Last year, I successfully renegotiated a labor agreement with the European

Union to allow free movement of people and payments for Vandorra citizens—vastly reducing unemployment and growing our economy by 2.5 percent. Since I have taken the lead on domestic and foreign policy initiatives, poverty is down, enrollment in universities is up, and our lower crime rates reflect that the needs of my people are being met."

Eric's eyes widened. "Seriously?"

Magnus closed his laptop. "In Vandorra, royals are not figureheads. The welfare of our people depends on us. From the time I could walk, I understood that the survival of my country would one day rest on my shoulders."

Eric looked mildly impressed, but that was huge for him. It gave Rachelle hope that Magnus could actually convince Eric to sign in to a clinic. It also made Rachelle glad she hadn't told Eric that she knew anything. The last thing the trip needed was another layer of tension. Eric said, "That's a lot of pressure to put on a kid. What if you had decided you didn't want the keys to the kingdom?"

Magnus shrugged. "I wasn't given the freedom of choice. My mother had only one child."

"Thankfully I was the second son in our fiefdom," Eric said. "Brett took over the family business, which allowed me to step away—far, far away—a move that was the best for all of us."

The sadness in his voice pulled at Rachelle's heart. "Not all of us, Eric. I needed as much help with Nicolette and Spencer as I could get. I still do."

Magnus nodded at Rachelle. "She does. Nicolette is a wild one."

"How do you—" Rachelle started to ask, then shook her head. "I don't want to know, do I?"

"Probably not," Magnus said with a shameless smile.

The three of them fell quiet again. She decided it might help for her brother to see, as he opened up, that she wouldn't come at him as if she knew all the answers. "Until recently I thought I was the only thing holding our family together; then I realized it was perfectly capable of going on without me." She touched Eric's arm. "I'm here because I love you, but also because I was hoping you could help me. I thought that getting to know you again might help me find a piece of myself I lost somehow."

Eric placed his hand over hers. "I didn't think any of you needed me."

Rachelle blinked back tears she thought would be too much for the moment. "Well, now you know we do." Magnus excused himself, saying he needed to use the facilities, allowing Rachelle and Eric to continue their conversation in private. The prince had two sides—one maddening and arrogant, the other surprisingly considerate and supportive.

Eric lapsed into silence before once again meeting her eyes. "I'm sorry I've been MIA since you arrived."

"I understand. It's not like I didn't spring my visit on you."

Let me in, Eric. Please.

"How's Mom?" Eric asked.

"Better now that she watches Linda twice a week. I had a hard time getting her out of her house before then. Spencer and Hailey have set a wedding date for November. They're hoping you'll come. We all are."

"It'll depend on my filming schedule."

Rachelle took a deep breath and leapt. "Why do you keep making those films if you hate being Water Bear Man?"

Eric withdrew his hand but didn't turn away. "Do you know how many people I employ? I'm not even sure I do anymore."

Since he'd opened the door to asking, Rachelle did. "Eric, who is Reggie?"

"What do you mean?"

"It's obvious he's more than an electrician."

"He's my friend. When I needed someone, he was there for me. I know he's hiding his wife and kids in the east wing. I don't even care—I'd gift him the whole damn house if I thought he could afford to maintain it. He's the only person I trust."

That last part wasn't easy to hear, but Rachelle couldn't let the moment become about her. It was good to hear that Eric had someone he trusted. "Maybe you should tell him you're okay with his family living there."

"No, if I do that, everyone will want to move their kids in. Some things are better left not discussed. Reggie only moved them in when his wife lost her job, so I gave him a raise. He could afford a new place now, but his kids like the pool. They're also doing well in school."

"How do you know that?"

"You don't want to know."

"Does everyone with money think privacy for others is optional?"

"Knowledge is power. You weren't raised with money, Rachelle, but now that you've been in the public eye, you'll have to learn how to protect yourself. When we were young, I thought it was cruel of Mom to not allow you access to your money, but now I see the wisdom in it. Never again will you know if people like you for who you are or for what is in your bank account. Some will want to get close to you because they want to use you—others will see you as competition and will befriend you long enough to learn your weaknesses. It will affect every friendship you have, every potential relationship. Go back into hiding, Rachelle, if it's not already too late. Otherwise, every move you make, every word you say, will be dissected and judged by people who will find you wanting. You can try to ignore it, but eventually, like slow-drip torture, it will change the way you see yourself."

Oh, Eric. "You sound as lost as I feel."

He grimaced. "I'm fine." He looked across the plane at Magnus, who was standing, speaking to one of his men. "Be careful with him, Rachelle. I don't trust him."

It wasn't surprising, considering what he'd just shared about trusting anyone. "At least he's not after my money. He runs several companies as well as his country."

Eric's eyebrows rose with humor. "And how do you know that?"

"I did a Google search on him." Rachelle defended herself with a smile. "It's totally different."

"Whatever you say."

Rachelle playfully slugged his arm just as she would have with Spencer. "Okay, okay. I'll try to be less quick to judge." Eric laughed, and the sound warmed Rachelle's heart. She couldn't help but add, "Please make it to Spencer's wedding. You don't know how much it will mean to him."

"I doubt that. We're not exactly a close family, are we?"

Rachelle swallowed hard before answering. "We could be. I barely knew Brett before he made an effort to be part of our lives again. It was painfully awkward at first—"

"Like this."

"Exactly like this. Maybe even worse. I didn't like his timing with Alisha. Spencer was still fake-engaged to her when he found out that Mark was his real father. I didn't see why he and Alisha couldn't wait for the dust to settle, and I was pretty vocal about it."

"The heart wants what the heart wants, I guess."

"I wouldn't know. I've never been in love. I thought I was, but those relationships never lasted very long. How about you?"

"No. I gave up on fairy tales like that around the same time I stopped believing in Santa Claus. Or in family."

That last part nearly gutted Rachelle. So many trite retorts came to mind, but she dismissed them. Eric needed something solid. "A year ago I would have said you and Spencer were cut from the same cloth. He was angry with all of us—especially Brett, Delinda, and Dad. The damage seemed irreparable, but they're all at least talking now. They still have issues, but Brett says family is his first priority, and that has gone a long way to mending bridges."

"Brett definitely drank Delinda's Kool-Aid. I can spend about two minutes with him before I remember why we don't talk anymore."

Someone else might have asked Eric why he called their grandmother by her first name, but Rachelle knew. She was a far cry from being a cookie-baking, kiss-your-boo-boo-when-you're-hurt grandmother. "Alisha has definitely softened Brett. If he hadn't been so busy at his wedding, you would have seen that side of him."

"I grew up with Brett. Trust me, I've seen all the sides of him I can stomach for one lifetime."

"That makes me sad to hear, Eric. I wish you had reached out to us. Why didn't you come to Mom's?"

"Why didn't you want to go to Dad's?"

Rachelle nodded. "I didn't feel like I fit in there." Rachelle finished her wine in one gulp. "If you'd known him, you would have liked Mom's second husband. Mark had a way of making everyone feel special. He would have done anything for us—even Alisha, who practically grew up at our house. When I don't know what to do, I still ask myself what he would have done."

"As long as it's not a matter of honoring someone else's marriage . . ."

Rachelle winced at that jaded, yet accurate, jab at a man she'd been closer to than her biological father and had more respect for, even though he'd been with her mother while she was still married. "Mark was a good man who proved his love for us time and time again. He wasn't perfect, but maybe that's another lesson he came into our lives to teach us. You don't have to be perfect to be able to bring good into the world. I wouldn't be who I am today if I hadn't known him. And every time I think about giving up on someone, I remember that he wouldn't have, and I open my heart to them one more time."

"How's that working out for you?"

His sarcasm stung, but with the memory of Mark fresh in her mind, Rachelle knew what to say. "It brought me to London to see you. It kept me there even though you wouldn't answer my calls. And now we're on a trip together to help a child and actually talking about things that matter. So I'd say it's working out pretty damn well."

"What are you going to do when you realize I'm too fucked-up for you to want in your life?"

Tears sprang back to blur her vision. "What are you going to do when you realize that we're all fucked-up but that we're better off together than apart? You're my brother, Eric. On your best days and on your worst days—that doesn't change. Nor does the fact that I love you."

"You really believe that?"

"I do." She sniffed. "I believe you love me, too, because I'm pretty fucking wonderful once you get to know me."

Eric chuckled. "How could I not love you? You're every bit as crazy as I am."

"I'll accept that, even though it was a bit backhanded." Rachelle wiped away a tear before it fell. "Would you like to hear how Magnus and I met?" She retold everything from standing still on the red carpet to hiding in the alley and brainstorming porno titles with Alisha. Normally she would have avoided the embarrassing parts, but Eric looked genuinely entertained, and it was good to see him smiling. She even told Eric about how she'd chewed Magnus out in private that morning, right down to how she'd poked her finger into his chest. The only part she left off was that Magnus had told her how he'd found Eric. Their connection was still too fragile for that.

When she finished, Eric smiled at Magnus and waved to him but kept his voice low enough so that his comment would only reach Rachelle's ears. "I was concerned for you, but maybe I should be for him. He has no idea who he's dealing with."

"Shh, don't warn him," Rachelle joked.

"Oh, I won't. Something tells me you're exactly what he deserves."

"Yeah, well, here's what *you* deserve." Rachelle playfully slugged him on the arm again, then burst into laughter that was a welcome release of tension. He joined in.

Magnus retook the seat across from them, and Rachelle smiled at him. He might not want more than a one-night stand with her and he'd called her a hot mess, but if it wasn't for him, she still might not know where Eric was. She definitely wouldn't know what Eric was struggling with or have a shot at being part of his support system. Her heart was bursting with gratitude, and it only heightened how intensely she was drawn to him.

For a moment she forgot they were not alone and let herself get lost in the desire in his eyes. It was too easy to remember the taste of him, the feel of his lips parting hers. For anyone beyond middle school, what they'd shared sexually had been tame, but it didn't feel that way. It felt decadent. The memory of his touch had her body warming, and craving more.

His cheeks flushed ever so slightly, making her wonder if he sensed where her thoughts had taken her. On impulse, she winked, and he coughed as if someone had sucker punched him.

He really does want me.

Wow.

I was wrong. I may be that grateful.

Chapter Nine

Holding true to most of his promise to Eric, Magnus arranged for their arrival in Vandorra to be unannounced. They'd landed at the private airfield of one of the smaller royal residences an hour away from Finn's hospital. Both Eric and Rachelle had retired to their rooms shortly after arrival. Rather than confine himself to the home's office, Magnus took his laptop to a table on a balcony that overlooked the lush gardens and pool.

He was in the middle of answering an e-mail regarding a policy change he'd proposed when he felt Rachelle's presence. Rather than turn around to immediately confirm her arrival, he took a moment to appreciate how his senses came alive for her. Being that aware of someone else was a novel experience.

She moved closer, and he could no longer fight the need to see her. He stood and turned to face her. She'd changed into simple white cotton shorts and a blue T-shirt. Free of makeup and shoes, with her hair hanging loose down her shoulders, he thought she'd never looked more beautiful. "Are you busy?" she asked, the hesitation in her voice revealing she didn't know that in that moment he was powerless to deny her anything.

He closed his laptop without taking his eyes off her. "Just finished." She smiled. "It's about tomorrow."

He motioned toward the steps. "Why don't we walk as we talk?" *Otherwise we may end up making love right on this table.* He flipped a switch, and the garden below became illuminated by decorative light posts.

She fell into step beside him. Once on a path in the garden, he offered her his arm. She tucked her hand around it, and the connection felt right. Another woman might have come to him in an outfit designed to turn him on. Or already have started to flirt outrageously with him. Female companionship came easily to a man with a title. Magnus was a healthy male in his prime. He'd accepted more of those appetizing offers than he cared to admit, but he couldn't remember any holding his attention for long. What was the old saying? Familiarity breeds contempt? For Magnus, it bred boredom.

Rachelle holds my attention with ease. Is it because we haven't been together yet? His gut told him she wouldn't be a one-night stand. Once would not be enough to know her the way he wanted to.

"I love this! It's an edible garden, isn't it? Funny, it didn't look it from far away, but these are mostly vegetable plants."

"My mother called it a kitchen garden, even though she didn't cook."

"I've never seen anything like it. I've seen beautiful gardens and I've seen vegetable gardens, but this mixture of colors and textures with the burst of flowers here and there—it's dazzling. I can't wait to see it in the light of day."

Her comment pleased him. "My mother put a great deal of planning into the design. She studied in France as a child and said it gave her an appreciation for all that is beautiful as well as useful. She often said we cheat ourselves when we choose one over the other."

"She sounds like she was an amazing woman."

"She was."

"How did she—I mean, if you don't mind my asking . . ."

"She was born with a weak heart valve. It never held her back, but it did take her from us too early."

"I'm sorry."

"Don't be. She is never far from my thoughts, therefore never far from me." It was something Magnus had once heard his father say about his deceased wife. Magnus had never repeated it, but he realized in that moment that it was also how he felt.

"That's beautiful, and how I feel about my mother's second husband."

"I know."

"You do?"

"Funny thing about small planes—sound carries better than you'd think."

She froze beside him. "You heard my conversation with Eric."

"We all heard it."

She closed her eyes as if remembering all she'd said. "Oh my God. You should have said something."

He shrugged. "What you were saying was too important to be interrupted. Except perhaps the last part about how we met. I don't believe you have my accent down when you do your impression of me."

She opened her eyes, looking pained. "And all your men were there. I'm so sorry."

He tipped her chin upward and ran his thumb lightly over her parted lips. "Stop apologizing all the time. It's not necessary. Do I look upset?"

She shook her head slightly, and desire once again lit her eyes. He much preferred that expression. "But your men—"

"Would not dare to have an opinion regarding a moment from my private life." He pulled her to him, wrapping his arms around her waist. "And I must admit, the story becomes more entertaining each time you retell it." People usually presented themselves in whatever way they thought would be most advantageous to them. Rachelle was refreshingly real.

She smiled then, relaxing against him. "Every time I think I know what to expect from you, you surprise me again."

"I could easily say the same about you. You are many things, Rachelle, but boring is not one of them."

She ran her hand over his chest in a light caress. "You might not say that if you knew me. My life back home was a quiet one. I taught six-year-olds all day, hit the gym most evenings, and spent a lot of time with my family. Before this trip, I hadn't even left the United States."

"And yet you came alone."

"Yes."

He kissed her then but kept it gentle and in control. She was a remarkable woman, and there was no need to rush. When she came to his bed, he wanted it to be completely without fear or regret. She melted against him, and his need for her challenged his decision to go slowly. Reluctantly he broke off the kiss while he still had the strength to.

They stood in each other's arms, breathing heavily. He remembered how boldly he'd spoken to her the first time he'd met her. It hadn't seemed to scare her. Despite being alone with him in a secluded garden in his country, she didn't appear intimidated by him at all. She might not consider herself daring, but she had a natural strength.

A man could make a partner of such a woman.

He frowned at where his thoughts wandered. A night with her—even a prolonged affair—was all he was looking for.

Wasn't it?

He stepped back and offered her his arm again while chastising himself for bringing her to his mother's favorite weekend escape rather than a more appropriate and less personal hotel. Rachelle was the first woman he'd brought here, and he didn't like what that implied.

Rather than taking his arm again, she searched his face. "What's wrong?" Rachelle Westerly surprised him. There were few in his daily orbit who took the time to read him. Her ability to read his disposition was disconcerting.

"Nothing."

She hugged her arms to her stomach. "Now that's an answer I no longer accept. It never mattered how bad things got in my family, they always said things were fine. They weren't, though. If there's a problem, just say it. I'd rather dig in and try to fix something than pretend it's not there."

Okay. "I like you."

"That's the problem?"

His shoulders tensed. He wasn't one who opened up to people easily. "I enjoy your company more than I thought I would."

"You say that like it's a bad thing."

"It is for me. If I have any intention beyond bedding you, I'm doing this wrong. You're currently a joke in the media. If it gets out that I've also made you my lover, it'll be another hit to your reputation, even though substantial damage has been done already."

"Wow, okay, remember when I asked for honesty? Feel free to deliver it in a way that's less of a kick to the groin."

Her turn of phrase amused, but the situation did not. "I care about your public image."

"Because?"

He frowned again. *I should have just kept kissing her. What am I doing here?* "Because I don't want to see you hurt by your affiliation with me."

She smiled then. "You're concerned about me. Despite all that tough talk, you're a worrier, just like me."

"We could not be less alike."

She lowered her lashes, then gazed up at him from beneath them. "You're a big softie, aren't you?"

"No."

"You don't have to be embarrassed about it. It's actually really sexy."

"Really?" That piqued his interest.

"Definitely. I'll admit that when I first met you, I thought you were attractive. I mean, all the 'I will have you' stuff was sexy, but I would never have slept with that man."

"No?"

"No, all he cared about was himself. Then you told me about Finn, and I saw how hard you fought to help my brother, and I thought, *Now there's a real man.*" She went up on her tiptoes and brushed her lips across his.

Nothing had prepared him for the tailspin Rachelle could send him in with one brief kiss that was both sweet and bold—just like she was. He groaned and gave himself over to the pleasure of her touch, of the way his body burned for hers.

What started gentle became more frenzied as the kiss deepened. She arched against him and moved back and forth against his bulging cock in an intimate, full-body caress. He slid one hand up beneath the back of her shirt, across her bare back, then down to cup her delicious ass. They ground against each other, and Magnus wanted nothing more than to free his cock right there in the garden and bury it deep inside her.

Not since his teenage years had he felt close to coming from foreplay alone. He needed to know that she was just as ready. He kissed his way down her neck and shifted her sideways just enough so he could slide a hand down the front of her shorts. With ease that came from experience, he slid beneath her panties as well and settled his thumb on her clit while his middle finger thrust into her wet sex. She gasped and gripped his shoulders tighter. He withdrew his finger, then thrust it in again, deeper. Withdrew it and went deeper still. "Oh yes," she whispered. "God, yes."

He took her mouth with his again, claiming her there as well. She met his passion with a hunger of her own that fanned the wildness in him. When her hands rubbed over his cock, he fought not to explode.

He increased the rhythm of his thumb across her clit until she was writhing and moaning against him. She was so wet, so ready for his taking, but he held himself back.

Soon.

This time he wanted her to be the one out of control. He pushed her shirt up and unclipped her bra, freeing those pert breasts for his mouth. When he circled one of her nipples with his tongue, she jutted against his fingers. Some women could orgasm from nipple play alone. He loved the idea that soon he would know all her pleasure points and how to use each to drive her wild.

He used his teeth to gently tug on her nipple while thrusting a second finger into her. She clenched around his fingers and cried out. When she shuddered and sagged in his arms, he withdrew his hand and brought it to his mouth. While she watched, he tasted her juices.

She watched and licked her bottom lip. He held her with one arm while using his other hand to unbutton his trousers. She took his lead and eagerly freed him, wrapping one hand around his cock while cupping his balls with her other hand.

He waited, and groaned with pleasure when she dropped to her knees and took him deeply in her mouth. God, her mouth was perfection. He dug his hands into her hair and watched her lave him with her tongue before taking him deeply again.

He was a man who enjoyed sex, but this was the first time he'd felt consumed by it. The things she did with her fingers and her tongue erased all ability to think from him. He wasn't used to feeling out of control, but had they stopped then, he surely would have died.

Too soon, an orgasm surged. He warned her gently, and she used her hands to finish him. As he slowly came back to earth, he knew he'd never forget the sight of her still on her knees before him. He shook himself off, adjusted his clothing, then helped her to her feet and pulled her into his arms.

For some time they simply stood there, holding each other. He hadn't meant to take it as far as it had gone, but it had confirmed what he'd already suspected—the more he had of her, the more he wanted her, and that meant that his plan required some adjusting. "Tomorrow, after we visit the hospital, I'll check you in to a hotel."

◆ ◆ ◆

They weren't the words any woman would welcome after what they'd shared. Rachelle stiffened in his arms. "That won't be necessary. I'm sure we'll be flying back to London."

"Not if Eric checks in to the clinic here."

Oh, shit. I forgot about that. "Either way, I am perfectly capable of making a reservation on my own." *What kind of sister am I? Where's my brain?* She remembered the intense orgasm that had rocked through her only moments before and shook her head in disgust.

"You're in my country and therefore you're my responsibility."

"I don't want to be anyone's *responsibility*." She attempted to pull away from him, but his hold on her tightened.

With a hand firmly on each of her hips, he said, "Why fight me, little Rachelle, when we both know you want to be mine?"

Her body clenched and clamored for just that, even as her mind rejected the idea. "What an outdated and sexist thing to say to a woman."

His hands slid around her waist, cupped her ass, and pulled her flush against him. "Then I definitely shouldn't say how beautiful you looked with your mouth wrapped around my cock." She shoved at his chest and would have torn herself away from him if his grip was not so strong. "Save your outrage, for I equally love the idea of burying my face between those thighs of yours. And I will taste you fully—tonight. We will make love until we fall asleep in each other's arms; then I will wake you with my tongue. Would you like that? Would you like to be fucked so completely that your favorite place will be on your knees for me?"

That's so wrong.

And so delicious-sounding.

His hand had already brought her more pleasure than half the men she'd had sex with. What would the full package be capable of? Still, his arrogance was over-the-top. She bit her lip as hunger surged within her and tried to remember why not taking things further with him was probably the sanest choice. Controlling men were sexy in movies and books, but Rachelle had come to London to find herself, not hand her independence over to a man. Not even a prince. "And what will *your* favorite place be?" *Above me?*

A lusty smile curved his lips. "Wherever brings you the most pleasure."

Holy shit.

The sound of a male voice broke through the silence of the night. "Excuse me, Your Royal Highness, but Mr. Westerly is looking for his sister."

Magnus released Rachelle slowly and turned to address a member of his royal guard, who remained out of view. "Tell him we'll meet him in the drawing room shortly."

"As you wish."

Blushing deeply, Rachelle adjusted her clothing and was relieved to discover it was mostly in place. She clipped her bra quickly and smoothed her hair down with shaking hands. She wasn't ready to face her brother.

Magnus tucked his shirt back into his trousers. "There's time to freshen up before seeing Eric."

How does he always seem to know what I'm thinking? "I don't want to look like I just—I don't want him to think we—"

Magnus kissed her lips gently. "That is why tomorrow you will be in a hotel." He groaned. "And why I can wait a little longer to have you. I told myself I would go slowly."

"The hotel is a good idea." She could hardly breathe as her body hummed for him again. *The heart wants what the heart wants, I guess. Only this isn't about love—it's sex, pure and simple. No, not pure or simple. This sex is carnal and complicated.* "Slower would be better." *Before I become someone I don't respect. All of this can wait until I know Eric is safe.*

Even as his eyes burned with desire for her, he nodded. "Then come. Let's go inside." As they walked together, he asked, "Did you have a question about tomorrow?"

"I did." Although it felt like a lifetime ago that she'd gone in search of him to ask. "I know there isn't much time, but the more I thought about our visit to the hospital tomorrow, the more I thought we should bring something with us."

"No clowns."

Rachelle laughed at his joke. "That's a given. No, what I mean is something to hand out to the children—especially if Eric is only willing to meet Finn. There will be a lot of disappointed children, and a stuffed Water Bear Man might appease them somewhat. Also, has anyone thought about his costume? Will he be wearing it during the visit? If you want him to, you may need to have someone fly it over. Since he's not actually a superhero, I doubt he travels with it."

"I did have the costume sent with some of his things, but I like the idea of having something for each of the children. They weren't exactly happy with my first visit."

Surprised, she stopped. She'd seen the public's reaction. It was difficult to imagine that children in his own country wouldn't also hero-worship him. "Tell me."

He stopped and pocketed his hands. The tension in his features made him look much harsher than she'd come to view him. "I didn't know some of them were afraid of clowns. They started screaming and making a production like a bunch of—"

"Children."

A corner of his mouth curved upward. "I settled them down, but it wasn't pleasant."

Oh no. He wouldn't have . . . he didn't . . . "You didn't yell at them, did you?"

"It was the only way to be heard."

"At a hospital for sick children?" He looked uncomfortable enough with the topic that she almost felt bad for chastising him. Almost.

He rocked back onto his heels. "My father usually handles such things, but he hasn't been feeling well."

"Oh no. I'm so sorry. Is it serious?"

"The doctor says everything at his age is serious. Lately, though, he tires easily, and it is more difficult to get him out of bed each day."

"Will he be there tomorrow?"

"There are too many unpredictable elements for me to want him there. If it goes well, he'll be pleased to hear about it. If it is a repeat of my first visit, I'll break it to him on a day when he looks able to handle the news."

There was a vulnerability about Magnus that was unexpected when glimpsed. Rachelle took his hand in hers. "Tomorrow will go well. I'm good with children. Just follow my lead."

He looked down at her hand around his and linked his fingers with hers. "So, you have a way with little brats?"

Although he was joking, she corrected him. "I doubt there is a brat in that place—just a lot of scared children who probably love you already and would show you if you let them see the softer side of you."

"I don't have a softer side."

Rather than take him at his word, she reviewed the many things he'd said to her, then snapped her fingers when the answer came to her. "Yes, you do. You have your mother in you, and she's always with you.

I bet when your father isn't sure how to act, he thinks of her. Tomorrow, try it and see if it changes how you see those children."

His hand tightened on hers. "I'm glad I was wrong about you being a prostitute."

Rachelle burst out laughing at that, and he joined in. "What am I going to do with you?"

He leaned down beside her ear and whispered a few suggestions that left her breathless and blushing. He gave her one last lingering kiss, then guided her to a washroom. "The drawing room is down that hall and to the left. I'll make a call about the stuffed water bears and meet you there," he said huskily before turning and leaving her.

A few minutes later, Rachelle stood before a fireplace in a turquoise-and-gold room and studied the painting of a king seated next to a queen with a young child between them. If not for the formality of their gold-embroidered attire, they might have been any family. The child, no older than three, faced forward as if taking on the world already. The king's attention, in contrast, was on the beautiful woman at his side, who was looking down at her child, but with a smile on her face as if she'd just shared a private joke with her husband. It was a loving family, and it made Rachelle wonder what had hurt the young boy in the painting enough that he'd hardened his heart. The loss of his mother? She wished she knew, because when she looked at the painting, she saw the Magnus she was truly drawn to. Not for a night, but on a deeper level that was as unsettling as it was exciting.

"Sorry," Eric said as he entered the room. "I had to take a call from my publicist. He didn't believe me at first, and then I regretted telling him. I threatened to fire him if he tells the press about tomorrow. Convincing him I meant it was what took so long."

Rachelle turned to face her brother. "You really don't do any appearances?"

"I really don't."

"You may find you like them."

"Pardon the interruption," a male member of the house staff said from the doorway. "Prince Magnus sends his apologies, but something urgent has come up. He will meet you for breakfast at eight. He requests you both be ready to leave for the hospital directly afterward."

Once they were alone again, Eric said, "I was looking for you earlier. Phillip said you were out for a walk with Mr. Call Me Your Highness. I don't know what I think of that guy."

"He's not so bad once you get to know him."

Eric's eyes flew to hers. "How well do *you* know him?"

Rachelle's cheeks warmed, but she held his gaze. "I met him at your premiere, just like I told you."

"I don't like the way he looks at you."

Really? Because I'm quickly becoming addicted to how I feel every time he does. "Are you applying for the role of overprotective brother?"

Eric went to stand beside her and looked up at the portrait above the fireplace. "He's hiding something. I don't know what. I'll feel better after tomorrow when we meet this kid he keeps talking about. If he even exists."

"Of course he does. Why would Magnus make something like that up?"

"It got me here. And you. People have done sicker things for less."

Who has Eric been spending time with? "Well, we'll know tomorrow, I guess."

Eric ran his hand through his hair. "I don't know if I can do it."

"You have to. You promised."

"As if that means anything."

Rachelle shook her head. "It does to me. And if it doesn't to you, then you need to take a good, long look in the mirror. People can do whatever they want to us, but they only change us if we let them. Maybe you've known some horrible people, but you're choosing to become like them."

"You don't know what I've seen."

True. I don't. And I can't admit to what I know. "Okay, then, tell me, are you a good actor?"

"As a water bear?"

"No, I don't mean in the movies you make, I mean in your heart. Mom says you wanted to be taken seriously as an actor when you first started out."

"I did."

"So, you're talented?"

"I used to think so."

"When you were your best onstage, what was it like?"

Eric sighed and walked away to look out the window as if he needed to spend a moment back in that time before he could describe it. "Like nothing else. I'd spend weeks, sometimes months, studying a character. Then practice my lines until I could say them in my sleep. When I took the stage on opening night, it was magic. For a short time, I wasn't me. I was Hamlet, Prospero, Valjean. So I suppose you could say that me at my best is someone else."

I hope one day you realize how untrue that is, but for now, maybe believing that can help you. "Then tomorrow, imagine the hospital is a stage, and become a character who brings joy to those children. I'll let you in on the secret to getting children to like you—simply like them. That's it. It's easy. You can fool them about a lot of things, but they know who doesn't like them. It's like a self-preservation sixth sense."

"That might work. Thanks." He looked toward the door of the drawing room. "It'll be interesting to see what the kids think of your prince."

"I'm sure they love him," she said in a positive tone, even though she had no idea how they saw him. She hoped his first visit hadn't been quite as bad as he'd described it, but so far Magnus had been brutally honest about everything else. She believed that he'd brought a clown and raised his voice in frustration, yet somehow that had led him to promising one of them that he'd deliver the impossible.

Magnus had gone to a lot of trouble to fulfill one child's wish. That didn't sound like a man who hated children.

But how well do I really know him? Her instincts told her he had a good heart, but she'd let the children's reactions to him prove her right or wrong.

Yes, tomorrow will be interesting.

Chapter Ten

The next morning at the hospital, Rachelle walked into the children's wing flanked by Magnus and Eric. Her stomach did a nervous flip. So far, the day had all the elements of a first day at school. Eric was defiantly refusing to wear his costume, stating that football players did not visit in their gear. Magnus had had his men bring the costume and was doing a poor job of concealing his disgust with Eric's decision. The two were in a pissing contest of royal proportion. Rachelle was ready to tell them both to grow up and remember that the visit was for actual children.

"Your Royal Highness, we are so pleased to have you with us again," the hospital administrator said—tall, thin, and stern-looking until she smiled. "I heard you have brought a stuffed animal for every child. Would you like us to distribute them, or will you be doing so?"

"We will, right, Magnus?" Rachelle asked.

The administrator's mouth rounded in surprise before she composed herself like lightning.

Magnus smiled at the flustered woman and spoke as if Rachelle hadn't. "Since Mr. Westerly is not encumbered by his costume, I'm sure he would like to do the honors himself."

Eric growled.

"It's a pleasure to have you here, Mr. Westerly. The children have talked about little else since we made the announcement this morning." With a bow of her head, the administrator added, "Please consider accompanying Mr. Westerly, Your Royal Highness. There will be a great number of children who will be disappointed if you don't. Tinsley in room five plans to propose to you."

"Propose?" Magnus's head snapped back.

"She's three," the administrator said with a smile. "And she believes you also have a palace at Disney. It's where she dreams of going when she feels better."

Magnus's expression sobered. "Will that be soon?"

"She's very ill, but we see miracles here every day." The woman looked at Eric. "Your presence is surely one of those. I did not think even our prince could convince you." As if realizing what she'd said, she quickly added, "No offense, Your Royal Highness."

"None taken," Magnus said. "It was not an easy feat."

The woman turned and greeted Rachelle. "And you are?"

Rachelle opened her mouth to answer and then didn't know how best to refer to herself. Eric's sister? Or simply Rachelle, the woman who had almost had sex with a prince in his garden last night? *I could probably leave that last part off.*

Magnus stepped forward and placed his hand possessively on Rachelle's back. "Miss Westerly is Eric's sister and a friend of mine."

"It's a pleasure to have you, Miss Westerly." She looked as if she wanted to ask about Rachelle, but didn't. "Why don't we stop in and see Finn first? I've never seen him so excited."

She led the way into the room of a young boy. Though thin and frail-looking, he was smiling. His smile faded somewhat when his gaze settled on Eric. "You're Water Bear Man?"

"I am," Eric said as he approached the boy's bed.

"Where's your suit?" Finn asked.

His mother instantly jumped in to explain how excited Finn was to meet his hero regardless of what he wore. It broke Rachelle's heart that her brother had disappointed the boy.

"No," Magnus said, "let Finn speak his mind. I have asked myself the same question."

"I heard you wanted to meet me, Finn. I didn't think you really wanted to have a conversation with a man in a spandex costume." Rachelle wanted to strangle Eric when he added, "You do know that Water Bear Man isn't real."

The room fell silent as everyone waited for Finn's response. His young chin rose. "I know he's not real, but I like him. He's strong and brave and he makes me laugh. I don't care if he's a lie. I tell my mother medicine tastes good even when it doesn't, so she won't cry. Maybe you could lie just a little to make me feel better."

Tears filled Rachelle's eyes, and she didn't know what she would do if Eric refused that brave little boy. She felt Magnus's hand tense on her back and glanced up at him. His expression was tightly controlled, but fury lurked in his eyes.

With all the charm of the star he was, Eric smiled at the boy. "So if I put my costume on and come back in, we can pretend this didn't happen?"

Finn reminded Rachelle of a young Magnus when he looked directly at Eric and said, "Only if you visit the other kids, too. I don't want to be the only one who meets him."

"You represent Vandorra well, Finn," Magnus said, and a huge smile spread across Finn's face.

"Did you hear that, Dad?" Finn turned to speak to the burly man beside his bed.

"I did." He leaned forward and ruffled his son's hair.

"Dad, tell Prince Magnus what you said about him."

The man looked uncomfortable before his prince.

Magnus graciously said, "I'm sure it was good."

Finn sat up straighter. "He said you're his hero because you fight for what we need. He used other words, but I can't say them because my mom's here."

Magnus laughed. "That's a smart choice."

Rachelle loved the admiration she saw in Finn's eyes as he spoke to Magnus. Eric excused himself from the room, taking a bag from one of the royal guards as he went.

"Is she your girlfriend?" Finn motioned toward Rachelle.

"Yes," Magnus said, then winked down at Rachelle. Even though Rachelle knew it was all a show for Finn, her heart was thudding wildly in her chest.

"She's pretty," Finn said.

"I think so." Magnus took a seat beside the boy's bed. He leaned in and spoke in a conspiratorial voice. "But I have to be careful with her, because when she gets riled up, she puts me in my place."

Finn's eyes widened. "How does she do that?"

Magnus wagged a finger and mimicked a woman's voice. "Magnus, don't you know better than that?" His voice returned to normal. "She calls me Magnus even though I'll probably have to throw her in jail for not showing proper respect."

"Would you really do that?" Finn asked with a gasp.

Magnus turned and gave Rachelle a long look, as if he was seriously considering the possibility. "It would be very difficult to date her if she were in jail, so I probably won't."

"What a relief," Rachelle joked as she fanned her face with one hand.

"Is there someone in here who wanted to meet me?" Water Bear Man, a.k.a. Eric, in a gray spandex suit and cape, boomed from the doorway. The room vibrated with energy, as if an actual superhero had entered.

Finn waved to him. "I did."

As Eric approached, he took up more of the room, and his acting was so convincing that it was easy to forget that just moments ago he hadn't wanted to do this. *He really is talented.* Eric made Finn laugh with a story of being late because he'd overshot Vandorra and accidentally ended up in Italy. With his chest puffed up and his voice dramatically deep, Eric announced that it's a crime to visit Italy without having a meatball. And no one could have a meatball without pasta. And who could have pasta without a loaf of bread? He gave his flat abs a pat, claiming that he'd had to fly around the planet three times to burn off all those calories.

Magnus gave up his seat to Eric and returned to Rachelle's side. Finn laughed at everything his hero said.

Finn's father and mother came over and thanked Magnus. Both had tears in their eyes. The father said, "Your Royal Highness, you don't know how much this means to my family. Finn has been strong for so long, but he was losing his fight. You gave him someone to believe in again."

"Water Bear Man," Magnus said.

Finn's mother touched her husband's arm. "No, you. We've always told him that your father feels like our father. He watches over us. We told him that one day you will do the same. To children, something like that can be difficult to imagine, but you've shown him that he's important to you. He'll carry that gift with him for the rest of his life. As will we."

Magnus shook both of their hands as if they were friends of his, and Rachelle fell a little in love with him as he did. Here was the strong boy in the painting, the man who'd offered to save her when he'd thought she was trapped in an immoral profession. This man would one day be an amazing king.

Eric looked over at Rachelle, and there was an expression of humility in his eyes. It was as if he hadn't understood until just then that only he saw himself as a pathetic joke. Spandex, cape, and all, he was bringing real joy to a sick child. He handed Finn a stuffed water bear, placed his hands on his hips, and said, "Finn of Vandorra, I want very much to meet the children of this place, but I require a guide. Are you up to the task?"

Finn looked to his parents for permission, who looked to the nurse beside them. She nodded and said he could wheel his IV with him.

"This is going to be great," Finn announced, "but I should put on some pants."

Eric raised a stuffed water bear in the air and boomed, "Yes, Finn of Vandorra, put on some pants, and we shall tour this place and leave mini-mes all over this land."

Finn waved for the nurses to pull his IV, then scrambled off the bed, gathered his clothing, and headed into the bathroom of his room. While he was in there, Rachelle took the opportunity to speak to Eric. "His family is so happy you're here. You've touched their lives."

Eric gave her a playful slug to the arm. "I wouldn't be here at all if it weren't for you. Thank you."

Magnus joined them. "The suit does make a difference."

Eric's eyes narrowed, but the anger from earlier was gone. When Finn entered the room again, Eric said, "Prince Magnus, that is hilarious. You should tell jokes to all the children. Finn, ask your prince to tell you a joke. He's so funny."

Finn stepped up and looked back and forth between his two heroes. "Do you know any jokes?"

Magnus looked stumped, then uncomfortable. Rachelle leaned toward Magnus and said, "Knock, knock."

"Who's there?" Magnus asked.

"Orange."

"Orange who?"

"Knock, knock."

"Who's there?" Magnus asked again.

"Orange."

"Orange who?"

"Knock, knock."

"Who's there?"

"Orange."

"Orange who?"

"Orange you glad we're off to meet another child instead of telling knock-knock jokes all day?"

Everyone laughed—even Eric and Magnus. For a moment they were on the same side.

Finn led the way, organizing the support staff, who were carrying boxes of stuffed animals. He shared his visitation route with the intensity of a child who had spent considerable time dreaming of exactly how the day would go. Eric walked at his side, waving to all the children while staying true to his superhero character.

Magnus remained at Rachelle's side, leaving her only to greet each child. They were as excited to meet him as they were Water Bear Man, and Rachelle loved watching Magnus become more and more comfortable with them. His humor was dry, but the children laughed, and their parents gushed their gratitude.

One mother said she traveled several hours each day because she could not afford to stay in the nearby hotels anymore. Magnus called the hospital's administrator over and asked if she knew of a successful program for providing short-term housing at hospitals. She said she did, but so far, she had not made headway getting the funds to maintain it. Magnus merely nodded, but that seemed promising enough for the administrator to look pleased. *His people trust him to care about them. Where do you see that in leaders anymore?*

The last room they visited held Tinsley, still bald from treatments, who left her bed as soon as Magnus entered the room and took his hand. Despite the dark circles beneath her sparkling blue eyes, she turned her eyes adoringly up at Magnus. "I have waited my whole life for you," she said so seriously that Rachelle swallowed the laugh she'd almost let out.

Magnus sat in the chair so he was at her eye level. "That's an awfully long time."

"Three years," Tinsley said.

The girl's parents stood off to one side, smiling. It was impossible not to. The little girl was absolutely adorable.

"I have good news and bad news for you," Magnus said in a serious tone.

The little girl's bottom lip jutted out in a pout. "No bad news."

"Okay, then I have good news and better news."

Tinsley smiled and clapped. "Good news."

"There are castles at Disney, but none that are mine, so there is no need to marry me."

The little girl's smile faded; then she looked at him with hope in her eyes. "Better news?"

"If it's okay with your parents, I will send you to the Disney park of your choice as soon as you are healthy enough to go. So you'd better get healthy soon. Mickey Mouse is waiting to meet you."

"Disney!" Tinsley cried out, and threw her arms around Magnus. Her parents came over to thank him. He looked up, and the smile he gave Rachelle stole another piece of her heart.

Eric chuckled from the doorway. "Nothing I could say will top that."

◆ ◆ ◆

Magnus said goodbye to Tinsley one last time and walked out of her room with Rachelle and Eric. He caught his reflection in a glass window and realized he was smiling. How had something that had been such a miserable experience just a few days ago become enjoyable?

Rachelle.

He could easily picture her by his side at other events. Her simple light-blue slacks and cream blouse would not gain the front page of a fashion magazine, but his people didn't need a fashion role model. They needed someone who would care about them, someone who would raise the next generation of his family with the same moral integrity his mother had.

For the first time in his life, Magnus had met a woman he could imagine as queen of Vandorra. She would be a pleasure to bed, she liked children, and she'd said she was at a crossroads in her life. It was at least worth further consideration.

"What are you thinking?" Rachelle asked softly, and Magnus realized he'd been staring at her with a big smile on his face.

Neither of them was ready for where his thoughts had wandered, so he shared a passing idea from earlier. "I was imagining you in a nurse's uniform, and then in half the uniform, and then in nothing."

She blushed, then swatted his arm. "Not here. Not with kids around."

Her words brought a fleeting image of her saying that to him because their own children were in a nearby room. He'd enjoy quietly convincing her that pleasure was worth the risk of waking them.

The ease with which he could picture Rachelle in his life was disconcerting. With his father's failing health, it was time to start thinking about continuing the royal line. Finding the proper wife and bearing heirs was a fundamental responsibility that could no longer be brushed aside. Despite the public image bashing Rachelle had taken, he was confident his people would embrace her—as long as he introduced her to them properly. The visit to the hospital, even though it was not covered by the press, would be spoken about and would go a long way in winning their approval.

Although there was still a lot to learn about Rachelle, he trusted his instincts in business, and a royal marriage was part business. Anyone who made a vow to him also made a vow to his people. She would have to love them as he did. Not every woman was capable of such devotion.

Rachelle's unwavering support of her brother demonstrated loyalty and commitment. The more he thought about it, the more he liked the idea of exploring this possibility more intimately.

While Rachelle was temporarily occupied by one of the hospital's staff, Eric walked over to speak to Magnus. He was still dressed in his formfitting suit. "Finn said that was the last one. I'd hire that kid when he's older. He's more organized than half the people I employ."

From across the hall, Finn waved before disappearing into his room. He'd looked tired but happy. "You gave the children a memory they will treasure for a long time, and for that I am in your debt." Magnus took out a card and handed it to Eric. "Now do something for yourself. The clinic is attached to this hospital. Go down to the service elevator, and take a left. Dr. Jonas Welsh is waiting to meet you. He will ensure everything is handled discreetly. If a cover story is required for your time there, we can say you are starting a children's foundation that was inspired by your visit today."

Eric pocketed the card. "He's there now?" He glanced over at Rachelle.

Magnus could have avoided the awkward truth, but he always had been a charge-forward-into-battle kind of man. "She knows."

Anger flared in Eric's eyes.

In explanation rather than justification, Magnus added, "She deserved the truth. Your sister's loyalty to you is a gift, not a burden."

Eric rubbed his hands over his face. "I didn't want her to worry."

"She was already worried, now let her be there for you."

"I don't understand why you're doing this. Nobody does something for nothing. What did you say yesterday? You want to help me so Finn and Rachelle won't be hurt. Well, Finn has met me now, so all that's left is Rachelle. Are you hoping that she'll stay here if I do?"

"She will stay, regardless."

"You are one cocky bastard."

"Let's not start slinging insults—I am in a good mood."

Eric's eyes narrowed. "I've gotten to a place where I don't care about much, but I care about Rachelle. If you hurt her—"

"I know—you'll kill me. You want to scare me? Go get your shit together; then come for me. Right now you're too easy a target."

"Fuck you."

"You disappoint me, Eric." Magnus straightened to his full height. "Life is full of allies and enemies. Learn to recognize the difference."

"You're my ally?"

"I'm not your enemy." Magnus sighed. "And right now you're more at risk of hurting your sister than I am. She's here because she loves you. You can piss on that or you can be grateful that you have someone like her in your life. It's your choice."

Eric frowned and folded his arms across his chest. He still looked conflicted when Rachelle rejoined them.

Unaware of the conversation's direction, Rachelle was all smiles. "I don't know about the two of you, but I'm ready to call today a success. Now we're off to meet King Tadeas. What a day, huh, Eric?" When neither Magnus nor Eric smiled, she cocked her head to one side, and her forehead furrowed. "What did I miss?"

"I'm not going with you to meet the king," Eric said.

"Why not?" Rachelle asked, her voice rising with concern.

The awkwardness of his movements looked out of place for a man in a superhero suit. "I have an appointment to keep."

"Do you want me to come with you?"

He smiled. "No, but I do want you in my life. I need to sort a few things out, but I'm glad you're here."

Tears filled Rachelle's eyes. "Me too."

Eric started to walk away.

Magnus called out, "Eric."

He stopped and turned.

Magnus waved for one of his men to bring him the bag containing his regular clothing. "You may want those."

Eric looked down, as if realizing only then that he was still in his spandex costume. He took the bag from the royal guard. "Good thinking, Your Imperial Highness."

Magnus shook his head, but a smile pulled at his lips.

Once he and Rachelle were alone again, she laid her hand on his arm. "You told him."

"I did."

She went up on her tiptoes and kissed him on the cheek. "Thank you."

His heart started a wild dance in his chest. Magnus had done many things during his lifetime he was proud of, but it had never felt this good. He chided himself for caring so much about one woman's opinion of him.

She'd called the day a success. Yesterday, his agreement would have hinged on whether it ended with him in her bed or not. There was still a very good chance that it would, but for now, having her by his side was enough. "Come, my father is waiting to meet us."

Chapter Eleven

Rachelle was all eyes as she and Magnus got out of a SUV in a large garage outside the walled area of a palace. The cars in it ranged from priceless to modest. "This is an odd entrance."

"Follow me," Magnus said, guiding her to the back of the garage. He pressed in a code on a pad beside an elevator door.

It was like something out of a spy movie. "It's a secret passage, isn't it? I knew this palace would be amazing."

Magnus smiled at her with indulgence. "Not everyone is excited by an elevator."

The doors of the elevator opened, but Rachelle paused before stepping inside. "My mother believed that money was what tore her marriage apart and was the root of all problems in our family."

"Do you?" He pushed a button to keep the door open.

"I used to. I've decided wealth doesn't change someone's core, just like getting drunk doesn't make a nice person into an asshole. But they both amplify certain characteristics."

"I can see that."

"Thank you for helping Eric. Some people would look at his life and think he has no right to be unhappy, but I sensed profound sadness when he came to Brett's wedding. It scared me, because I didn't know how to reach him."

Magnus placed his hand on her lower back and ushered her inside the elevator. "Well, he's in the right place now to get help. I hope he chooses to."

"Me too." The elevator opened to a long, well-lit hallway. "What is this place?"

"You could call it a secret passage, but it's not as secret as it is secure. Had we come through the front gate, we would have been met with photographers, and you would once again have been in the media."

"Linked to you." Rachelle knew she wasn't a trophy date, but it was a little insulting to be sneaked in a back door. "I understand."

Magnus swung her to face him, backed her against the wall, and leaned in. "This is my preferred way to enter the palace, because I don't like every move I make to be on display, but if you wish, I will walk out the front door with you on my arm."

His breath warmed her cheek. The desire in his eyes made her wish they were alone. It might be easy for him to forget the guard who had walked ahead of them or the one who trailed behind, but they were not as invisible to Rachelle. Still, his mouth was painfully close to hers. The temptation to throw her arms around his neck and pull his mouth to hers was nearly irresistible. She croaked, "That won't be necessary."

He leaned closer until his lips hovered just above hers. "If you're having any doubt about how I feel about you, I'll gladly spend the night showing you. And if you still aren't sure, I'll show you again in the morning."

Rachelle's breath caught in her throat. A thousand witty responses would likely come to her later, but just then she couldn't think of anything beyond how much she wanted to say yes to him—to every wicked fantasy being close to him fired in her. She bit her bottom lip, and her eyes began to close.

He gave her a swift, deep kiss as if they were already lovers, then growled, "Why did I bring you here first?"

"You said your father wanted to meet me."

"Oh yes. Originally I planned to introduce Eric to him."

"Is your father a fan?"

Magnus kissed her forehead, then stepped back and took her hand in his. "My father is slowly withdrawing from everyone. I try to bring new people to meet him to force him to leave his bed."

"I'm so sorry. That can't be easy. How old is he?"

"Eighty. I came late to my parents. For a while the doctors believed my mother couldn't conceive, but then I arrived."

"What would have happened had you not?"

"My uncle, Davot, is next in line."

"Wow, so if you don't have children, his family will rule Vandorra?"

"Yes. Or if anything happens to me."

"Happens to you?"

"History is full of ill-fated princes."

"Are you saying your own family would kill you for the crown?"

He looked as if he might say more on the subject, but did not. "How did we get onto such a morbid topic?" They stepped into the second elevator. "When we enter the main hall, I will show you to a sitting room. My father said he is up to receiving guests, but I will confirm that before taking you in to meet him. I hope you understand."

"Of course."

◆ ◆ ◆

As they rode upward, Magnus marveled at the calm of the woman by his side. She was neither preening herself nor fidgeting nervously, as many did. Not that he had brought a woman home in such a manner before, but he had certainly introduced women to his father in the past. Even though Rachelle had been raised modestly, it was obvious that she was accustomed to meeting people of influence, because she was more impressed by the idea of a secret passage than his title.

When the doors of the elevator opened, Magnus nearly stumbled. The sight of his father, perfectly groomed and dressed in one of his finest suits, took him by surprise. "Father."

The king grinned. "Magnus, you're late." He gave Magnus a back-thumping hug completely out of character for his formal father.

"My apologies, Father. The children's hospital took longer than I anticipated."

His father looked Rachelle over. "You must be Rachelle Westerly."

Looking unsure of how to greet him, Rachelle stepped forward. "Yes, Your Highness, uh, Majes—"

"You may call me Tadeas, at least while we're not in public. Then Your Majesty will do."

"That's very kind of you." Rachelle held out her hand to shake his.

Normally, the king held to the etiquette of not touching unless he initiated the contact, but he seemed to understand that Rachelle meant no offense. He clasped his hands around hers in a warm handshake. "An American rose, if ever I've met one. Just stunning. And a schoolteacher, too. I've always said intelligence is important in a woman."

Magnus knew before she opened her mouth that Rachelle could not let that comment slide. "One might argue that intelligence is as important as tact."

The king laughed heartily and released her hand. "A woman of spirit. I like her. As did everyone at the hospital."

Magnus was relieved to see his father up and showing interest in something. "The report traveled fast," Magnus said lightly.

"I'm still the king. I should know everything."

"Indeed."

"I've arranged for lunch to be served on the lawn overlooking the pond. The weather is perfect for enjoying the outdoors, wouldn't you say?"

"I suppose," Magnus said slowly. He and his father normally dined in the smaller formal dining room when alone and the larger one when they entertained, although it had been a long time since his father had welcomed guests to the palace. *Has he been double-dipping in his medication?*

As they made their way through the palace toward the door that would lead to the pond, Magnus watched his father closely, trying to determine the source of his unusually good mood. "Have you seen the doctor, Father? You seem different today." Perhaps he'd been put on an antidepressant?

"No. No doctor necessary. I feel too good to see one."

"I'm happy to hear that, Father." Even though it was disconcerting to see a sudden, dramatic change in his father's demeanor. Was this mania?

Tadeas stopped and addressed Rachelle. "Your brother was unable to come today?"

"He had an important meeting he couldn't put off."

Tadeas arched an eyebrow at his son. "That's disappointing."

They arrived at a table set for five. "Father, are you expecting someone else?" Once his father sat, Magnus held out a chair for Rachelle, then took his own seat.

"I am," his father said, but didn't elaborate. He turned his attention once more to Rachelle. "You have your grandmother's eyes."

"You know my grandmother?" Rachelle asked.

"We've met," his father said. "Truly lovely woman."

Magnus was intrigued. He and his father spoke about nearly everything. "I don't remember you ever mentioning her. How long ago was that, Father?"

"Yesterday."

Rachelle gurgled, then choked on the water she was sipping. "Yesterday? You met my grandmother yesterday?"

His father smiled. "She extended an invitation to join her for tea. Imagine, a woman bold enough to summon a king."

"That sounds like Delinda," Rachelle said with a groan.

"She has a passion for life that is invigorating, and a presence that makes a man sit up straighter. I did not think I could feel anything for a woman after your mother, Magnus. She took my heart with her when she died. But I feel twenty years younger today. The sun is shining brighter. Food tastes better. I have a lot to live for, Magnus, and it took meeting Delinda Westerly to remind me of that."

Magnus watched the blood drain from Rachelle's face but felt no sympathy for her. Would her story be that she hadn't known her grandmother was in Vandorra? He didn't believe in coincidences. What did Delinda Westerly want with his father? Had she sent her granddaughter as a distraction? His temper rose, but he kept his expression carefully blank.

Is my cousin coming for the crown again? If so, how would Rachelle and Delinda Westerly play into such a scheme?

Oh, my little Rachelle, this changes everything.

Chapter Twelve

Rachelle tried to remain calm as she digested the news that her grandmother was in Vandorra. Delinda didn't do anything without an agenda. *She obviously knows I'm here. Why would she meet with King Tadeas?* "Did she say why she's in Vandorra?"

When Magnus had described his father, Rachelle had imagined a frail, small man. The man seated at the head of the table might be thinner than Magnus, and his hair steel gray, but his shoulders were still square and his eyes as sharp as his son's. He looked at his son while he answered Rachelle's question. "She was concerned with a clip of video and a series of articles that followed it. After seeing the video myself, I completely understood. Of course, I promised our cooperation with repairing Rachelle's reputation. I was disappointed, Magnus, to see how far you had allowed the story to go unchecked."

"It has only been two days, Father, and the video was obviously doctored. Nothing more than a splash in the media, quickly forgotten."

"Magnus, you know as well as I do that nothing is forgotten in this day and age. Mrs. Westerly is joining us for lunch so we may discuss how to best rectify the situation."

"Rectify?" Rachelle and Magnus asked in unison.

"Ah, here she is now." The king rose to his feet. Magnus did as well, and Rachelle followed suit.

Magnus looked angry, but he kept silent.

Delinda approached the table with her head held high. The king walked to meet her halfway and offered her his arm. Despite Rachelle's irritation with her grandmother, she had to admit Delinda didn't look at all out of place. Her pastel-blue dress and jacket were perfect for a formal garden lunch, as were her pearls. Rachelle felt distinctly under-dressed in her slacks and blouse, but feeling inadequate around her grandmother was par for the course. Had Rachelle been offered a million dollars to cite a time when she'd done something her grandmother approved of, she doubted she could.

According to Delinda, Rachelle had always been too thin, too sensitive, too concerned with the business of others. Although they had recently reconciled, for most of Rachelle's life, Delinda had made no secret of her dislike of Rachelle's mother. Rachelle thankfully had endured limited interactions with Delinda, but Eric had practically been raised by her. It was no wonder he had run half a world away as soon as he'd been able to.

Magnus offered his hand in greeting. "A pleasure to meet you, Mrs. Westerly."

"The pleasure is mine, Your Royal Highness," Delinda answered smoothly, as if meeting royalty was part of her daily routine. Rachelle hadn't doubted for a second that her grandmother would have impeccable etiquette.

"Grandmother," Rachelle said stiffly in greeting.

"Rachelle," Delinda said. No warmth rang in her tone, but Rachelle hadn't expected any. Whatever Delinda said, she wasn't there for Rachelle. The only reputation her grandmother worried about was her own.

The king held out the chair beside him. "Please, sit beside me."

Even Rachelle knew that the king normally sat first, and the deference to her grandmother grated. The last thing Delinda needed was a larger ego. Once they were all seated, Magnus having held her chair for her, staff began to deliver bowls of chilled cucumber soup. Rachelle's stomach churned from nerves, so although it looked delicious, she didn't touch it.

"Is Eric arriving late?" Delinda asked.

The king answered, "Unfortunately, he had a meeting that could not be postponed."

Delinda pursed her lips, then turned her attention to Rachelle. "Your visit to the hospital went well this morning. Of course, I'd expect nothing less from Eric."

"He was amazing," Rachelle agreed.

"Public engagements can be difficult to navigate at first. I heard your son's first visit at the children's hospital was not as well received," Delinda said to the king before taking a delicate sip of her soup.

The king didn't seem to take offense at the comment, but Magnus's hand clenched beside his plate. "I heard the same," the king answered.

"Rachelle has a natural way with people, especially children." Delinda looked across the table at Magnus in direct challenge, then back at his father.

"I couldn't agree more. My son's public image would benefit from her softer touch," the king said.

"Father," Magnus said between gritted teeth, "may I have a word with you alone?"

His father frowned. "Magnus, we are in the middle of a conversation. Whatever you would like to discuss shall have to wait."

Magnus stood. "I disagree, Father."

"Sit down, Magnus."

Magnus remained standing. "Father—"

The king rose to his feet and said, "Respect me, Magnus, or leave my table. You are not king yet."

Magnus and his father shared a long look that ended with Magnus returning to his seat. "Of course."

When the king was once again seated, he turned to Delinda. "My apologies. As my only child, my son has too often gotten his own way, and I have allowed it. It is time, however, for him to take on more responsibility." He turned back toward his son. "We have spoken regarding you cultivating a humanitarian role. This is the perfect opportunity to do just that."

Wait, am I a humanitarian project? "I don't understand," Rachelle said aloud.

Delinda remained surprisingly—or strategically—silent.

The king said, "Rachelle, if it so suits you, do my son the honor of accompanying him on his next few public engagements . . . as a personal favor to me."

Rachelle's eyes flew to Magnus's. The same man who had talked about little else beyond wanting to get into her bed now looked put off by the idea of spending time in public with her. Part of her wanted to say yes, just to stick it to him, but she'd never been a spiteful person. It was, however, a wake-up call regarding how he actually felt about her. "Although I am flattered by the idea that I could help your son's image, there are many better-suited *escorts*, I'm sure." She hadn't meant to stress that one word so bluntly, but she'd never been good at hiding how she felt.

The king's eyes narrowed with displeasure, all of which he directed toward his son. "Magnus, what have you done that a guest of ours would refuse such an offer?"

Delinda interjected, "Your Majesty, I'm sure the fault is not your son's. My granddaughter has always been shy."

Shy? Really? I was doing fine before you arrived. I don't need your help, and that's what I'll tell you the first chance I get.

The king sent Magnus a pointed look.

Magnus smiled, but it looked more like a baring of teeth. "Rachelle, it would be my pleasure."

No, it wouldn't. You don't like being forced. Neither do I.

"It's settled, then," the king said. "I'll have arrangements made. How long will you be in Vandorra, Rachelle?"

Rachelle opened her mouth to say she wasn't sure, but her grandmother answered for her. "She has taken a leave of absence from her job, so there's no rush for her to return. I'll remain as well. I do like to stay busy, though. Idle hands and all that."

"What sort of things do you like to do?" the king asked.

"I would love an excuse to gather some of my dearest friends. I spent a great deal of time in Europe when my husband was alive. Do you know of anything coming up?"

Slapping his hand down on the table, the king said, "It has been nearly twenty years since Vandorra has had a royal ball. Would you be interested in helping me plan one?"

Delinda lowered her eyes as if she hadn't essentially planted the idea, and Rachelle wished she could call bullshit right then and there. Delinda was neither meek nor unsure by nature, but she was playing so for the king, and it was working. "I haven't planned a ball in years, and those were always charity events. Is there a local cause that could benefit from such a thing?"

What the hell, if the crazy train was pulling out of the station, it might as well do some good. "The children's hospital was looking for funding to build long-term housing for families."

"An excellent idea, Rachelle," the king said. "Magnus, Mrs. Westerly and I will plan the ball. Why don't you and Rachelle look into suitable housing locations near the hospital?"

"I would love to," Magnus said, but his eyes told a different story. Like her, he was holding his opinion in check, but he wasn't actually planning to go along with any part of this.

He turned to look at her. Rachelle's stomach lurched painfully. *He's not happy—not with the situation and not with me.* She raised her chin and met his gaze. *Well, I'm not happy, either. Get over it.*

I'd tell Delinda to go home, but my opinion on anything has never mattered to her.

Rachelle had gotten so lost in her thoughts that she'd stopped listening to the conversation. When she tuned back in, it was to hear her grandmother's preliminary invitation list. The king looked impressed by the names she was dropping. Magnus looked skeptical that she had those connections. Had it been possible to speak to Magnus without being heard, Rachelle would have assured him that if her grandmother said she knew someone, she did. *I don't know what her goal is, but the one thing you shouldn't do, Magnus, is underestimate her.*

◆ ◆ ◆

Magnus kept his silence only out of respect. His father was obviously enamored of Delinda Westerly, and she was using it quite shamelessly against him. It was hard not to admire the skill of her technique. She hadn't come with demands, but certainly an agenda. Had she told his father what she wanted, he might have agreed or he might not have. The genius of her method was how she made his father believe each idea was his own.

Magnus was willing to let her think she had fooled him as well until he determined her endgame. One of her goals appeared to be that he spend time with Rachelle.

It was possible that she was fishing for a title for her granddaughter. She wouldn't be the first. The ever-shrinking pool of monarchs had some seeking a title for the novelty of it.

What made him think she might have a surreptitious secondary goal was her list of influential invitees to the ball. He would have expected her to pull from the families who were most closely linked to her: the Andrades, the Corisis. She could have claimed affiliation with other royal families in an attempt to validate Rachelle's suitability. Either might have impressed his father, but instead, she'd chosen political leaders who held influence over Vandorra. Some had signed agreements with Magnus recently, while he was still in negotiations with the others. It was as if she was reading from Magnus's contact list, claiming each as her own. Her list was not a vain act of name-dropping, it was a veiled threat—and his father did not have enough information about Magnus's recent dealings to recognize it.

Watching Delinda in action made Magnus reassess every interaction he'd had with Rachelle. Apples didn't fall far from their trees. He was forced to ask himself a difficult question: *Did she dupe me?*

From meeting him on the red carpet to nearly having sex with him in the garden—how much had been orchestrated as part of a larger plan? When seen through that lens, many things made sense that hadn't before.

When something seems too good to be true, it usually is. Rachelle would have him believe that money and power were of no consequence to her, that meeting him had been a coincidence. She was all loyalty, sweetness, and fucking rainbows. Of course it wasn't real. No one was that nice.

Was even Eric involved? His pain had seemed real. It was more likely that Rachelle and her grandmother had seen Eric's condition and used it to their benefit.

Magnus shook his head. He'd love to have dismissed the entire idea as paranoia, but the reality was that his jaded view of people had saved his father in the past. *Let them believe they have us duped. And I'll do what I always do—whatever it takes to protect my family.*

He smiled at Rachelle and liked that her confidence wavered in response. *Want to spend time with me? You will, but on my terms.*

Chapter Thirteen

After an excruciatingly long lunch that had felt more like a hostage situation, Rachelle sat across from her grandmother in the back of a Bentley Mulsanne Grand Limousine in the front drive of the palace. Everything she'd held in for the last few hours was ready to burst out, but she struggled to choose where to start her rant. She wondered if Magnus was in a similar state now that he was finally alone with his father.

"Delinda—"

"Since when am I Delinda to you? You've always called me Grandmother," Delinda said. She leaned forward and instructed the driver to take them both to where she was staying.

"No," Rachelle said. "I'm staying at the Royal Hotel."

"You most definitely are not. Michael, do not listen to her. I'll use the drive to talk some sense into her."

Her driver sat back and turned the engine off. Rachelle turned to meet his eyes in the rearview mirror. Michael drove Delinda when she traveled, but normally he was her house butler—one who had worked for her for decades and become sort of part of the family. Evidently he was not afraid to act as if he were one.

Delinda let out a dramatic sigh. "Rachelle, dear, with your public reputation teetering, do you really believe that the best place for you to stay is a hotel?"

"Magnus—Prince Magnus arranged a suite for me, and I don't see any problem with the arrangement."

"She doesn't see any problem with it, Michael. Rachelle, people will treat you with as little or as much respect as you demand from them. When a man procures a hotel room for a lady, he is asking if she is of easy persuasion; it is best not to prove him right."

Rachelle fisted her hands at her side. "Why are you here?"

"You heard what I said to King Tadeas: I was concerned for you."

"No." Rachelle shook her head vigorously. "You're not here for me. If you were, I would feel a lot less humiliated."

"I would think that feeling came from being snuck in the back door like some common whore. Had I not arrived, they might have had you serving the lunch."

"Stop it, Delinda. I'm not a child who will allow you to speak to me any way you choose."

"What has come over you, Rachelle? You've always been the sensible one."

"Why?" Rachelle ground out. "Because I never challenged you? I did that out of respect for my mother and because we were in your home. But I didn't ask you to come here, and I don't want you here. I don't know how to express that to you in a *sensible* way."

"Michael, do you hear the way she is speaking to me?"

"Yes, ma'am."

"I don't know why I try as hard as I do when they are so ungrateful."

Michael cleared his throat. "Perhaps she is not in need of your assistance."

"Not in need? Not in need? First, the prince allows high society to call her trash; then he invites her to his bed as if she is. And she sees no problem with that arrangement. Well, you'll both have to excuse me for believing I am very much needed here."

Rachelle turned away and saw paparazzi taking photos of them from outside the gate. "Could we discuss this somewhere else?"

"You mean somewhere private or at a hotel where any visitor you have will likely be fodder for gossip?"

"Michael, just drive, okay? My things are already at the hotel. We'll at least have to swing by there."

Michael started the car and drove down the driveway. "Of course, Miss Rachelle."

Delinda clasped her hands on her lap. "I would be cross with you, Michael, if I didn't know your stubbornness is out of love for my granddaughter. How do we show her that mine is as well?"

Rachelle met her grandmother's eyes. Love from anyone as controlling as Delinda was complicated. "If you want me to believe that, tell me why you're really here."

Delinda looked away, then back. "To help you, Rachelle. I understand how this world works. With a wave of my wand, you could be the most beautiful woman at a royal ball, the envy of everyone, and the only woman Prince Magnus can imagine at his side. You could be queen of Vandorra or the woman who was asked to be and decided it wasn't enough for her."

"I don't want to be queen of anything," Rachelle protested even as a part of her soared at the idea of Magnus wanting her by his side.

"No? You'd prefer to be used and tossed aside instead? Because that is where this is headed. Not sure? Tell me, what has he done to prove me wrong?"

He helped Eric. He didn't need to do that.

I don't want to do this. I don't want to look at Magnus through her eyes. He wasn't going to use and toss me aside.

He was—

"I can't stay at the Royal Hotel."

"Thank goodness you're coming to your senses."

"And I won't stay with you." Rachelle turned in her seat to look at Michael. "Michael, could you take me to a modestly priced hotel near the children's hospital? I'll figure out how to have my things sent over."

"Absolutely, Miss Rachelle. I can arrange for your things to be brought to you."

"Thank you, Michael."

They rode in silence for several miles before Rachelle said, "You're not here for me, Delinda, you're here for you. I won't call you Grandmother again until you realize that."

Delinda pursed her lips in thought, then said, "I'm sure you'll feel quite differently when the prince proposes."

Rachelle counted to ten—twice.

When Michael pulled up in front of the midrange hotel, Rachelle stepped out of the limousine, relieved that Delinda hadn't asked about Eric. She didn't know what she would have said if she had.

Funny how things came full circle. A week ago all that had mattered was helping Eric. Somehow, along the way, Rachelle had begun to believe there was something between her and Magnus that could matter as well. Delinda had brought that to a crashing halt. Even if Rachelle wanted to see him again, it wouldn't be the same.

Rachelle leaned back into the limo to say, "Go home, Delinda. If you really want to help me, go home."

Michael closed the door of the limo. "She loves you."

"Does she? Sometimes I'm not so sure."

He tipped his head. "I am. She's here." He turned to open the driver's door. "She won't be forever. Think about that before you push her too far away."

With only her purse in hand, Rachelle walked into the hotel and checked herself in. A short time later, her suitcase arrived. Her head was spinning with everything that had happened over the past few days.

She didn't want to view any of it through Delinda's judgmental lens, but she couldn't shake the doubt her grandmother had planted. Magnus had taken her to the children's hospital with him. That was public.

Of course, the visit was all about Eric. My presence didn't hold any meaning.

He convinced Eric to seek help. Not for me, though. That was probably for Finn.

"When a man procures a hotel room for a lady, he is asking if she is of easy persuasion; it is best not to prove him right." Delinda's voice echoed in Rachelle's mind.

Easy persuasion? First, that was completely outdated and sexist. Labels were for small-minded people.

He just saw me as a woman who dreamed of starring in a porno with him.

Oh my God, I am such an idiot. What did I think a prince would want with me? She changed into workout clothing, found the hotel's gym, and started running on a treadmill. "I'm not princess material."

And I hate that Delinda might be right.

Rachelle ran faster. Sweaty and disheveled, she glared at herself in the mirror.

He didn't ask me on a date. He didn't even bring me through the front door. He essentially offered me nothing, and I was ready to gobble it and him up.

Sorry, Eric. I usually am the sensible one. You should be my first—and only—priority.

Chapter Fourteen

"You're not a child anymore, Magnus. It's time for you to choose a wife," King Tadeas said as they took a slow walk around the palace after Rachelle and her grandmother left.

"I have plenty of time for that, Father. You were just shy of forty when you met Mother." Magnus was relieved that his father was out of bed and wanting to exercise. Dr. Stein had become concerned as of late. Pain had led to his father's withdrawal, but lack of movement was what the doctor had said was quickly adding to his ailments.

"And look at me, not certain I'll meet your children before I go."

"You're not going anywhere, Father."

"We are all going somewhere, Magnus. I would like to see you settled before I do, though. What do you think of the American?"

"I thought your heart was set on Princess Isabella," Magnus chided gently. His father had been advocating that match since he was a child.

"I must say I was disappointed to learn she was linked to the petty video about Rachelle. That sort of behavior hints at a jealous soul I wouldn't want raising my grandchildren."

Finally, something we agree upon. "Thankfully, she has never been a serious consideration for me."

"Has anyone?"

Magnus hesitated briefly as he remembered how Rachelle had been at the hospital. She'd been the first woman he'd ever seen in that light. Too bad he'd learned she wasn't the angel she presented herself as. Speaking of that: "Regarding Mrs. Westerly. You seem taken with her."

"She is a rare combination of beautiful and brilliant."

"Yes, well, she is not above using your high opinion of her to her advantage."

His father laughed. "I don't doubt that for a second. It is a joy to watch her in action."

Magnus didn't share his humor. "Be careful with her, Father. The list she cited was straight from my recent dealings. She wanted you to believe that the ball was your idea, but the guest list was intended to prove to me that she has the ear of many powerful people. She's dangerous and cunning."

"She may prove to be if you continue to treat her granddaughter the way you have. What you saw at lunch was an American mama bear rushing to defend her cub. She absolutely will take a swipe at you—at us—if she feels Rachelle is threatened."

"Then I will send her scuttling back to the United States before she has a chance to."

The king stopped and turned to face his son. "Not everything is a battle, Magnus. This is a dance, and one that I find invigorating."

"A dance? Father, I think you're confused."

"No, I see things more clearly now than I have in a while. Delinda Westerly is a proud woman who believes her granddaughter has been treated unfairly. I agree with her. Rather than sneaking Rachelle into the country, you should have announced her arrival and shown her more respect."

"It was not that simple."

"It will be from now on. I will arrange several public appearances, all of which you will attend with Rachelle. Your behavior will be above reproach. Are we clear on this?"

There was no one else who would dare speak to Magnus in that tone—except possibly the woman his father was commanding him to spend time with. "What are you hoping to gain by this? Are you trying to appease Delinda Westerly? Because I assure you, I can resolve the situation much faster."

His father shook his head and began walking again. "You will do no such thing. I will deal with Delinda. As far as this *situation* is concerned, your responsibility will begin and end with her granddaughter and the engagements you will attend with her."

"For what purpose?"

They came to a grassy place that had been Magnus's favorite playground as a child. "When you were young, your mother argued that we should keep you innocent as long as possible. So we tried, but you could not be contained. You didn't want to play with trucks—you had a wooden sword and were determined to slay your share of dragons. Well, you've done that, Magnus. Now it is time to prove your dedication to Vandorra in another way. Honor my request to spend time with Rachelle Westerly. If she is not to your liking, you will have two months to choose another bride."

"Or?"

"Is there a need for a threat, or will you honor my wishes?"

The strength of his bond to his father was that he could be honest with him. "You know I have never liked being forced to do anything."

"Then abdicate your throne, Magnus. Find an island somewhere and live off the land. Perhaps then, and only then, you will be able to live in such a free way. Although I believe even that lifestyle is ruled by the laws of Mother Nature. For as much as we feel in control, we are not. You have done great things for Vandorra, but to secure its prosperity, you must marry and produce an heir. My request is that you announce taking a step toward doing so at the ball."

"So the ball is to be a forum to announce my engagement?"

"Yes."

Magnus ran a hand through his hair. "This is no small request."

"But nor will it be as bad as you imagine."

"If I am to do this, why obligate me to spend time with the Westerly woman?"

His father smiled. "Because your search should start where your heart is already leading you." He told Magnus he would see him the next day and walked away, leaving Magnus alone and shaking his head.

He was attracted to Rachelle, but he didn't have feelings for her. And if there had been a spark of any kind, it had been extinguished. She might be beautiful, and her body might have the power to set his aflame, but his father was wrong—his heart was definitely not involved. She was nothing to him. Less than nothing now that she'd arranged to have her presence forced upon him.

Just thinking about how Rachelle had done both sent blood rushing to his cock, and he groaned. It was time to start preparing for a full-out war.

Although his father had claimed this was a dance and not a battle, Magnus saw trouble coming. *I don't know if I can spend time with Rachelle without fucking her.*

But that doesn't mean I'll marry her. The woman he would choose would be far less trouble. Offhand, he could think of three with the right pedigree who were both beautiful and quiet in nature. None of them would dare raise a hand to him or correct him.

His dick twitched and strained as his head flooded with images of Rachelle, the scent of her, the feel of her wet sex contracting around his fingers. And that mouth. He groaned as he remembered the pleasure she'd brought him and imagined how much more they could bring each other.

He headed toward the palace and made his way to the elevator exit. He chose to drive himself, although the royal guard followed, as they always did. They were a presence he was accustomed to. Ever since there had been an attempt on his father's life and the threat had been traced to his cousin, Magnus had been vigilantly guarded. There wasn't a single part of being forced to choose a wife that Magnus was happy with, but he understood his father's motivation. Single Magnus meant his line of descent was vulnerable.

Back at the office in his own palace, he called the clinic to check if Eric had actually admitted himself. He had.

He asked Phillip to dig deeper for any and all information about the Westerly family. If Delinda did start trouble, he wanted to know exactly how to shut her down.

Finally, he called the Royal Hotel to confirm that Rachelle had checked in. She had not. It made sense that she would have gone to stay with her grandmother, but on impulse Magnus asked Phillip to confirm that as well.

"Your Royal Highness, I have located Miss Westerly. She is not with her grandmother."

"Then where is she?"

"It appears she has checked in to a hotel, but not the Royal."

"I don't understand her."

"It is directly across the street from the hospital. Proximity to her brother, perhaps?"

"Thank you, Phillip."

Was her concern for her brother real, or was this move as strategic as each of her grandmother's had been?

He tried to put her out of his head, but she crept repeatedly back into his thoughts, making work impossible. Eventually he walked out of his office and slammed the door behind him. "I'm going out," he growled.

"Out?" Phillip asked, trotting beside him. "Should I have a car brought around?"

"No, I'll drive myself."

"Of course, Your Royal Highness. May I ask where you're headed?"

Although Magnus did not like having to answer to anyone, especially when he couldn't justify where he was going to himself, he understood the reason for Phillip's question. His was not to judge, but to protect. It was a role to be honored rather than resented. "To see Miss Westerly."

Chapter Fifteen

After a short visit with Eric, Rachelle wandered down the street in search of a pastry shop. Her brother had looked uncomfortable, but he said he was staying. She assured him she was right across the street if he needed her. She didn't mention that their grandmother was in Vandorra, but she was conflicted about whether not preparing him had been for the best.

Lately, no choice felt like the right one.

She stopped in front of a café and stared at a piece of chocolate cake on display, losing herself temporarily in the promise of it. She didn't want to think about whether she should or shouldn't tell her family about Eric. She didn't want to remember any part of seeing Delinda that day. She definitely didn't want to wonder what Magnus had thought of that lunch. Had it left him as confused?

Rachelle placed her hand on the glass and sighed. Maybe it was for the best. Where could time with Magnus have led except disappointment? Even if he had been good in bed—*an amazing, once-in-a-lifetime, orgasm-until-I-couldn't-move kind of good*—what would they have done next? A date?

Sure. Why not?

Movies.

Maybe minigolf.

I'm sure he enjoys all the same things I do. Yeah, not likely.

What had he said? *"We could not be less alike."* That about summed them up.

So, thanks, Delinda. I suppose you did me a favor.

"One would think you've never seen cake before," Magnus said from behind her.

Rachelle spun around. She almost asked him what he was doing there, but instead said, "Go away," and turned back toward the glass display.

Magnus leaned close to her ear and said, "Is it difficult to pretend not to be interested in me after you and your grandmother essentially trapped me into spending time with you?"

She glared at him over her shoulder. "Oh my God. Poor you. I would ask how you're holding up, but I'm a little preoccupied right now with worrying about my brother. And just so you know, regardless of my grandmother's performance, I have no intention of going anywhere with you. So you're not trapped at all. Go away. You're free."

"I wish it were that easy," he growled. "I can't get a damn thing done. All I can think about is you and tasting you again." He pushed her hair aside and kissed the curve of her neck.

Lust punched through her, and she placed a second hand against the glass to steady herself. *Yes,* her body screamed.

No, her mind argued.

Meanwhile, she stood frozen, neither pulling away nor responding to his kiss. His lips trailed up to just behind her ear. "Come with me. No one needs to know. It'll just be you and me and this . . ." His breath caressed her cheek. He hovered close enough behind her to warm her. "Say yes, Rachelle."

The temptation to give in was nearly overwhelming. Her body hummed for him, but her need was deeper than purely sexual. It had been a long week, and she was in a foreign country, alone and worried. *How can I want to be with anyone right now?*

She turned in front of him, leaning back against the glass while looking up at him. His lips were mere inches above hers. The same desire that raged within her was reflected in his eyes. It would be good with him. So good.

But then?

I can't believe I'm going to say this—but my grandmother is right. I don't want to be the one he uses and throws away. "No," she said, nearly choking on the word.

He blinked several times, as if her refusal was difficult for him to process. "I don't chase women."

"I'm not asking you to." She slipped out from beneath his arm. *Women. Not even specifically me.* After their intimate romp in the garden, it would have been tough to sell that she wasn't interested in him at all, so she didn't try. Physical distance from him allowed her to think clearer. "I appreciate what you've done for Eric. Today was amazing and something I'll never forget."

"And last night?" he asked, holding her captive with the intensity of his gaze.

She took another step back. "Also amazing, but not something we should repeat. I'll be in Vandorra as long as Eric is here. That could be one week or several. If he checks himself out tomorrow, I'm going back with him."

Magnus pocketed his hands and frowned. "Your grandmother—"

"Is not here because I asked her to be. I had no idea she was even coming. The video of you and me embarrassed her, and that is something my grandmother will not tolerate."

"So she's here to repair your reputation."

Rachelle shook her head and laughed without humor. "You don't get it yet. This is about her pride."

"And getting you a title?" he asked with enough arrogant smugness that Rachelle's temper began to flare.

"She doesn't care about the title. She's trying to use me to knock you down a notch." As soon as Rachelle said it, she knew it was true. "How I feel is irrelevant. No different than how you used me to manipulate Eric."

"A moment ago you thanked me for what I did for Eric." Magnus was offended, but that only reinforced Rachelle's resolve.

"I did, but that doesn't mean I'm foolish enough to think you care about me. You and my grandmother are both used to getting what you want, and you don't care who you have to hurt to get it. Well, I'm not playing her game or yours."

She turned to walk away, but Magnus grabbed her arm. "My intention has never been to hurt you."

She pulled her arm free. "Then respect what I'm saying. I don't want to do this. I don't want to be what my grandmother uses to humble you. And I don't care if you find it inconvenient to want someone you can't have. I'm not an appliance. I'm not here to make your life easier. You want to prove you care about me at all? Stay away from me."

◆ ◆ ◆

The woman Magnus had thought would spend the night with him walked away without hesitation or a single glance back. Only after he saw her enter her hotel lobby did he check to see where his men were. When he located Phillip, he nodded for him to approach. "She claims she had no idea her grandmother was even coming." Magnus's attention was drawn back to the entrance of her hotel even though there was no reason to believe she would reappear through it. He sighed. "I believe her."

Phillip's expression remained respectfully blank.

Magnus continued, "She said if I care about her at all, I should stay away from her. How does that make any sense?" Normally, Magnus would not put as much thought into what a woman said, but Rachelle's feelings mattered to him, and her request had put him in a no-win situation. To get what he wanted, he needed to disregard her wishes. To respect her wishes, he needed to deny what he knew they both wanted.

Phillip was quiet for a moment, then said, "My wife once told me she did not want to celebrate her birthday, so we didn't. I didn't buy her a card. I didn't take her to dinner. I pretended as if that day were any other day. I regretted that decision for the entire twelve months that led up to her next birthday. Women are complicated creatures."

"Why not just say what they want?"

"They do, but they say it as only another woman can understand it."

"Absurd."

"Would you like it translated?"

"Excuse me?"

Phillip took out his phone. "You could ask my wife."

Magnus shook his head. "I will do no such thing." In the brief time it took Phillip to repocket his phone, Magnus gave in to his curiosity. "You will ask her, but do not tell her it is for me."

"I can't tell her it's for *me*," Phillip joked, but he sobered when he realized Magnus was serious. "I'll be vague." A moment later Phillip greeted his wife, then asked if he could have her opinion on something. She agreed.

Phillip said, "One of my friends is interested in a woman who told him to stay away from her, and he's looking for advice." Phillip shook his head. "No, this is not like that. She was interested in him yesterday. She said—" Phillip turned to Magnus. "How exactly did she say it?"

"She said, 'You want to prove you care about me at all? Stay away from me.'"

Phillip repeated it to his wife. "How certain are you?" Then he nodded. "That's pretty certain. Thanks, my love. I'll see you tonight."

"Well?" Magnus demanded after Phillip hung up.

"I'd rather not share what she said. She didn't know we were referring to you."

"Phillip, your honesty is as valuable to me as your loyalty. Say it. I will not be offended."

"You know my wife is blunt."

Magnus folded his arms across his chest and waited.

As expected, Phillip caved. "She said you screwed up big-time. Translated to womenspeak, it means: I've decided you're a jerk, but I'll give you one last chance to prove you're not."

"That makes no sense. How could I prove what I am or am not by staying away from her?"

"I don't know. I didn't ask that part. Should I call her back?"

"No." It already felt ridiculous to have entertained her opinion at all. Magnus not only didn't chase women, he also didn't sit around and try to decipher what they wanted from him. There had always been too many women in the world to waste that much time on one.

He told himself Rachelle was no different. Instead of spending another moment on her, Magnus decided to contact a couple of the women who were already considered a good marriage match for him.

I don't have to prove myself to anyone.

He'd known from the first time he'd met Rachelle that indulging in her would be messy and complicated. He hadn't predicted it would be *this* complicated, but hers was a gift that just kept giving. First a needy brother, now a manipulative grandmother. The path to sex with Rachelle was a minefield of drama.

As he drove himself back to his palace, he couldn't stop thinking about how dejected Rachelle had looked as she'd spoken of her grandmother. It reminded him of how she'd been hurt by her brother's rejection. Part of him wanted to protect her even while another part was pulling away.

What is my fascination with her?

Is it because she doesn't want to see me?

A royal prince—a powerful one at that. Yet she would rather spend the night alone in a cheap hotel than with him.

Similar thoughts plagued him even after he'd arrived back at his palace. He told himself her opinion of him didn't matter, but that didn't stop him from rehashing their conversations in his head.

Rachelle was a proud woman who spoke her mind—he liked that.

Wealth and power were not her goal, or she would have followed her grandmother's plan, perhaps even to the point of attempting to trap him into marriage. Instead, she'd turned her back on her grandmother and him.

Memories of her in the garden were impossible to keep at bay. They circled and nipped at him until he could no longer ignore them. There was no other woman, suitable or not, who held his interest the way she did. It would be a waste of time to contact other women before he resolved this issue.

Why would a woman be so open one day and then want nothing to do with a man the next? He dismissed Phillip's wife's theory. *Which part did I screw up? When I helped her brother? When I honored her by taking her to see my father? I've been honest with her about what I want. I would think that would be applauded.*

He remembered how she'd looked on the way into his father's palace. *She wasn't turning me away before her grandmother arrived.*

A thought came to him that put a smile on his face. *She's embarrassed by how eagerly she would have come to me.*

I can work with that.

Perhaps I should be giving advice to Phillip.

Chapter Sixteen

The next morning, shortly after Rachelle had finished getting dressed, even though she had nowhere to go, a letter was delivered to her hotel room. She sat on the edge of the bed and opened the formal envelope by peeling off the royal seal. It was an invitation written in calligraphy on thick cream-colored stock paper. "The Master of the House has been commanded by His Majesty to invite Rachelle Westerly to a reception by the King for the Orphanage Development Committee at Pavailler Palace on Tuesday." Rachelle skimmed the rest for the date and time. "Dress: Lounge suit/day dress. Guests are asked to arrive between six p.m. and six twenty p.m. A reply is requested . . ."

She threw the envelope onto the bed beside her.

Fuming, she called her grandmother. "I'm not going, but I can't believe you would sink that low. Orphans? Really?"

"Well, hello, Rachelle. Good morning to you as well."

"There is no good morning that starts with being blackmailed into doing something."

"I agree. Now why don't you tell me what has you in a tizzy?"

"As if you don't already know."

Delinda sighed. "Must we go round and round? I don't know what you're upset about this time. Either explain it to me, or call me later when you've calmed down. I have neither the time nor the patience for guessing games."

Rachelle read the invitation aloud. "Are you saying you didn't orchestrate this?"

"It's genius, but I can't claim it as mine."

While talking to her grandmother, Rachelle searched the Internet for how to politely decline going but found nothing. "Are you kidding me?" she muttered. "Doesn't anyone decline a royal invitation?"

"I don't believe they do, dear. Especially not to receptions regarding orphans." Rachelle could hear the smile in Delinda's voice.

"I'm glad you think this is amusing, *Delinda*. I don't. And I refuse to be manipulated. I told Magnus yesterday that I didn't want to see him again, and I meant it."

"You did? Well played, Rachelle."

Breathe. Count to ten. Think of all the reasons why swearing doesn't help a situation. "I'm not playing. Maybe that's what you don't understand. I don't care what's all over social media. I don't care that your pride was dented and that you think sticking it to the prince will make you feel better. Do you care at all about how I feel? Let me tell you why you can't answer yes. You don't know me well enough to know what I care about. That's the tragedy here. Not my reputation. The real tragedy is that you don't see how much you hurt the people you claim to love." Rachelle hung up the phone and fell backward onto her bed. *Well, that went well.*

Was it past time for me to say that?

Or should I have kept it to myself?

I don't know why I think I can help Eric or anyone else when I don't even know what the hell I'm doing most of the time.

A knock on her door jolted her out of bed. She shook her head in resignation when she opened the door and saw a member of the hotel staff holding a bouquet so large only the person's legs were visible beneath it. She directed the young man to put it on the floor and tipped him before hunting through the bright, exotic flowers for a card.

I tried. I can't stay away. Magnus.

In a few minutes, Rachelle would remind herself why it was wrong for Magnus not to have respected her request. She'd muster up some indignation. However, she let herself bask for a moment in how good it felt to see that he hadn't immediately moved on to another woman.

Pathetically, wonderfully good.

Her phone rang. She scrambled to retrieve it from beside the bed. Magnus.

Do I answer it? I told my grandmother I didn't want to play games.
"Hello," she said in a husky voice.

"How are you today?" He sounded genuinely concerned.

She considered telling him not to call her again, then decided to be honest with him instead. Hell, that might be an even better deterrent. "I'm a mess. A wreck. I'm angry. Scared. Confused. Tired. Have you ever been in a situation where you feel like there's no right choice?"

He was quiet for a moment, then said, "Come to lunch with me."

"No."

"You cling to that word as if it were a shield. What would happen if you said yes instead of no all the time?"

"Really? And I suppose the first thing you think I should say yes to is sleeping with you?"

He chuckled. "In my fantasy you're awake, but we could try it your way, too."

She laughed, then caught herself. "It's not going to happen. Not awake. Not asleep."

"See. All that negativity is making you unhappy. Want to improve your mood? I'll ask you something simple, and all you have to do is say yes."

Bad idea.

Very, very bad idea.

But I do want to hear his question. "Okay."

"Come to lunch with me."

She almost immediately said no, but this time didn't. Instead, she paced her small hotel room and mentally listed all the reasons why she shouldn't go with him. *One, all he wants is sex. Two . . . isn't reason one enough? I'm better off staying here at the hotel. Alone. With nothing to do. Waiting for Eric and hoping he wants to see me when he gets out.*

What the hell? "Yes."

"Perfect. Come down now. I'm parked in front of the hotel."

"It's only ten o'clock."

"I thought you'd like to see some of the area before lunch."

"Wait. You're downstairs? What if I had said no?"

"Come down, Rachelle." He hung up.

Rachelle rushed to the mirror in the bathroom to check her appearance. She hadn't planned on going anywhere except for a walk, so she was casually dressed in jeans and tennis shoes. Her hair was loose and a little wild. She'd chosen her plain light-blue T-shirt for comfort rather than style.

Not exactly attire fit for a royal outing, but it's the real me.

She squared her shoulders. *I came here to find myself. Well, here I am. Not perfect. Not wise. Just me. Somehow that will have to be enough, because I don't know how to be better than this.*

A moment later, Rachelle turned from closing her hotel room door and screamed when she realized there was a man standing just behind her. He waved his hands at her nervously, and she calmed as she realized who he was. "Reggie. Oh my God. What are you doing here?"

Oddly, his reappearance reassured her. "Eric called me. He didn't like the idea of you being alone in a city where you don't know anyone, so he asked if the wife and kids wanted a mini vacation. We've got a suite over at the Royal Hotel. What are you doing in this shitbox?"

Rachelle laughed nervously as she came down from an adrenaline rush. "I like it here. Have you spoken to Eric?"

"You mean, do I know that he's in a clinic across the street? Yeah."

Good, I don't need to pretend. "Then you know why I'm here. I wanted to be close by."

"I walked over from the Royal Hotel."

"Yes, well, I didn't want to stay there." She wasn't willing to say more on the subject, since it would have involved both Magnus and her grandmother's lecture about him.

Reggie looked around and made a face. "Whatever you say. Anyway, I just thought you should know that we're down the street if you need anything."

"Thanks, Reggie." Rachelle stepped away from her door and started toward the elevator.

"Oh, and are you aware that you're being followed?"

Rachelle froze. "Followed?"

Reggie hit the elevator button as if he hadn't just said something shocking. "When you went out yesterday, the kids and I thought it would be fun to see if we could trail you without being seen. It was entertaining for about a minute until we realized there was a man who went everywhere you went."

"A man? You mean Prince Magnus?"

"No, some other guy. Short blond hair. Real tall and skinny. He was dressed to blend in. I didn't notice him at first, but my son said he was everywhere you were, and damned if he wasn't right."

Breathe. It's probably one of the royal guard. Maybe Magnus is making sure I'm safe?

Reggie continued, "He was a little on the creepy side, so I sent my kids back with my wife and kept following you."

Okay. That's also a little creepy, but I'm going to try to see it as sweet. Don't they say never ask questions you don't want to hear the answers to? But I have to. "Did you see anything else?"

"This is where it gets weird—"

This is? This is? Rachelle kept silent, both because she wanted to hear what else he'd seen and because her head was spinning.

"There was a woman following the man who was following you. No shit. When you were in front of the café, about to make out with your prince boyfriend, did you think you were alone? They were both there, just standing around pretending they weren't watching you."

Lurch, you're freaking me out. Rachelle rode down the elevator with Reggie. "Why would anyone be following me? I'm no one."

"You're an heiress to billions, the sister of an A-list movie star, and you're dating a prince—not a no one. I bet you're about to be kidnapped and ransomed."

Rachelle gasped. She remembered how she'd initially felt about Magnus's guards. "I'm paranoid enough without any help. Don't joke like that."

"Who's joking?" Reggie said with a shrug.

Grabbing Reggie by both arms, Rachelle said, "I'm going out with Prince Magnus now. Do you think he's involved?"

Reggie pried her hands off him. "Now you're letting your imagination run away with you. Not everyone is out to get you."

"Just the two people who are following me around?" Rachelle asked in a high pitch. She looked around. "Do you see them now?"

"Listen, I wouldn't have told you if I thought it was going to upset you. It could be nothing."

"You said I was about to be kidnapped."

"I shouldn't have said anything. I don't know. It's just a feeling."

Rachelle hugged her arms around herself. *How could I not have noticed someone following me?*

Where was my mind? Chocolate and Magnus.

What great final words those would make.

Eric had been right about money changing a person's life—and not all in good ways. She was beginning to see what he meant. "Reggie, do you think I need a bodyguard?"

He made a face. "I'd get one. I'm willing to watch out for you, but take a bullet? Eh. I have kids. You know?"

Rachelle nodded. *Note to self: Reggie—not a hero. At least, not mine.*

The elevator stopped before the lobby, and Reggie stepped out.

"Where are you going?" Rachelle asked.

"Not on your date. I've seen how the two of you drool all over each other. It'd be awkward."

"I shouldn't go, either." She went to step out, also, but Reggie held up a hand to stop her.

"You want my opinion? You're safer with him than you are alone."

The door of the elevator closed a few inches in front of Rachelle's face. She stepped back and almost lost her balance. *Safer with Magnus? If we're at that point, shouldn't I go to the police?*

And say what? "My brother's electrician was covertly following me and noticed he wasn't the only one doing it"? "Oh, where's my brother? I can't say. Who's following me? I don't know."

Am I losing my mind?

Probably.

She took out her phone and considered calling her grandmother. *I can only imagine what she'd say if I tried to explain this to her.*

And then I'd have to tell her why I won't leave Vandorra yet. Eric would never forgive me for involving her.

When the elevator door opened at the lobby, Magnus was right there—smiling.

Rachelle took a shaky step toward him.

Magnus tensed when he saw how pale and unsteady Rachelle was. He took one of her arms and guided her to a bench near the elevator, then sat beside her. "Are you feeling okay?"

She shook her head. "No. I might throw up."

Phillip took a step back. Magnus didn't budge. "Are you ill?" He placed his hand on her forehead. No fever. He took one of her hands in his. It was cold. "Did something happen?" This wasn't at all how he'd imagined seeing her again would go, but he didn't care. He needed to make sure she was okay. "Tell me."

"Can I trust you?" Large, scared eyes sought his, and his heart began a wild dance in his chest.

Her question hit him like a punch. He'd come to her thinking mostly of himself and what he wanted, but when she looked at him, none of that mattered. "Yes."

Her eyes shone with emotion. "We have to make sure Eric is safe without letting everyone know where he is or what's happening."

"Eric is safe, Rachelle. I spoke with him this morning."

She shook her head. "That's not enough. I need to know he is. I need to know I am."

She was genuinely upset, and he was filled with an anger that had nowhere to go. Something had spooked her. Whether the threat was real or imagined, he would do whatever it took to make sure he never saw that look in her eyes again. "I should not have allowed you to choose your own hotel. Phillip, have her things packed and brought down."

"No," she protested. "It's not the hotel."

He nodded for Phillip to do as he asked, then turned his attention back to Rachelle. "Women shouldn't travel on their own."

She stood. "Don't go there. Don't get me all upset with you, too. I can only freak out about one thing at a time."

Magnus rose to his feet. "What happened?"

She rubbed a hand over her forehead. "First, could you just apologize for that comment about women? I can't be rescued by a sexist pig . . . not even if he's a prince."

Well, then. Her mind went on curious tangents. "Which part was wrong?"

She sighed and waved her hand. "Forget it. You're right, it would take too long. I don't need to move to another hotel, but I do need to hire a security guy . . . a bodyguard . . . something. One for me and one for Eric. Are they expensive? I have money in my savings if we're talking about a couple thousand, but I've tied up a lot of my money in a retirement fund. I can't ask my family for help. Not until I know if I actually need it. And I'm fine. I can do this on my own. Is there an Uber app for goons?"

"Rachelle Westerly, if you don't start making sense soon, I will be forced to call your grandmother."

"You wouldn't."

"I would."

She glared at him. "Oh, yeah? Then I'll call your father."

"And say what?"

She wilted somewhat. "I don't know. I don't even know why I said that." She sat back down. "This is stupid. I'm arguing with you about nothing when I should be doing something."

"Because?"

"I'm being followed."

Her words shot through Magnus. "Why do you think that?"

"Reggie told me."

"Who's Reggie?"

"He's my brother's electrician, but he's here in Vandorra. Eric asked him to watch over me."

"And discovering that this electrician is following you is what upset you?"

"No, while he was watching me, he saw a woman watching a man who was watching me."

"Have you been drinking?" Was she even in danger, or did she need to speak to a professional as well?

She flew back to her feet. "I don't know why I thought you'd help me with this." She paced in frustration. "Go back to your palace and your orphan receptions, and I'll figure it out on my own."

She moved to walk away, and he pulled her to him. "Stop."

She froze against him.

He struggled to keep his thoughts straight as his body went haywire simply from having her so close. "Who is following you?"

"I don't know," she said, and her eyes reflected her confusion. "Reggie could be wrong and there's no one. Or he could be right—"

"What did he say he saw?"

She relaxed somewhat within the circle of his arms and told him exactly what Reggie had said her pursuers might want. "Crazy, right? Stuff like that doesn't really happen, does it?"

He debated which she needed more: the truth or comfort. People absolutely were kidnapped for ransom. The world could be an ugly place—even in Vandorra. "It does, little Rachelle. Unfortunately, it does. I'll send two of my royal guards to watch over your brother."

She nodded and met his eyes. "And me?"

"I'll protect you." He pulled her closer. If someone actually was following her, his men would find them and deal with them accordingly.

She leaned back and said, "The driver who took me from London to you gave me a black card with only a phone number on it. He told me to call it if I ever needed help. He said I'm never alone."

How did Phillip miss this? "Did you recognize the man?"

"No. I'd never seen him before."

"Where's the card now?"

"In my purse."

"Give it to me and I'll find out who he is."

147

She hesitated, then stepped back, dug the card out of her purse, and handed it to him. "Who do you think is following me?"

Magnus pocketed it and chose his next words with care. The real possibilities would only scare her, so he kept those to himself. "Probably photographers hoping to get a shot they can sell."

She didn't need to know that Reggie's guess was a very real threat—especially since she was now in the public eye. Sadly, it was impossible to have something without someone also wanting to take it from you. He would never forget the day he'd discovered his cousin Davot had hired a man to kill his father. The attempt had failed, but there had been no way for Magnus to reclaim his childhood innocence. The world would forever be a different place for him. One in which he needed to be strong enough to fend off any threat at any time. Despite only being seventeen, he had gathered enough evidence that he could have had his cousin convicted; then he and Phillip, who at that time had been new to the royal guard, had gone to threaten his powerful cousin. Together, armed with evidence, they had backed the man down. His father still did not know the real cause of his boating accident. At the time, he had been reeling from the death of the queen, and Magnus had not wanted to add betrayal to his grief. From then on, Magnus had cleared the way for his father. King Tadeas's strength as a leader had always been his ability to inspire his people, and Magnus made sure nothing stood in his way for long. Together they had moved Vandorra forward. As much as the world needed warriors, it also needed people like his father and Rachelle to make sure society was something worth defending.

Rachelle smiled in relief. "I hadn't thought of a photographer. That makes sense."

Magnus placed his hand on her lower back and guided her out of the hotel and to a waiting car. "Now tell me, what's your issue with orphans?"

Chapter Seventeen

After the way the day had started, Rachelle hadn't expected to enjoy a moment of it, but as Magnus whisked her away in a sports car, excitement surged again. When he wasn't being insufferable and arrogant, being with him was a heady experience. Everything else faded away when he looked at her. When he took her hand in his and rested it beneath his on his thigh as he drove, she could barely concentrate on anything else.

To cover her nervousness, she talked. She explained in detail that her desire to decline the invitation from his father had nothing to do with the cause and everything to do with not liking to be forced to do something.

"I understand that feeling well," he'd said.

"Of course, I'll end up going to the reception anyway. I can't say no."

"Unfortunately, that has not been my experience with you," Magnus said with dry humor.

A laugh burst from Rachelle. "I'm here, aren't I?"

He brought her hand to his lips. "Yes, you are."

Her heart did a funny flip. He hadn't said where they were going. Erotic sex-dungeon fantasies warred with more mundane possibilities. Although she enjoyed reading about wild escapades, she tried to imagine what her reaction would be if he actually brought her to one. *I'd probably faint. Or let out a nervous fart. You never read about those happening.*

She studied the strong profile of the man beside her and wondered if the women he normally dated were so sophisticated they didn't even worry about such things. "Where are we going?" she asked.

He glanced at her, then back at the road. "You shouldn't get into any car without knowing. I could be taking you anywhere."

She went to pull her hand free, but he held it firmly. "That's not funny."

"It's not meant to be. You need to be more careful, Rachelle."

This time she did tug her hand free. "I am careful."

"Are you? Who knows you're with me today?"

"Reggie. Why are you doing this? I just started to relax, and you're making me nervous again."

"My goal is not to scare you, but to prepare you, because your life is about to change."

What? "Take me back to the hotel. Never mind about lunch."

"Your things are no longer at the hotel."

Rachelle turned more toward him. "You knew that wasn't what I wanted, and you did it anyway?"

"Yes," he said without a hint of regret.

"I'm done. Take me back right now."

"I will not. I will, however, offer you a choice. If you wish to be deposited where your grandmother is staying, I will drive you there and inform her why you require the royal guards I have assigned to you."

"I'm not limited by whatever choices you come up with. I'm an adult woman. Drive me back to the hotel now." *See, that's why I don't think I'd like the sex dungeon. In theory, giving a man control sounds sexy—until you see how he reacts to having a little power.*

"Your second option is my own preference. I have a business meeting in eastern Vandorra. You see some of my country, then stay at my family's riverfront home in Domovia. It is a historic, rural town. You could sleep in or go shopping and meet me in the afternoon."

"No."

He smiled. "Do not worry. There are plenty of bedrooms at my family's home. You will be allowed to choose one of your own—unless you decide to share mine."

Rachelle folded her arms across her chest. "I don't think you're reading my mood correctly. I'm imagining strangling you, not having sex."

He roared in laughter. "You are a delight."

"And you're delusional."

He pulled the car over to the side of the road and unclipped his seat belt. "Am I?"

Her breath caught in her throat. The desire in his eyes seared through whatever resistance she had. He wasn't an overbearing prince who had just offended her by brushing off her demands. She wasn't an independent woman driven to correct him.

As they sat there, their breathing becoming more and more shallow, each fighting the same battle. Reason and resolve crumbled in the face of their desire.

"Come here," he commanded.

She clutched her seat belt and glanced around. There was an SUV pulled over a hundred feet before them, and another about the same distance behind them. "No."

He traced her cheek with the back of his fingers. "They are trained to look away."

She slapped his hand away. "That's disgusting."

He chuckled. "Honestly, I forgot they were there. I can tell them to pull back farther."

"That's not necessary, because nothing is going to happen."

He leaned closer. "So none of this?"

She sat frozen, wanting his touch more than she wanted to refuse him. When his mouth descended upon hers, it did so with gentle expertise. His hands dug into her hair, but his kiss remained an almost tender invitation that was impossible to resist. She closed her eyes and parted her lips for his. He groaned with pleasure.

Rachelle had been kissed many times before. She'd even been kissed deeply by *him*, but not like this. He was barely touching her, but they were connecting so intensely that her body burned for his. Every flick of his tongue against hers, every leisurely, artful tease, challenged what was left of her resolve. Her hands sought his muscular chest, and she no longer cared who might be watching. He ended the kiss with another groan but remained close enough so that their breath mingled.

The slow smile that spread across his face was a lusty one, like a pirate looking over the bounty of his raid. His eyes went to her still-parted lips. "What keeps you saying no to me when it is clear that you want to say yes?"

She fought to regain her composure. Manipulation even when it felt as good as this did was still wrong. "Your ego, for one."

His smile widened, and his voice was a hot caress on her cheek. "Then rein me in." His hands tightened in her hair. "Make me yours as completely as I will make you mine."

Barely able to breathe, Rachelle released her seat belt and turned toward him. The bulge in the front of his trousers confirmed his statement. This was no insecure, still-living-with-his-parents boy. This was a powerful man who was used to getting what he wanted—and what he wanted was her.

And his challenge rocked through her.

Make me yours as completely as I will make you mine. What did that even mean? People didn't own each other. They met, fell in love, had a few kids, and divorced, then learned to be civil for the sake of the children. That's how the modern world worked.

Magnus didn't live by those rules.

Had he sought to simply control her, she would have found him easier to resist. What did he want? Even as she tried to figure it out, part of her knew. She wrapped her arms around his neck and pulled his mouth back down to hers. There was nothing gentle about the kiss this time, and that was her choice. She arched against him and slid a hand down to his cock, loving how he shuddered from pleasure beneath her touch.

She kissed him until she sensed he was as close to losing control as she was. When she broke off the kiss, she felt shattered, but in a wonderful way. She wanted to be his. It was too late for her already. Even if she ended it now, even if they never took this further, he had already ruined her for other men. She would never again endure a bland kiss and wonder if the problem was hers. She'd never sit across from another nice man and hope she became more attracted to him. How could she, now that she knew what it should feel like?

Even if this doesn't last, even if this is a huge mistake—I'd rather live with the regret than spend the rest of my life asking what it would have been like to say yes to him. Yes to being his and yes to trying to rein him in. "We should go," she whispered.

"Where? Have you made your choice, little Rachelle?"

"Yes," she said huskily while sitting back and reclipping her seat belt. "I want to see your riverfront home." His answering smile was a little too smug, so she added, "But don't call me little. I don't like it."

He swooped in with one last deep kiss that left her far too turned on to care what he called her. "You will learn to."

◆ ◆ ◆

It was painfully difficult not to end the day early and take Rachelle somewhere private where they could finish what they'd started, but Magnus had a second agenda for the day. His men were looking into who might have been following Rachelle as well as securing his home. Her safety took precedence over his passion.

He pulled his car back onto the road and stole a glance at her. She still looked flustered by his last comment, and he was tempted tell her it had been a joke, but it was too much fun to see how she would respond.

He didn't want to spend his life with a woman who was afraid of him, nor was he looking for someone who would agree with everything he said. How boring would a life with such a woman be?

He glanced at her again. Rachelle Westerly was certainly not boring. Was she the woman for him? That was still to be determined, but the journey toward that decision promised to be quite enjoyable.

"Just because I said yes to your family home doesn't mean I said yes to anything else."

He arched an eyebrow and tried not to smile. "I believe your agreement to everything else was clearly stated by your hand on my cock a moment ago, but we can circle back to that later. If you'd like to deliver your answer in the form of deep throating, I'm open to that as well."

She huffed and folded her arms across her chest. "You're such an asshole."

He laughed. "Give me your hand."

"No."

Intrigued, he tried again. "Then let me offer you mine."

A hint of a smile twitched the corner of her mouth. She looked down at his outstretched hand and then met his eyes again. "I don't want to encourage your bad behavior."

She brought out a playful side of him he didn't know he had. "Should I apologize? It's not something I'm good at, but for you I'll give it a go. I sincerely regret my obsession with wanting to rip your jeans off and kiss my way up those delicious thighs of yours. It's inappropriate for me to keep imagining how wet you'll be for my cock after I've made you come again and again with my tongue. Forgive me?"

He loved the flush his words brought to her cheeks and how she smiled as she placed her hand in his. Her words, however, took him by surprise. "I hope you don't apologize to my grandmother in such a manner. You'll give her a stroke."

"You're evil. Pure evil." He pulled her hand to his lips and nipped it gently. "But you've found a quick cure for a boner."

She laughed. "You deserved it."

"I did." He laced his fingers with hers. The SUV in front of them turned onto a driveway, and Magnus sighed. "We'll have to continue this conversation later, because we've arrived."

"Where?"

The long dirt driveway wound through a thickly wooded area that opened to a grassy field and a small, stone building he knew well. "I thought you might like to meet my mother's sister."

"You're taking me to see your family?" Rachelle looked down at her jeans. "Like this?"

"I'm the one who is not correctly attired. You'll understand once you meet her."

Magnus only had time to open Rachelle's door before he heard his aunt exclaim, "Magnus. You're early. I thought you were coming tomorrow." As she approached, she wiped her hands on a towel tied to one of the belt loops on her jeans. She was a tiny, slender woman, with a short mop of salt-and-pepper curls. She could have chosen to live in any of the palaces in the country, but she preferred the simpler life of tending to her flower farm. She and her botanist husband were the reason Vandorra was known for exporting hardy and richly colored flowers. The science as well as the beauty it produced was a labor of love for her. She waved to Magnus and called for her husband, Aiden.

She approached quickly and gave him a hug so full of love he felt his mother was there with them, if only for the briefest of instants. When she released him, his uncle Aiden took her place with a back-thumping hug. Just under six feet, his uncle looked healthy and fit despite his sixty-plus years.

"Change of plans," Magnus said after his uncle released him. "I hope you don't mind that I brought a friend. Aunt Nissa, Uncle Aiden, this is . . . my friend Rachelle Westerly."

His aunt looked Rachelle over from head to toe, and Magnus was surprised by how much he wanted her to like Rachelle. He could marry a woman his father didn't approve of, but if Nissa didn't like someone, neither would his people.

Rachelle held out her hand in a shy greeting. "It's a pleasure to meet you."

"Yes, a pleasure, and an unexpected one at that." His aunt shook her hand but continued to look her over. "Aiden, she's American. I did not see that coming."

His uncle ducked his head down and offered his hand to Rachelle. "Don't mind my wife, Rachelle. Magnus doesn't bring women around for us to meet."

Rachelle shot Magnus an odd look. "He doesn't?"

"Westerly. You aren't related to that movie star, are you?" Nissa asked.

"He's my brother."

"Are you an actress, too?" A frown wrinkled Nissa's forehead.

"No, I'm a first-grade teacher. I took time off, though, to visit with my brother."

A smile lit Nissa's face, and she put an arm around her husband's waist. "She teaches young children, and she's close to her family. I like her already."

Magnus added, "Her grandmother is staying with Father's friends the Wimbleys. You may know her. Delinda Westerly."

His aunt's eyes widened, and she looked Rachelle over again. "Your grandmother has caused quite a buzz in our social circle. I've heard her name several times in the last few days. She's a woman of strong opinions, isn't she?"

"That's an understatement," Rachel said.

The smile returned to his aunt's face. She turned to Magnus. "How did you manage an unchaperoned outing with Delinda Westerly's grandchild?"

Magnus wiggled his eyebrows. "She doesn't know I have her yet."

His aunt patted her husband's arm. "Isn't he funny?"

His uncle smiled politely. "I don't believe he's joking."

Rachelle rolled her eyes skyward. "I am an adult, and my grandmother has never had a say in what I do or who I do it with."

"Oh," his aunt said with rounded lips.

Uncle Aiden waved toward the house. "How bad are our manners? I'm sure Magnus didn't bring Rachelle here to see our driveway. If you haven't had lunch yet, why don't we eat overlooking the main field? It's in full bloom at this time of year."

"That sounds wonderful," Magnus said.

"We'll gather up the food and meet you on the patio. Show Rachelle around, Magnus. We won't be long," Nissa said as she began to step away, pulling her husband with her.

"Would you like any help with it?" Rachelle asked.

Nissa paused and looked up at her husband. "She's sweet, too." Then to Rachelle she said, "Run along with Magnus."

As they walked away, Rachelle said, "I feel bad about not helping," under her breath.

Magnus took her hand and began to lead her up a steep path toward a spot his aunt had always said had the best view of the farm. "They'll be fine. When Aunt Nissa says she'll gather up the food, she means she'll run into the house and send her kitchen staff scrambling to prepare something."

"Kitchen staff. Of course," Rachelle said. "She just looked so—I thought—I guess I should have known, considering she's part of the royal family."

"Aunt Nissa doesn't consider herself anything but a regular person. Her husband, however, made a fortune before they met. He owns a lucrative shipping company but gave up that life to live here with her, with the stipulation that they would always have a fully staffed kitchen. He says the one time he tried her cooking was enough."

"That's awful," Rachelle said with a smile.

They reached the top of the hill, and he knew the exact moment she raised her eyes to take in the view. Her hand tightened on his. "I've never seen anything like it. There must be thousands of rows of flowers. It looks like it goes on forever."

Magnus moved to wrap his arms around her from behind. "And not a vegetable in sight. My mother would have hated it. Well, not all of it. My aunt is passionate about educating people about the declining global honeybee population. This is not only a floral garden, it's also a working laboratory for university students seeking natural ways to control pests and weeds without harming the bees. Since you can't normally grow vegetables without bees, my aunt argues she's doing her part to keep my mother's vision alive."

Rachelle leaned back into his embrace. "It's absolutely breathtaking."

Her body fit so perfectly against his. He couldn't be this close to her without his imagination going into lusty overdrive, but it wasn't the time or the place, so he didn't allow himself to act upon it. "Did you like the flowers I sent you this morning?"

"I did." She smacked her forehead lightly. "I didn't thank you, did I? I'm sorry. I forgot."

He nuzzled her neck. "Understandable. I took a chance that if you liked a bouquet, you would love this place."

"I do." She turned in his arms and looked up at him. "Is it true that you don't bring women to meet your aunt and uncle?"

He ran his hand up and under her hair, then combed it down through it. "You're the first."

"Why am I here?"

There wasn't a simple answer to that. "Nissa is all I have left of my mother."

Rachelle smiled. "Who are you? Will the real Prince Magnus please stand up?"

He pulled her closer to him, linking his hands together behind her lower back. "I am who I need to be." He kissed her then, savoring the feel of her soft lips. "But sometimes, when I'm with you, I'm who I want to be."

Her eyes fluttered and she melted against him. "You're not just saying that so I'll sleep with you tonight, are you?"

He kissed her lightly again. "Sleep? No. What I have in mind has nothing to do with resting." He winked.

She blushed, but desire lit her eyes. Whatever she might have been about to say was lost as one of the staff called out that lunch was served on the patio. On the way back down the path, she stopped and said simply, "Thank you for sharing this with me."

And in that moment, she stole a piece of his heart.

Chapter Eighteen

Later that evening, Rachelle buried her face against a warm wall of muscle and sighed. A voice in her head told her to wake up, but she didn't want to. She felt herself being lowered onto a cool, soft cloud but didn't want to go there alone. She clutched at the warmth, desperate to keep it with her.

"Not tonight, little Rachelle," Magnus said gently.

Too comfortable to resist the lure of sleep, Rachelle let herself drift away. When she woke, it was with a dry mouth and a headache. The room she was in was dark, but dimly lit by a table lamp. The bed as well as the rest of the room was comfortably modern. She sat up, regretted having moved that quickly, and lay back down, but not before seeing that she wasn't alone.

Magnus, shoes off and shirt half-undone, was asleep in a chair beside the lamp. Rachelle rolled onto her side, tucked a hand beneath her head, and took the sight in. Even in his relaxed pose, he exuded power—like a sleeping lion, one with more depth and humor than she'd imagined when she first met him.

His eyes opened and he sat forward. "How do you feel?"

"Like a deceptively sweet-looking older couple drank me under the table." *Yeah, 'cause that happened.*

"I should have warned you that they love their wine. You seemed to be holding your own until suddenly you weren't." He ran a hand through his slightly tousled hair. "I put a glass of water and aspirin next to your bed."

"Thank you." Rachelle popped two pills in her mouth and chased it with several gulps of water. "I don't drink. Now I remember why." As she settled back down, she realized she was still fully dressed, tennis shoes and all. "I hope I didn't embarrass you—or myself."

"They loved you, said you were quite charming. My aunt has a theory that you don't really know someone until you see them soused."

"So you got me drunk to see if I become an asshole?"

He smiled. "It wasn't my idea to have you sample wines from each region of Vandorra, and you could have said no at any time. I'll admit, I was curious to see which side of you it'd bring out."

"And?"

"You shared a few too many stories about a cat you had when you were five, but outside of that, you were actually sweet and cuddly. A little too cuddly for me to be able to even take off your shoes. It was flattering, though, to be told you have high expectations of how good sex with me will be."

"I did not say that."

"You did. Once in the car to Phillip. And again to me when I carried you up to my bed. Some men might be intimidated, but I'm confident I can deliver."

She groaned again. "I'm too hungover to come up with a good comeback for that, but I want you to imagine that I did, and it was a zinger."

He placed a hand over his heart. "It cut me to the bone. Left me a humbled man."

Rachelle wasn't sure she wanted him humbled. Part of his charm was his confidence and the realization that he was a man who might never be tamed. And yet, he'd stayed and watched over her. "Are we at your family's riverfront home?"

"A.k.a. what I'd imagined would be a sex den last night."

"You'll live." She moved to sit up but felt nauseated when she did. "Will you?"

"The jury is still out on that."

Magnus picked up the phone beside him and made a short call. Despite the time of night, he requested a continental breakfast as well as an assortment of juices—and a Moody Tuesday.

"What is that?"

"It's a hangover cure from my college days. Steadman kept the recipe for emergencies, although I haven't needed it in years. Age has taught me that sampling a wine does not require downing the glass."

"I don't think I can keep anything down."

"You will try."

"Is that a royal command?"

His eyebrows arched. "Do you respond to those? If so, I definitely won't waste them getting you to try something that will have you feeling better within an hour."

Still flirting, still hot for her, and Magnus didn't appear at all upset with how the night had gone. Was this the real Magnus? "I really liked your aunt and uncle. They were surprisingly down-to-earth and funny."

"They liked you, too. Very much."

A light knock on the door announced the arrival of a member of his house staff with a silver serving tray. "Your Royal Highness," the woman said. "Would you like it near the bed?"

"Yes, thank you," Magnus said. "You may place it beside her."

Rachelle pulled herself into a seated position. "Thank you."

"You're welcome, Miss Westerly," the woman said before quickly departing.

In place of a tall Bloody Mary, as Rachelle had expected, there was a short tumbler of dark liquid on ice. She picked the glass up, sniffed the contents, and made a face. It smelled like alcohol but looked like mud. "What is it?"

"Fernet-Branca. The Italians swear by it as a hangover cure. Some put it over espresso, but I find that adding crème de menthe lessens the bitterness."

Her stomach churned just looking at it. "I'll stick to water."

"Playing it safe? You disappoint me, little Rachelle."

She chose a piece of bread with honey and bit into it. *Delicious.* "I've never eaten dirt, but I know I won't like it."

He walked over to the bed and moved the tray so he could sit beside her. "Once you give in to fear, you've decided exactly how small your life will remain."

If he weren't so absolutely gorgeous, even more so in his disheveled state, he would have been easier to be irritated with. As it was, her body was doing a wild scramble to decide if it could ignite with passion even while still uncomfortably ill. "Peer pressure only works on children."

He lifted the glass to his own lips. "No pressure, merely an educated suggestion. You'll hate the taste if you've never had it. It's bitter. Revolting. Not a drink for the meek. But if you dare more than a sip, it will warm its way through you." He took a generous gulp of it. "Much as you're doing to me."

Swoon.

He held the beverage out to her, and she accepted it. How could she not after that?

Wait. "It's bitter and revolting but will grow on me, just like I'm bitter and nasty but growing on you?"

He chuckled. "Perhaps I worded that poorly. At first it doesn't seem to your taste, but the more you get to know it, the more difficult it is to imagine a time before it."

"Is that actually better?"

"Drink, Rachelle."

Her first sip had her gagging in disgust. Bitter medicine. Thick. Oily. With just a hint of mint as a reprieve. She almost replaced the glass, but he was watching her closely. To prove something to herself as well as to him, she downed the rest of the glass.

The initial shock of it was followed by a lingering taste similar to licorice. She expected her stomach to refuse it, but oddly enough it didn't. There was a punch to it, but not like she remembered from her one and only whiskey shot.

"So?" he asked.

"I don't think I'm going to throw it up," she said, because that truly had been her fear a moment earlier.

He laughed. "Eat your honey toast and finish your water. You'll feel better."

Rachelle lifted a piece of toast to her mouth, then stopped. "Do you phrase everything as an order?"

"Do you always fight for control, even when something is for your own benefit?"

"I don't know." She looked at the bread, then back to him. "My mother blamed the end of her marriage to my father on how controlling his mother was. Delinda had all the money, and she held that power over my father. Not over us, though, because my mother thought we were better off without the money."

"So your mother raised you to not trust half your family."

"No. No, she wasn't like that." Even as Rachelle said the words, she wondered if there wasn't some truth to them. She loved her mother and for most of her life had taken her side without question. That didn't mean her mother was perfect—hell, she'd hidden an affair and the parentage of one of her children. Was it possible that the only way for Rachelle to find her way back to her family was to admit that her mother was human—flawed? "Maybe she did divide us without realizing how it would change all of us. Those of us who stayed with Mom wondered why our father didn't care more about us. Those who went with Dad wondered why Mom found them easy to leave behind. It didn't have to be that way."

"It didn't, but you are building bridges over that divide. I admire your dedication to your brother, especially since he has little toward you."

There was no denying that one, even though it hurt not to be able to. "Brett tried to explain our different upbringing to me. He said he and Eric were raised without the laughter and open expression of love that we were." She placed the bread down on the plate and hugged her stomach. "You don't want to hear this."

"Yes, I do," Magnus said, caressing her arm gently before dropping his hand. "I want to know you, Rachelle. The good and the bad."

She met his eyes and saw only sincere interest there. However this turned out, Magnus was part of this journey to understand herself. His opinion would help, because it was a fresh look at situations she was too close to. "My understanding of my family has been shaken lately. I used to think my grandmother was a horrible woman, that my father had cheated on my mother, and that Brett and Eric thought they were better than us. Then my grandmother turned eighty and offered all of us grandchildren access to our inheritance on the stipulation that we marry and invite the family to the weddings. I stupidly suggested that my best friend, Alisha, marry Spencer. He needed money, and she's always been part of our family. I didn't see the harm."

"And they married?"

"No, but they did get engaged. Then she met my oldest brother, Brett."

His eyebrows rose.

She continued, "Exactly. It wasn't good. Alisha and Brett fell in love just after Spencer found out his father was not my father."

"So, your mother was unfaithful."

"Yes, and none of us knew. We all assumed it was our father who had cheated."

"And then she took half of his children from him." There was disgust in Magnus's tone that made Rachelle wish she hadn't shared the story.

"Her second husband was an amazing man we all loved." Magnus didn't need to say anything for Rachelle to see even that in a new light as well. "Which could not have been easy for my father." As Rachelle looked back with new eyes, the line between right and wrong blurred. "Brett always says that our family's divide was like cracks in glass that could be traced back to one defining event."

Magnus took her hand in his.

Although everything Rachelle was sharing had been disclosed to her months earlier, it was the first time she was truly facing it. "My grandfather Oliver killed himself, and Delinda considered it her fault for not preparing him better when he took over her family's business. When he died, my father, Dereck, took his place, and Delinda was determined he would not fail. Brett says Delinda's greatest fear was losing her son or one of us the way she'd lost her husband. So she made it her goal to toughen us up. I try to like her, but I don't know that she's ever said anything nice to me."

"I wondered why you wouldn't tell her where Eric was."

"I want to see the good in my grandmother, but life is always a battle to her, and we are soldiers she's trying to prepare for it." Rachelle thought about what working with so many children had taught her. "Tough love can be a good thing, but sometimes people need a kinder touch. Sometimes you have to consider what the other person needs. My grandmother doesn't do that."

"Yet." His voice dipped.

Her gaze flew to his.

He said, "You're a natural teacher, little Rachelle. You will be the one to show her."

Rachelle wiped a tear away from the corner of her eye. "On my cockiest days, I don't know if I believe I can."

He leaned over and kissed her. "Then you need to see yourself through my eyes."

Whether it was the Fernet or the man seated beside her on the bed, Rachelle felt better than she had in a long, long time. "I'm sorry I ruined last night," she blurted, then blushed.

He chuckled. "I don't want to leave you this morning, but I must, at least for a few hours. You'll have a driver and one of my guards at your disposal if you decide to go shopping in town. I'll be back early, and then you can show me exactly how sorry you are."

She would have laughed, but the heated way he was looking at her filled her mind with X-rated possibilities. "I always apologize best after being apologized to," she said cheekily.

He kissed her again and growled, "I'll keep that in mind." He stood. "I should go while I'm still able to."

Rachelle couldn't stop smiling after he left. She ate everything on the tray, called to check on Eric, then took a long, hot shower. At first she wasn't sure she wanted to go out, but the lure of seeing a new town in a country she knew very little about was strong. Besides, it would give her a chance to buy lingerie. She'd never been the type of woman who wore it, but Magnus made her feel sexy, and she wanted to explore that side of herself.

Now, all she had to figure out was where a woman would buy lingerie in a small Vandorran town and how to ask to be brought to such a store without looking like she was looking for . . . well, what she was looking for.

The original meeting scheduled for that day would not have been enough to pull Magnus from Rachelle's side, but early that morning Phillip had texted that he'd received new information regarding the people shadowing her. It was a conversation Magnus didn't want Rachelle to overhear until he had a better idea of who it was and what they wanted. As was his practice with his father, his goal was to eradicate any problem without her ever knowing.

They met at Phillip's parents' home a mile down the river, a place Magnus knew well from childhood. Before Phillip had become a royal guard and while Magnus had still been unhindered by the responsibilities of his title, they had played together. Magnus's mother had wanted her son to have a normal childhood, at least as much as possible. She'd brought him to this area to encourage him to kayak, ride his bicycle, and make friends. Several of his friends from that time had joined the royal guard, and he was as loyal to them as they had proven to be to him. It was those men Magnus would not only trust with his life, but defend with his own, if need be.

Seated across from him in the living room, Phillip said, "It's a complicated mess, Magnus."

"So, uncomplicate it for me."

"I'll start with the black card with the white phone number. It belongs to an American security expert, Alethea Narcharios. She's big-league. Until a few years ago she was testing the physical and online security of major companies. Lately, she's been a private hire for wealthy families in the United States. My guess is she's on Delinda Westerly's payroll. Possibly to protect her granddaughter."

"Possibly? Why else would she be here?"

"That's what I asked myself for no other reason than my gut told me to. I looked for any attempted hacks to your server, any unusual hires, anything that might indicate interest in your business rather than Rachelle's."

"And?"

"And I found all of that. If you were not as paranoid—"

"Diligent."

"—as you are about safeguards, she would not only have access to your bank account but to your dresser drawers as well. I am combing through every staff change we've had in the last month, but I may have to go back further. This woman is an insidious weed once she has a toehold. Thankfully, we're a step ahead of her now."

"Why would Delinda Westerly want to hack my server?"

"This is solely speculation, but it might be the same reason she's making a show of inviting your contacts to the ball she's planning with your father. She is not happy with the public treatment Rachelle has received because of you. Revenge? Blackmail? Hard to say."

He didn't want to return to seeing Delinda or Rachelle in that light. "Is there any evidence that Rachelle is aware of what her grandmother is doing?"

"None that I've come across."

"Good. Then bring me the Narcharios woman."

"I haven't been able to locate her. She uses disguises, pays in cash, and she's well funded. I can tell you she's here, but that's it."

"That's not good enough."

"Understood."

Magnus rose to his feet and paced the room. "Eric's man said there were two people following Rachelle. Have you identified the man?"

"Yes. Goran Petek. He was in prison in Slovenia for murder until his conviction was recently overturned."

"Someone bought his freedom. Where is he now?"

"Back in Slovenia. He returned yesterday and was picked up by their police. It seems evidence regarding his involvement in a second murder has come to light."

"Neutralizing him without killing him."

"Yes."

"I don't like that this has been playing out on our soil, yet this is the first I hear of it." Magnus didn't let himself fully process that a known killer had been stalking Rachelle. Emotion clouded his judgment, and he needed a clear head to protect her. "Who had Petek released in the first place?"

"We're still investigating that."

"I want someone in Slovenia today. I don't care what it takes. I want to know who he was working for and what they wanted with Rachelle. This is a top priority. Are we clear?"

"Yes."

"No one gets close to her unless they've been thoroughly checked. No one."

"Understood."

Angered that there was not more he could do, Magnus slammed his fist sideways against the wall. "She's important to me, Phillip."

"I know. We'll keep her safe."

Magnus swore. "I sent her into town."

"Don't worry, she's far from alone."

Chapter Nineteen

For someone who had been nearly invisible for most of her life, the trip into town bordered on the ridiculous. Magnus had said he would provide a driver as well as a guard for her, but somehow that had grown into four men in suits escorting Rachelle down the cobblestoned main street. So much for fitting in.

As she walked, people came out of their homes to meet her. She was tempted to tell them she wasn't anyone of importance, but they seemed so excited that she didn't have the heart to. One woman introduced an entire herd of children to her. Rachelle took the time to ask each a question based on their age. She knew from experience to ask the littlest about their toys and the older ones about themselves. There were many, many times in Rachelle's life when she wasn't confident, but meeting people and putting them at ease was what she did well. She liked people, and somehow, more often than not, they liked her.

It was natural when a conversation with a plump, older restaurant owner named Zinnia led to following her back to her kitchen to sample the woman's *ribollita*, a vegetable soup thickened with bread. When Rachelle attempted to pay for the soup, the woman refused and said it was an honor to have her in her restaurant at all. Only then did Rachelle say, "Please, let me give you something. I think you have me confused with someone else."

"No. No. I know who you are. You're Prince Magnus's woman."

I wish that didn't sound quite so much like he owns me, but I'll allow it for cultural differences. "We're friends, yes."

The woman continued, "Maybe one day his bride."

Whoa. "I don't know about that."

"He would not bring you here unless you were very important to him. We helped to raise him. We are his home. His trusted friends. You understand? Four guard you today. One is my nephew. One I had to beat with a stick to keep out of my garden every year until he joined the royal guard. Desi, I have not forgotten where all my ripe tomatoes went." She turned toward the grown man, who smiled sheepishly at her reprimand.

"Yes, but my wife needed to practice, and now she makes the best sauce in Domovia. You said so yourself."

"That is the only reason I allow your son to take my roses for his girlfriend. He's in love."

Desi frowned. "My son is fifteen. What does he know of love?"

"You were about his age when you started stealing my tomatoes."

The other men laughed.

Desi did not.

In that instant, Rachelle's impression of the guards changed. They were no longer intimidating strangers in suits. They had names, families, and a place in this loving community.

"Thank you, Zinnia, for a beautiful lunch," Rachelle said. "Your warm welcome means more to me than you know."

Zinnia nodded as she walked with Rachelle back out onto the sidewalk in front of the restaurant. "Be good to our Magnus. He does not open his heart easily, but there is no one who would fight more fiercely for Vandorra—or for you if he chooses you."

If he chooses me.

Like it's that simple.

"How did you become queen?"

"Oh, he chose me."

Relationships are so much more complicated than that.

Standing on the curb with Zinnia, Rachelle wished it didn't have to be. Imagine how simple life would be if nothing else mattered besides wanting to be with someone who wanted to be with you? For just a night, Rachelle wanted to experience that. Even if it didn't last. Even if something that good couldn't.

One night.

One perfect night. Then I'll go back to reality.

On that note—"Zinnia, where do women buy clothing in this town?"

"Like a dress?" the woman asked.

"And other things."

"Other things?" Zinnia smiled knowingly. "Like a pharmacy?"

Rachelle tried not to die right there of embarrassment. "No, a clothing shop." She glanced down at her jeans, then back at Zinnia. "I'd like to get something more feminine."

"One minute," Zinnia said. She turned and called back into the restaurant, right over the heads of the patrons. "Niko. Where does your wife buy those little nighties you blame your five children on?" He called back the name of a shop in a larger neighboring town. "Oh yes. Do you think you could send her quick to buy something nice in a size"—she looked Rachelle over—"eight? Something that would have you propose to her all over again."

One of the men offered to go. Zinnia told him he was too young to have good sense in such things, but she would tell his father that he offered. The room fell quiet after that. Desi might not have been the only one she'd ever taken a stick to.

A moment later, Niko said his wife welcomed any excuse to shop and would be happy to go.

"Oh no. Please tell him it's not necessary."

Zinnia thanked Niko and closed the restaurant door as they exited. "It shouldn't be until your wedding night, but I've given up lecturing the young. You'll do as you please anyway."

"Nothing is happening. I simply was looking for something besides jeans."

Throwing her hands up in the air, Zinnia said, "Why do the young lie? I was never your age? Never in love? How do you think all of you got here if we didn't first do what you're planning? Your generation invented the Internet, not sex."

Okay, then. I may have overbonded with the townspeople. "It's probably time for me to head back. Thanks again for lunch."

"You are a natural beauty. You don't need makeup, but your hair could use a trim and maybe a good brushing. My sister is the best stylist in all of Vandorra. I will call her. She also does manicures. Beautiful and fast."

You don't by any chance know my grandmother, do you? Rachelle smoothed a hand over the curls she hadn't straightened that morning.

"You'll need a dress," Zinnia said. "Men love dresses. I know just the shop. My cousin Abri travels once a month to the city to fill her shop with the best of the season. She is who we go to when we want something special."

"I don't want to be any trouble. Really. I have clothes."

"No trouble. It is a memory we'll all treasure when you marry our Magnus."

"M-marry? I don't really know him all that well."

Zinnia frowned, but a moment later her smile returned. "Hopefully the right dress will change that." She stepped away to make a few phone calls.

Rachelle looked at the men who still flanked her and realized they had probably heard the conversation. It didn't show on their faces, but Magnus had said they were trained to look away. Still, she felt she needed to address the awkwardness of the situation. "I know what you're probably thinking, but it's not like that. Well, maybe it's exactly like that, but I live a very ordinary life. I don't travel to Europe. I don't meet princes. I went to prom with my brother's friend because he felt bad for me when he heard I didn't have a date. So let me enjoy this, okay? Even if it reinforces your impression of me, I don't care. I'm probably going right back to my regular life after this, but not today. Just give me today."

A long silence followed.

Desi cleared his throat. "My wife showed me the video clip of you and Prince Magnus in London. She said he'd bring you here. She was right. She's always right."

"She makes him say that last part," one of the other guards joked.

In a move that was so fast Rachelle almost missed it, Desi punched the other man on the arm, then went back to standing as if nothing had happened. It took Rachelle by surprise, and she laughed.

Zinnia returned just then. "Did I miss something?"

"No, not a thing," Rachelle said.

"My sister said she has time if we go now. Ready?"

Rachelle tucked her hands into her jeans pockets. "Yes. Thank you for doing this, Zinnia."

Zinnia linked arms with her and guided her down the street. "It's my pleasure. Now let's talk about those tennis shoes. Are you planning to play tennis today?"

◆ ◆ ◆

It was late afternoon before Magnus drove back to his family home. He sat in his car to give himself time to calm down, because his temper was still hot, and he wouldn't want to show that side of himself to Rachelle. She didn't need to see the rage that had filled him when the man he'd sent to Slovenia reported Petek was dead. The car transporting him to court that morning had been involved in a hit-and-run crash that had left him and the driver dead. He'd been erased. Whoever was behind this was covering his tracks, but that wouldn't save him.

His frustration with the situation was not Rachelle's fault. He and his men needed to act fast and decisively. With Phillip's help, Magnus designed a plan to lure Delinda's security expert out into the open. They used their own experts to create duplicate servers, planted information, orchestrated opportunities, and made everything challenging enough for a breach to be believable. If she was as curious as Phillip thought she was, she would follow clues that would lead her right to a time and place they controlled, and they'd have her.

Delinda Westerly was a problem. It was one thing to engage in harmless matchmaking. It was quite another to hack someone's server. She would soon discover why Vandorra's borders were safe, despite their limited military capabilities. Magnus didn't wait for a fight to come to him, and if he went to battle, he didn't back down until he won. For that reason, he also sent his people more aggressively to uncover anything he could take Delinda down with if it came to that.

A car pulled up behind his. Magnus got out to investigate, then relaxed as soon as he recognized them as local musicians from town. Ones he'd known since they used to race their bikes up and down that very driveway. "Benito, good to see you."

"Your Royal Highness," Benito said in greeting before the two exchanged a warm handshake.

"What are you doing here?"

"Every dance floor needs music."

"I'm sorry, my friend, but there has been a mistake. We don't have an event planned for tonight."

Benito wiggled his eyebrows. "I forgot. It's a secret. If anyone asks, I said nothing."

"What is a secret?" Magnus growled, his patience already thin after the day he'd had. The three other musicians scurried into the house with their instruments in hand.

"You put me in a difficult spot, no? I would be forever grateful if you let me run inside while you pretend to be surprised."

"Look at my face, Benito. Do I look like I want to be surprised today?" If his friends had organized some kind of party for him, they had chosen the day poorly. All Magnus wanted was to lose himself in the heaven of Rachelle's body.

"Trust me, this will put a smile back on your face."

"Benito."

Benito looked around instead of immediately answering, which pushed Magnus from impatient to angry. Who did Benito fear more than his prince? "Zinnia asked me to be early, but you know how the band is. One of us is always late. Please, don't tell her. I swore we would be here before you."

Zinnia? What the hell was going on? Magnus strode away from Benito to direct his questions toward someone who knew better than to hedge around the truth. "Desi, what is going on here?"

Desi shot a quick look at the guards and stepped forward. "Your Royal Highness, it is a dinner for you and Miss Westerly."

Still running on the frustration of the day, Magnus asked impatiently, "Then why is Benito here?"

Desi's expression turned pained. "We took Miss Westerly to town this morning, as instructed."

"And?"

"Everyone liked her."

On any other day, Magnus might have found this mildly entertaining, but not that day. "I didn't ask you what people thought of her, I asked about Benito."

Desi straightened to a military posture. "Yes, Your Royal Highness. He is here to play music while you dance with Miss Westerly after dinner."

"By my command?" Magnus demanded.

"No, Your Royal Highness."

"Surely someone thought to ask my permission."

"No, Your Royal Highness."

Temper flaring, Magnus growled, "So, to clarify: I have spent the day determining and planning a defense against a real threat, while, instead of assisting in that, my royal guard has been occupied how?"

"Preparing for this evening, Your Royal Highness."

"Preparing how? I'm guessing it wasn't by patrolling the perimeter. Nor by questioning everyone in town to confirm there are no suspicious persons." It was a sharper tone than he normally used with his men, but too much had been happening in Vandorra for them to not be extra vigilant.

"No, Your Royal Highness." The remorse in Desi's eyes was genuine. "It will not happen again."

"It can't, Desi, for the sake of my life as well as yours."

Desi nodded respectfully.

Magnus turned and strode up the steps. Desi must have radioed ahead, because by the time he stepped into the house, his staff was in a panicked scramble. He walked from room to room, shaking his head at what they had wasted their time on. The dining room, as well as most of the first floor of the home, was full of white roses and lit candles. A quick glance out one of the windows revealed that a square dance floor had been created on the lawn facing the river. Benito apparently hadn't gotten the news, because he and his band were still setting up.

Just as he returned to the foyer, Phillip appeared. "A moment, Your Royal Highness."

"Did anyone clear this with you? They brought in food, flowers, entertainment. Do they understand how many unknown elements they introduced to my house? My house. Nothing happens here without my knowledge and my permission."

"It appears this was a spontaneous idea they collectively went with."

"Unacceptable. This will not happen again. We need to do better than this, Phillip. How can I protect her if my own men become unpredictable?"

"I will speak to them."

"Where did they get the flowers? The candles? Were they delivered? And if so, by whom? I want to know the name and description of every single person who stepped into my home."

"I'll have that information for you shortly, Your Royal Highness."

Magnus ran his hands through his hair. He knew he sounded like an asshole, but nice didn't keep people safe. "Why? What is the purpose of all of this, anyway?"

Phillip hesitated, then said, "It's my understanding that Miss Westerly met Zinnia in town today, and the two got on well enough that they hatched this idea in an attempt to please you."

"Well, get it all out of here."

"Are you sure? Miss Westerly obviously went to a lot of trouble—"

"You know what I didn't need today, Phillip? Another fucking surprise. I don't care how much work went into this. I want it gone."

A gasp echoed through the foyer. Magnus turned and was sucker punched by a completely different version of Rachelle than he'd left that morning. Dressed in a strapless dark-blue gown that fit her like a second skin, her hair piled on top of her head in a sexy knot of curls, she stood halfway down the stairway, taking his breath away. He'd waited a long time for her, and there she was, wrapped up for him like a candy begging to be devoured. The anger in her eyes only fueled the wild passion burning within him.

"You don't care about anyone but yourself, do you? And you don't even bother to hide it."

Phillip wisely withdrew, as did the rest of his staff.

Magnus spoke as he crossed the foyer to the bottom of the stairway. "You appear to be feeling better."

"I am—well enough to be able to drive myself back to the city, if you could lend me a car."

"That's not how I see tonight going," he said as he advanced up the steps. He was done playing games. She'd obviously dressed with the intention of pleasing him, and it had worked. He didn't need roses, candles, and pretty dresses to want her—but he appreciated the effort.

She stood her ground, her chin raising the closer he came. He would have told her how long the move made her neck look but decided the kisses he'd rain on it would deliver that message. She said, "It appears we'll both be disappointed tonight, because I'm leaving."

He came to a stop on the step below her, still towering over her by a few inches, but her mouth was deliciously closer. Her breasts swelled with each deep breath she took, reminding him of the first night he'd met her. "Keep the dress on the first time I fuck you." She raised her hand to deliver a slap, but he caught it easily. "I don't mind if you like it rough, but let's take it somewhere private." He pulled her closer. "You look so fucking hot in that dress. Good choice."

"Let me go. Are you deaf? I'm not staying. Not now."

He grabbed her chin and forced her to look him in the eye. "Because I didn't like the flowers? Because I don't dance? I don't give a shit about those things. If you're looking for someone to romance you and read you poetry, that's not me. I'm not that man." He ran a thumb over her lip and loved how it opened for him almost against her will. "You don't care. All you want is my cock again. Say it."

Her eyes raged with the same desire flooding him. "No."

He tasted her lips, teasing them with his tongue until she opened them for him. He lifted her into his arms while continuing to plunder her mouth. Her arms wound around his neck, and their kiss tasted of anger and fire. He didn't know if he could trust her, and she was obviously furious with him, but none of that mattered, because their need for each other consumed all else.

He carried her up the rest of the steps and down the hallway to his room, kicking the door closed behind him. He walked to the bed and tossed her down on it. Standing over her, he said, "Now is not the time to lie to yourself or to me. We both know this is what you want. All you have to do is say yes." He stepped out of his shoes, then pulled his shirt free of his trousers. "Yes to me bringing you pleasure." He dropped his shirt on the floor. "Yes to pleasing me." He unbuckled his belt and removed the rest of his clothing smoothly. He stood before her, naked and fully aroused. "One word, but you have to say it. Give yourself to me."

Despite the passion in her eyes, she said, "And if I say no?"

"You won't," he said, slipping her shoes off and taking each of her stockinged feet in one hand. "But it is always your right to." He slid a hand beneath her gown, up her leg, and discovered the stockings ended midthigh. "These stay, too."

She licked her bottom lip. "You like them?"

"Oh yes." With one strong move, he pulled her to the edge of the bed and held her legs up and apart at his sides. He followed with the other stocking, then went higher to the satin that covered her wet sex. He lightly ran his hand back and forth over the material. "Did you buy this for me as well?"

"Yes," she whispered, her eyes fluttering and glazing with need.

He eased the material aside and dipped his finger gently inside her. "I like that word on your lips. Say it again."

"Yes."

He rewarded her by circling her nub until he found just the pressure and rhythm that made her squirm against his hand. She gripped the sheets on either side of her as he caressed her intimately. He wanted to see all of her, kiss every inch of her, but first he wanted the fantasy from that first night. As he touched her, he told her exactly how much he wanted to fuck her, how beautiful she was, how this was only the beginning of the pleasure they'd bring each other.

When her face was flushed with excitement and she was wet and ready, he hauled her to her feet and kissed her deeply. She was wild for him, her hands grasping for more of him. He stepped back, hiked her gown up, and unsnapped the satin crotch.

"Wait." She reached into the bodice of her dress, pulled out a condom, and tossed it at him. He caught it and smiled.

It was all on then. He sheathed himself, then lifted her so her dress bunched and her legs wrapped around his waist. He kissed his way down her long neck and across the mounds of her eager-to-be-released breasts. Her sex hovered just above the tip of his cock, teasing, ready. She dug her hand into his hair and raised his mouth to hers. The kiss they shared shook him to his core. Never had he wanted a woman more.

They kissed until there was nothing but a painful hunger that could no longer be denied. With a step, he backed her to the wall and thrust up into her. She gasped into their kiss, then met his thrust with one of her own. Deeper and harder. Faster and more wild. The only sound in the room was her calling out for him not to stop and him swearing because it was that fucking good.

When he felt her giving herself over to an orgasm, he joined her with one last powerful thrust. He kissed her gently as they both came back to earth slowly.

Reluctantly, he lowered her back to her feet and disposed of the condom before returning to her side. Her clothing fell back into place. He wrapped his arms around her from behind and nuzzled her neck. "You have good taste in dresses."

"Thank you." She melted back against him. "I still think you're an asshole."

He chuckled. "We'll see if you're still saying that by morning." He kissed his way across her shoulder while unfastening the back of her dress. She stepped out of it, and he turned her, appreciating every curve the tiny satin outfit clung to, as well as those it revealed. "I like the idea of getting to know the many layers of you."

Her hand sought his cock and encircled it. "As opposed to stripping right down and putting yourself out there."

"I'm not as complicated as you are." Remembering what they were talking about had become nearly impossible as soon as she'd touched him. "This is who I am."

She brought her other hand around to caress his balls while she rubbed her beautiful tits, still covered with satin, across his chest. "Too bad, I was hoping there was more."

He gripped her ass roughly. "What else do you need?"

She shook her head. "It's okay. I'll settle for a night of good sex."

If all his blood hadn't been pouring back into his cock, he might have known what to say to that, but he was already finding it difficult to concentrate on anything beyond having her again. He picked her up, carried to the bed, and this time rolled onto it with her.

They made love again, and it was every bit as good as the first time. He stripped her bare for their last, leisurely romp. By the time she fell asleep in his arms, they were both sexually sated, and he knew every inch of her body. What he didn't know was what more she'd expect from him—and it bothered him enough to keep him awake.

He tucked her to him beneath the blankets and frowned at her as she slept. Now that his head was clear, he replayed his arrival home and didn't like the way it had gone. She didn't know he'd been as angry with himself as he'd been with his men. He wasn't a man who failed, and he'd already failed to protect her. He'd left her unprotected and vulnerable to whoever had hired Petek. It didn't matter that he'd had no reason to believe she was in danger. Magnus knew how to protect what was his—and she was. She had been since their first kiss.

In the darkness, her gown formed a lump on the floor. He remembered how beautiful she'd looked on the stairs. She'd wanted to be beautiful for him, and she had been.

Had everything else been her idea as well? Was his rejection of it what had disappointed her? Without knowing the nature of his day, she wouldn't have understood his reaction.

He was not a man who spent much time worrying about what those around him felt, but the idea of hurting the woman in his arms didn't sit well with him. He rolled over and, despite that it was one in the morning, texted Phillip to order Benito to return.

Did he leave something? Phillip texted back.

No. I have changed my mind. Arrange for flowers, candles, music. Everything that was planned earlier. Use only trusted people.

It will take time. I had the flowers given away in town.

You have an hour.

Rachelle shifted against him, cuddling more closely to his side, and he dropped the phone. Phillip would make it happen. "Are you sleeping?" he asked.

"Are my eyes closed?" she asked with groggy sarcasm.

"I've been thinking about what you said."

She opened one eye, then shut it. "Any chance we can talk about this in the morning?"

"I'm awake now."

"Yes, you are. I, however, am not."

"Then you are remarkable at maintaining discourse while sleeping."

Her eyes opened then. "Fine. What did I say that you actually heard?"

"That I was not thinking about you when I canceled what you had planned for me. I was still preoccupied with my meeting. You and I will shower, get dressed once again, and go have the dance you wanted earlier. As well as whatever else you arranged."

"I'm sure everyone is gone."

"They are on their way back."

She rolled over to check the clock beside the bed. "At this time of night?"

"Yes."

"Just like that? No one is even upset that you essentially threw them out?"

"They would not dare to be."

"Of course not, because of who you are. You don't think that makes you a dick?"

"Do you not want them to return?"

She sat up, and he was momentarily distracted by the bounce of her bare breasts. "No, I do not want them to return. That whole dance thing was stupid. I shouldn't have been angry with you last night. That's just who you are. It's not like you've tried to hide it. You've been blunt about what you want from me. My mistake was letting Zinnia get into my head."

"I don't understand."

She gave him a long, sad look. "I know."

He sat up. "Get up. As you said, it's late. We don't want to make everyone wait too long for us."

"I just said I don't want them to come back. I'm tired. I'm going back to sleep." She lay back down and rolled away from him. If she truly wanted him to feel anything resembling remorse, she shouldn't wag her sweet ass at him.

He picked her up and carried her to the shower. "I don't require a woman to translate this for me. You're upset that I didn't dance with you, and you will continue to be upset until we do. So we shall dance."

He deposited her in the shower and turned the water on—full blast.

She shrieked and jumped away from him in the stall. "Are you crazy? That's freezing."

He laughed and shielded her from the water until it warmed, then pulled her toward him. "Now, you're awake." He wiggled an eyebrow in challenge.

She threw a facecloth at him. "Jerk."

"Still upset?" He placed his hand flat on her chest and pushed her back against the wall of the shower. "Luckily I know how to sweeten your mood." He dropped to his knees, lifted one of her legs, and swung it over his shoulder, then sought her nub with his tongue.

She gripped the back of his head with one hand, steadying herself with her other. "Oh yes. Oh, God, yes."

Sometimes the best way to talk to a woman did not involve talking at all.

Chapter Twenty

The embarrassment Rachelle felt when she walked down the main staircase fully dressed in an evening gown at three o'clock in the morning faded as soon as they reached the foyer. Whether it was the glow from more orgasms than she'd ever had in one night or the warmth of the candlelight the house and grounds were bathed in, Rachelle felt as if she were stepping into a dream. There were flowers everywhere, not the same as before, but just as beautiful. If his staff felt inconvenienced at all, they hid it well.

Magnus led her out onto the lawn where the band Zinnia had introduced Rachelle to in town was now playing soft music. She waved to Benito and mouthed, *Thank you.*

Benito smiled and nodded.

As they reached the dance floor, Magnus expertly spun her and began to lead her in a polished waltz. She recognized the tune only because she'd attended dance lessons with Alisha leading up to her wedding. Brett had also gone, but Alisha had said she wanted to keep it fun, and having her best friend there accomplished that. Strange how it took traveling so far away to appreciate all the ways she and Alisha had remained close despite how much had changed.

Magnus spun her again, and her attention returned to him. "I thought you said you couldn't dance."

"I said I don't, not that I couldn't."

"Then why are we doing this?"

He pulled her closer. "Because you wanted to."

She tipped her head back to see his expression. "And that matters to you?"

"We are dancing, aren't we?"

She glanced around. "You don't feel guilty at all about everyone who had to make this happen twice? They might be smiling, but I bet they all wish they were sleeping."

He spun her around again. "I have given up many nights of sleep to ensure these same people have what they need. I would take a bullet for them, as they would for me. My life is dedicated to them, just as theirs are to me."

"That's actually beautiful." And a level of commitment outside of Rachelle's experience—at least when it came to men. Did he carry that sentiment over into his relationships? "Have you ever been in love?"

"No," he said confidently enough that her heart cringed.

Well, that clears up any misconception I might have that he's falling for me. She tensed in his arms. "I don't want to meet more of your family or your so-close-they're-like-family friends." He effortlessly swung her around again, and she matched his steps naturally. Here, as well as in bed, they fit. It was just every time he opened his mouth that she wondered what the hell she was doing.

"Why are you upset with me now, little Rachelle?" He didn't look particularly concerned by the possibility.

But since he asked . . . "I'm not upset with you. I'm upset with myself. I'm okay with this being temporary, but I don't want to get hurt. I don't want to get confused."

"Temporary." He repeated the word as if mulling it. "It doesn't have to be. You're the first woman I've considered marrying."

"M-marrying?" She tripped over his foot and stumbled against his chest. *Does that mean he—? Didn't he just say he'd never been in—?* "We barely know each other."

He leaned down and murmured in her ear, "I wouldn't say that after last night."

Her heart went into a wild panic in her chest. "Marriage is more than that. You don't know anything about me, really. Not even my favorite food."

"That information would be best given to whichever chef we employ."

"Or my interests. Or what I want to do with the rest of my life."

"The rest of your life would be here in Vandorra. Your interests would be me, our family, and our people."

She froze. "And what would your interests be?"

"That depends on how well you continue to please me in bed."

She shoved at him. Of course he didn't move. He was an irritatingly strong wall of muscle. "Of all the egotistical . . . sexist . . ."

He roared with laughter and pulled her flush against his chest. "It was a joke. You're so easy to rile. Smile, little Rachelle. It's not every day you receive a proposal from a prince, is it?"

She snorted. "That was not a proposal. At least not one I'd ever say yes to."

His hold on her tightened. "I have never met a more contrary woman."

She held his gaze. Holding out against the fire in them took effort. On a purely primal level, she wanted to be his, but not on his terms. "What a relief it must be, then, that my answer is no."

His expression darkened. "I retract my proposal."

"Too late. It's already out there and has already been declined."

He frowned a moment longer; then his humor returned. "How did I miss it? You were joking. Touché, little Rachelle."

Is this what Cinderella had to work with?

What had he said? *"Rein me in."*

He needs someone who can, but is that me? He started to dance again, and she easily fell into step with him. She thought about how poorly her family communicated with one another. If her father had been open about the fact that *his* father had killed himself, would his marriage have survived? If her mother had been open about her affair and about who Spencer's real father was, would their family have healed instead of growing further apart? Was what a person hid more destructive than what they shared? One quality she admired about Magnus was that he said what he thought.

"This is who I am," he'd said.

And I have never been more myself than when I'm with him.

As they spun around the dance floor, Rachelle asked herself why, despite how he drove her crazy, she couldn't imagine returning home and going on a date with anyone else. *"Make me yours as much as I will make you mine."* He'd issued that challenge to her.

I don't know how to, but my gut tells me it doesn't happen by agreeing to a proposal that doesn't include love. "Magnus, don't you think love should be a prerequisite to proposing to anyone?"

"Love is a weak base to build a marriage on."

"You're wrong. It's the only base strong enough to sustain a marriage."

"Did your parents love each other?"

His question cut deeply. "Yes."

"My parents married before love came to them. What they had was commitment to each other and to our country."

"I'm not your mother, Magnus." As she said it, she realized something else as well. "I'm not mine, either. I want it all—the love, the promise, and the forever after. If I find that, I'll fight for it, but I wouldn't marry for less."

They danced for several moments without speaking. There was a beauty and a sadness to the way they connected without truly connecting.

"I'm not looking for my mother. Nor am I interested in one like yours. You are the first woman I can imagine ruling beside me. If love is what you require, we'll find it first."

Find it? She chuckled, half convinced he was joking again. "That's not how love works."

He stopped then and kissed her as if she already belonged to him, was already a part of him. Lust and longing swept through her until there was nothing beyond him. When he raised his head, they were both breathing raggedly.

Breathlessly, she said, "But we could give it a try."

◆ ◆ ◆

Around noontime, Magnus woke to the satisfying feeling of a once-again-naked Rachelle cuddled to his side. Although he'd had many relationships in his life, he hadn't encouraged any of those women to spend the night in his bed. Normally he preferred to wake alone, but Rachelle had turned that on its head. She was where she belonged.

He grimaced as he remembered his proposal. By nature he wasn't an impulsive man, and he'd taken even himself by surprise with his talk of marriage. Their marathon of lovemaking must have softened his brain. He was lucky she'd turned him down.

Even though he didn't feel lucky.

Logically, he knew it didn't make sense to move forward with Rachelle before the issue with her grandmother was resolved. He didn't believe she was involved, but there were still too many unknowns to be certain. He had a high success rate when it came to setting and achieving goals, because he gathered facts before he acted. There were fewer surprises that way. In his experience the unexpected was never good.

Except in the case of Rachelle. Nothing about her or what she brought into his life was predictable, and yet he couldn't imagine waking up the next day without her in his bed. Was that the love she sought?

Many women would not have turned him down, regardless of how he'd phrased it. She expected more from him. Her happiness was already important to him. He enjoyed making her smile and could easily imagine raising children with her. Infidelity would never be a problem, since Magnus did not make a vow he was not prepared to honor.

She wants all that, and love, too. Not just any kind of love, but the romantic Americanized version of it. Am I capable of that?

Would I be happy with any less from her?

It was a question he hadn't thought to ask himself until just that moment. He turned and studied her peaceful expression as she slept. He didn't want her to agree to be with him out of convenience or because he was the best fuck she'd ever had. He wanted her heart as well as her body.

Without waking her, he gave her temple a gentle kiss. *I understand now.*

I will propose to you again, little Rachelle, but not until I can say the three words you will soon proclaim to me.

Her eyes opened slowly. "Do you ever sleep?"

"Should I respond with something romantic?"

She smiled. "You could try."

He lightly slapped her rump beneath the bedsheets. "Perhaps I would do better with some instruction. What does an American man say after a night of good sex?"

"Are you still here?" she joked dryly.

He threw back his head and laughed. "Men are the same everywhere."

"Sadly, yes," she said with a twinkle of mischief in her eyes.

He rolled onto his back, pulling her on top of him as he went. "Give me a day to recuperate and I will remind you of our differences as well."

She kissed him. "What makes you think I'll give you the chance to?"

"This," he said, kissing her back, deeper and slower. When the kiss ended, her cheeks had flushed beautifully. "My bed is your bed from now on."

She cocked her head to one side as she looked down at him. "Some men might phrase that as a question."

He dug his hands into her hair and brought her lips to his again, this time for a possessive kiss. Nothing separated her skin from his, so he felt how his words affected her. Her body, although well loved, tightened with excitement. He shifted beneath her so his quickly hardening cock was cupped by her wet sex. "Other men do not matter to me, and they will no longer matter to you." Before she had a chance to respond, he angled his pelvis back so his tip parted her folds. "You're mine, Rachelle."

She brought her lips back to his, opening her mouth to him, her body to him again. He was hard and ready. She took him deep inside her, then arched so her breasts danced before his mouth. He worshipped them with his tongue and teeth while she moved up and down on his cock. He loved the moment his independent woman followed her own pleasure and sat up. She steadied herself by holding his outstretched hands and ground herself against him, taking him deeper and deeper. His pleasure this time was found in the pleasure she brought herself. She came before he did and then sagged with a pleased smile. He rolled her gently beneath him and found his orgasm in the sweet warmth of hers.

It was only later when she was once again beneath the covers and in his arms that he realized they hadn't used a condom the final time. With any other woman, he would have been furious with himself, but in his mind, she was already his. Only the details of how and when it would become legal were still under negotiation.

Chapter Twenty-One

There were few times in Rachelle's life she considered so beautiful, so perfect, she tried to ingrain them into her memories. The week that followed her early-morning dance with Magnus was one of those magical times.

They stayed at his family home for a couple of days, long enough to have gone into town as a couple. The wonder of seeing Magnus with the people in the town was that he didn't act like a royal with them. He sat with them, laughed with them, even traded playful insults with a few. Just like the rest of the men in town, he also sat up straighter when Zinnia spoke to him. Rachelle asked him if she'd ever gotten him with her switch. He'd laughed, but he hadn't denied it.

In the town he called his home, he and Rachelle ate sinfully rich foods, drank too much coffee in cafés, and spent hours talking in the corner of a bar while Benito played modern pop music. Magnus asked her endless questions about her childhood, her interests, her current bucket list. She countered with questions of her own and loved that he held nothing back. Every day she handed a little more of her heart over to him; every night she found pleasure in his arms.

When they finally returned to the capital city, Magnus left her each morning to work but gave her his afternoons and evenings. And, of course, his nights.

Every piece of what had seemed like an impossible puzzle was beginning to fit together. She and Magnus visited with Eric and the children on the other side of the hospital. They met with architects to design housing for families of the sick children and chose a nearby lot that presently housed only a warehouse. Even Delinda was supportive. Well, if the definition of supportive was not actively trying to destroy or devalue her relationship with Magnus, as Rachelle had expected her grandmother to. They hadn't yet returned to see his father, but the reception for the orphans was that night, and they would see him then. She was attending as Magnus's official date. Magnus said he would present her to his father again and announce his intentions.

Although Rachelle wasn't entirely sure what intentions he was referring to, she trusted Magnus. The more time she spent with him, the more she saw that he expressed his feelings with actions rather than words. He didn't fawn over his people or try to win them with charm, but he delivered each and every time they needed him. They loved him for it in a way that almost no one loved a leader anymore.

How could she not fall for him?

He still said ridiculously sexist things that made her eyes roll skyward, but he wasn't bothered when in private she took him to task for them. In fact, more than once she'd wondered if he said some of them simply to get a rise out of her.

He was never the type to gush words of love and flattery, but Rachelle had been with a man like that, and none of it had been sincere, anyway. When she'd needed that man, he hadn't wanted to be bothered with her problems. However much Magnus might sometimes frustrate her, she was beginning to believe he might show his feelings for her the same way he did with his people—with actions rather than words. Measured that way, he put to shame the men who'd come before him.

She smiled as she sat in a chair while having her hair and makeup done. She met her eyes in the mirror and realized she'd never seen herself look happier or more beautiful. Right or wrong, love or only lust, what she had with Magnus was giving her the confidence she'd lacked.

He could have chosen any woman, but he chose me.

Take that, all you girls who got dates every Friday night in high school.

I may have bloomed late, but look at who it brought me.

◆ ◆ ◆

The past week should have been one of the best for Magnus, but outside of his time with Rachelle, it had been riddled with frustration. He had not planned to return to the capital city until he'd cornered and questioned Alethea Narcharios. Unfortunately, she had proved more elusive than anticipated.

Left without other options, Magnus had gone directly to the source of one of his issues—Delinda Westerly herself. It hadn't been easy to catch her without his father by her side. Another point of irritation for him.

When he finally caught her alone, he could have asked her what she sought to gain by attempting to hack his life, but instead he'd explained how boundaries were important in any family. At first she'd puffed up like an angry cat, but when he explained that he wanted this clarified before he again asked Rachelle to marry him, she became agitated for another reason.

"Again? You've already asked her?" Delinda had asked in a hurt tone. "Why am I hearing this from you and not her?"

"Would the truth change how you behave? Rachelle has told me all about your relationship. Not much of it was good."

She'd been offended, of course. There were the expected threats, some even involving the contacts she was inviting to the ball she was still organizing with his father.

"What brought you here, Mrs. Westerly? What's your endgame?"

"I told you—Rachelle."

"She doesn't believe that, nor do I."

"I don't care what you believe."

He'd finally lost his patience and growled, "Rachelle loves you, but she won't let you near anything she cares about. If I were you, I'd ask myself why."

Their exchange had ended on that sour note. Like everything else he'd tried to accomplish that week, it hadn't gone as well as he'd hoped. His people had followed a money trail connected to Petek's death back to Vandorra, but they were still working on who had hired him and then killed him off. Which meant the threat to Rachelle might come from any direction. She was presently better protected than he was, but Magnus wouldn't sleep well at night until he knew why Petek had been hired to follow Rachelle.

All that was forgotten, though, each afternoon when he held Rachelle in his arms again.

In a week that felt like he could do nothing right, she was his reason to keep trying. The more he got to know her, the more he could not imagine his life without her in it. Tonight at the orphan reception, he would present her to his father in an official capacity. Magnus had made his choice, and if their week together was anything to go by, Rachelle had made hers as well.

He had little experience with labeling his emotions, but the more time he spent with her, the less he wanted to be away from her. Often while he was sitting in a meeting, his mind would wander to her, and he ached for her. Ached. He hadn't known something could feel so good and so bad at the same time.

As Magnus drove toward his palace and Rachelle, he decided he'd attempt to put that feeling into words for her. She'd like that.

Or she'll tell me how I should have said it.

He hoped she never made things easy for him. She was perfect just the way she was.

And since there was very little chance that he would change, he saw a future full of fiery debates and passionate makeups. The images that followed that thought had him speeding back to her. If he played it right, there was time for one more argument before the reception.

Chapter Twenty-Two

That evening Rachelle and Magnus entered his father's palace through the front gate, met by surprisingly respectful photographers. After she thought about it, she realized she should have expected nothing less. His family made the laws here.

A member of the royal household welcomed them into the palace and briefed them on the location of the guests as well as the order of the planned events. There would be time to mingle with the guests before the arrival of the king. King Tadeas would say a few words, then circulate as well. Dressed in a dark-blue suit, Magnus looked like the businessman she'd grown accustomed to him morphing into each morning, but he held himself differently in this space. He became who he needed to be—someone of sophisticated etiquette and composure.

The reception was not, as Rachelle had originally feared, an act of manipulation. Planning for the event had started months before she and Magnus had even met. This formal cocktail party honored those who had completed building several satellite orphanages in the rural communities of Vandorra. Magnus had explained to her that their ultimate goal was to keep children, unless there was a reason to remove them from the area, as much a part of their original community as possible. Their goal was to build networks of support around the most needy rather than yanking them away from everything they'd known because it was easier. Magnus never took the easy road, and he didn't look away from those who needed him. One day he would be a hell of a king.

Being on the arm of such a man would have intimidated Rachelle a month ago. She would have wondered why he wasn't with a more beautiful woman or someone with better social graces. She would have felt like a fraud had he draped her with diamonds, but she'd chosen a modest, long-sleeved, dark-floral dress from a department store and paired it with classic pointed designer pumps. Yes, it was more formal than what she normally wore, but enough of her personal style that she felt comfortable in it.

As they made their way into the reception area, Magnus lowered his head and said, "Your grandmother is likely already inside. If you wish to show her respect, we should start with her."

Although Rachelle had done her best to avoid Delinda for the last week, not wanting to give her a chance to fill her head with negativity, she nodded. At the end of the day, Delinda was family. "I'd like that."

Rachelle introduced herself to each of the staff she encountered until she caught Magnus watching her. Only then did she realize the staff looked surprised by her friendly greeting. "Was that wrong?"

He smiled. "No, it was pleasantly right."

Upon their entry, the volume dropped significantly. No one rushed to greet their prince, but several looked as if they wanted to. Some of the house staff dispersed around the room, and Rachelle guessed they'd instructed the crowd to wait to be approached by Magnus.

As expected, Delinda was not standing alone. She was surrounded by a healthy number of men and women, both young and old. Even in Europe, Delinda's name opened doors, and the flock around her seemed to understand that well.

Magnus greeted her warmly. "Mrs. Westerly, it is a pleasure to have you join us."

"Thank *you*, Your Royal Highness. The pleasure is mine," Delinda said with all the polished etiquette of a woman who was not new to attending such events. She turned her attention to Rachelle. "Rachelle, you look lovely in that dress."

Rachelle stepped forward to kiss her grandmother's cheek. "Thank you." When she stepped back and took a closer look at her grandmother, she was surprised to see the circles beneath her eyes that makeup had not fully concealed. Her grandmother looked her age that evening, and Rachelle was filled with guilt for having avoided her. "I'm sorry I've been so busy."

In place of the cutting sarcasm Rachelle expected, Delinda smiled and gave her hand a pat of support. "And yet you made time to see me each day. No matter how short the visits were, they warmed my heart."

Her comment confused Rachelle until she realized how many eyes and ears were focused on their conversation. *We're onstage. I can't forget that.* "I always have time for you, Grandmother. Always."

Magnus greeted each of the people around Delinda. Although he introduced Rachelle by saying, "It is my pleasure to present Miss Rachelle Westerly," and nothing more, it didn't seem that more was needed. The mere fact that she was on his arm seemed to be a statement of its own.

After a few minutes, Magnus excused himself from the group and led Rachelle toward another. Once again, he presented her with simplicity, then spoke to each person in the cluster. Although several seemed nervous as he approached, he put them at ease. He had informed conversations, as if he knew a great deal about everyone in attendance, and expressed sincere gratitude to each in turn. Rachelle was impressed with how he left each of them feeling as if their presence that evening mattered more than his.

When they finally had a moment alone, Rachelle motioned for Magnus to bend so she could say something softly in his ear. "Magnus, I'm worried about my grandmother. She doesn't look well. Will there be a break during the events tonight when I could take her aside and ask her how she's feeling?"

His gaze flew to Delinda, who was now seated with a circle of people around her. "She does look tired. After my father speaks, he will do just as we did. It would be simple enough to slip away then. Should I accompany you?"

"No, she'll be more honest without an audience."

"Yes, I can see that." He looked her over again. "If you are very concerned, take her aside now."

As Rachelle watched Delinda holding court, she told herself she was worrying about nothing. Her grandmother was the strongest woman she knew and would probably be healthy as a bull until she was well over a hundred. "It can wait. She seems fine right now."

"Come, then. There are more people for you to meet." He took a step toward another group, but Rachelle halted him.

He looked down at her with concern.

She felt a bit silly but wanted to express what she was feeling. "I'm proud to be here with you. You've changed the way this American views royalty. Your people are lucky to have you."

He didn't bend to kiss her as he might have when they were in his hometown. His smile, though, also shone from his eyes and made her glad she'd told him. "And I am lucky to have you with me. I have attended hundreds of these events, but this is one I shall always remember."

She blinked back tears. For Magnus that was practically a declaration of love. "Me too." She floated, not walked, with him to meet the next group of people.

A short while later, King Tadeas entered the room, and a hush of excitement ran through the crowd. He thanked all in attendance for coming and made special mention of several for exceptional dedication to the cause. When he finished speaking, Magnus brought Rachelle over to him.

Here, before his people, Magnus bowed his head to his king. "Father, it is my pleasure to officially present Miss Rachelle Westerly to you."

His father smiled with approval, then turned his attention to Rachelle. "It is good to see my son with someone who is teaching him to smile again. You are always welcome in my home, Miss Westerly."

Rachelle bowed her head, although she wasn't sure if she should have curtsied. "Thank you, Your Majesty. The honor is mine for being included in a celebration for such a worthy cause. I did not expect to enjoy my visit as much as I have, but Vandorra is an easy country to fall in love with."

"Easier than my son?" King Tadeas joked in a tone low enough for others not to hear.

Rachelle blushed and said as softly, "He's growing on me as well."

The king laughed and nodded with approval again. "Dine with me on Sunday, both of you. Something tells me we have much to talk about."

"We do, Father. Sunday it is."

With that, Magnus and Rachelle seemed to be released from official duties. All attention turned to the king. Rachelle searched the room, startled when she didn't see Delinda. She was probably in the washroom. "Magnus, I'm going to slip out to speak to my grandmother now."

"I'm here if you need me," he said.

"I know, thank you." The wonder of the man she tore herself away from was that he meant it when he said that. Never had she dared to imagine having someone in her life she could lean on, believe in. Love wasn't supposed to be this good, was it?

And love was what Rachelle could no longer deny feeling for Magnus. Waking up in his arms made each day feel like a miracle on its own. Alisha had told her love changed everything, but she hadn't believed her until Magnus. With him on her side, she felt like she could handle whatever life threw her way—even a lecture from Delinda.

When she didn't immediately see Delinda, Rachelle made her way down the hallway to peer into the other rooms. She was about to step into one of the rooms when she heard a male voice say, "Prince Magnus is brilliant. You'll never see Vandorra selling off palaces to the public."

"But an American? And one that has been mocked on every website, in every newspaper? How desperate for money is he?" a female voice asked.

Rachelle's chest tightened painfully. She wanted to walk away, but she couldn't. She didn't want to hear what else they'd say, but part of her had to.

The man said, "Call her whatever you want, that woman is set to inherit billions when her grandmother kicks the bucket. Did you see the way he was fawning all over her? I wouldn't be surprised if he rushes her to the altar. Hell, when a deal is that sweet, you close it fast."

"Do you think she's even his taste?"

"Prince Magnus is a pragmatist. A chinchilla would be his taste if it came with the dowry she has. Royal marriages are always business first, pleasure with lovers after she pops out a few children. Who cares if she's angry then?"

"Must you be so crude, Joel?"

"Must you be so naïve, Tatiana? I almost feel bad for her. Unless she's trading her freedom for a title. Some women are into that."

Sick to her stomach, Rachelle forced herself to walk away then. She didn't recognize their names, but that made it worse in a way. They were just voices in the night, slapping her in the face with a potentially ugly reality. All her earlier doubts came crashing back. From the first moment she'd seen Magnus walking down the red carpet toward her, she'd known he was out of her league. Except when it came to an inheritance bigger than his country's GDP. Eric had warned her that once people knew she had money, she would never again be able to trust anyone.

Every relationship would be doubted, he'd said. Rachelle rushed blindly away from prying eyes. She needed air and a moment alone to think. She ran through the kitchen and out a side door.

In a most unladylike way, Rachelle spent several moments bent over a trash can, fighting to gain control and hoping she didn't vomit right down the front of her dress.

Luckily, she had her phone with her. "Alisha?"

"What's wrong, Rachelle? I thought you had a reception tonight. Oh no, Delinda didn't do something, did she?"

Crap, she never had found her. "No, it's not her. It's me. I just heard something, and I don't want to go where it's sending me."

"Are you back in an alley?"

Rachelle looked around at the long three-sided area lined with trash bins. "Yeah. I'm back to that."

"No. Really?"

Speaking to Alisha calmed Rachelle as only a best friend could. "So, I told you how well things were going."

"Yes, you did. Magnus sounds amazing."

"What if he's not? What if he's only with me because I have a substantial inheritance in my future?"

"Did he say that?"

Rachelle headed out of the alley. She needed fresher air than the trash area was providing. "No, I overheard some people saying he was brilliant to marry someone like me. You should have heard them talk about Delinda's money. It was ugly."

"Fuck them," Alisha said.

Rachelle let out a surprised laugh, since her friend never normally swore. "So you think I should just forget what they said?"

"That would be impossible, wouldn't it? Once you've heard something, you've heard it. What you need to ask yourself is if you believe it."

"He's perfect, Alisha. He's sexy, attentive, funny—even when he's not trying to be. I've met his friends, and they all love him. We've worked together this week on real projects and he has valued my opinion at each step. It is good with him, Alisha. So good. Too good?"

"So you'd rather be with an asshole, because that's the only kind of man who you believe could love you?"

"No. I don't believe that."

"Then you think Magnus is a manipulative liar who is driven only by money."

"No, that's not how I see him at all." She thought about the way he cared for his people. He was arrogant, but not greedy. Although he and his father had palaces, he didn't take money from his people to support them. He was a successful businessman as well as a prince.

"So, what are you going to trust? Two nasty strangers who are probably insanely jealous of you and Magnus? Or your heart? Because I know you love him."

"I do." She continued walking down a grassy path. "I just don't want to wake up a year from now and feel like a fool. Eric warned me that people would want what we have. That has never been true for us, but what if it is now? How awful am I that I'm even considering this?"

Alisha sighed. "Love makes potential fools of all of us. It's a leap of faith. Brett could come home from work any day and tell me he's found someone else, but I can't live afraid that he will—because that's not living. I'm going to believe in him and in us with every ounce of myself until he gives me a reason not to. I've never met Magnus. I can't tell you if he's worth the same kind of faith. That's for you to decide. Is he?"

Rachelle walked on and thought back over the last few weeks. Even at his most infuriating, Magnus had always done what he thought was best for her. From suggesting she leave prostitution to moving her out of a hotel he didn't think she was safe in, from practically kidnapping Eric to visiting him daily at the hospital—he showed he cared.

"Yes, he is worth that kind of faith. I panicked when I heard those people talking about why they thought he's with me, but they don't know me."

"No, they don't."

"And they obviously don't know him."

"That much is sure."

"Eric is so sad right now because he doesn't let anyone close to him. I know exactly how lucky I am to have you in my life, Alisha. I'm going to let myself believe in Magnus, too. And if anyone wants to question our relationship—fuck them."

"That's the spirit."

Rachelle looked around and realized she'd wandered out of the view of the house. "I've got to let you go, Alisha. I think I went back one path too many, and I may be lost now. I'm going to retrace my steps and head back into the reception. Thanks again. I miss you."

"I miss you, too. Text me later when you get back to the house, okay? Just so I won't worry."

"Sure thing."

With that, Rachelle chose a path she hoped led back to the house. Her high heels made the going slower, especially now that she wasn't distracted from how sore her feet were getting. She looked around, realizing she was alone for the first time in a while. Normally there was a royal guard somewhere nearby. She called out in the hope that one was. "Anyone there? I've gotten a little turned around, so if you're out there, speak up. I need a little direction on how to get back." A man in a suit with the insignia of the royal guard appeared. "Oh, good. I'm sorry. I know I shouldn't be way out here, but I was walking and talking—then, poof, I was lost. You know how that happens."

The man nodded as if to someone behind her, and she quickly followed his gaze. Another royal guard stepped out of the bushes. Then another. None of these three looked familiar, now that she saw them all together. The hair on the back of her neck rose, and she fumbled to dial Magnus on her phone.

The first man grabbed her phone and threw it in the woods. The other two grabbed her from behind. Duct tape was slapped over her mouth before she had a chance to scream. More was used to expertly secure her hands and legs together. The first man threw her over his shoulder. With tears born from fear, she tried to meet the eyes of the other men, plead with them not to do whatever they were about to, but they did just as Magnus had said they were trained to—they looked away.

She fought the best she could but only succeeded in dislodging her shoes. As if she were nothing more than a rug, the man deposited her in the back of a black SUV flanked by two other guards. They secured her with lap belts so tightly she could barely breathe. A lone driver got in and slammed the door behind him. He touched an earpiece and said, "The bird is in the cage and ready for delivery."

As the car pulled away, Rachelle prayed for her life. *The bird is in the cage? This was planned. By the royal guard? Why? I thought they liked me.*

If they even are the royal guard. They could be the people Reggie saw following me. Oh, God, was he right? They're going to ransom me?

I should have stayed where everyone else was. Magnus told me to be more careful, but I didn't listen. I didn't think something like this could actually happen.

She thought about all the things she had put off doing, everything that would be left undone. She didn't want to die without telling Magnus she loved him. She wanted to tell Delinda she forgave her. She didn't want to be the reason Eric gave up hope.

This isn't how it ends for me. It can't be.

It can't be.

Magnus checked his watch. Rachelle had been gone long enough that he was concerned. He certainly didn't want to intrude on whatever conversation she was having with Delinda, but his instincts told him it was time to check on her.

He had just stepped out of the reception area when he spotted Delinda sitting in a side room with a cup of tea in hand. He strode and looked around. "Where's Rachelle?" He hoped she hadn't upset her.

"I haven't seen her," Delinda said quietly.

"She told me she was coming to find you."

Delinda put her tea aside. "Well, she did not. I was not feeling well, so your father suggested I rest in here. Had she asked, she could easily have found me. Evidently something more important came up."

Magnus called to Phillip, who was out in the hallway. "Phillip, where is Rachelle?"

Instantly on alert, Phillip radioed that question to his men.

Magnus took out his phone and called her. No answer. He saw one missed call from her about twenty minutes earlier. Was she angry? Upset? Scared? She hadn't seemed any of those things.

Phillip said, "She was seen going into the kitchen a while ago."

"A while? How long is a while ago? A minute? Thirty minutes?"

Delinda joined them. "Is something wrong?"

Magnus walked away from her because he wanted to keep his focus on the only thing that mattered. "Phillip, I want her found, and I want her found now. Search the palace room by room. Sweep the garden. We have security tapes—have someone review them. Now."

"She might simply be talking with someone and ignoring her phone, but we will find her."

Magnus began his own search, uncaring that Delinda called out for him to stop so she could join him. If she was offended by his indifference, she could voice her complaint later. Phillip was right—Rachelle might simply be distracted by a conversation with someone. They'd all laugh about this later and agree Delinda was best left out of a search that wasn't even necessary.

The problem was, his gut was churning. He trusted his instincts, and they were screaming something wasn't right.

Phillip found him as he was about to enter the kitchen. "Magnus."

One look at Phillip's face and he knew it was serious. He braced himself for the worst. "You found her?"

"No, but we have video of her being taken from the party. She didn't go willingly."

"What do you mean, taken?" Magnus's hands fisted at his sides.

"We have a motion-activated clip of video from the south path. She encountered a man in a suit with the royal guard emblem, but I didn't recognize him. I sent men, Magnus, but I doubt she's still there. It looked planned. He had her bound by two others with what looked like duct tape."

"Oh my God." Magnus could have given in to the rage nipping at his heels. He could have asked Phillip how this was possible when so many were supposed to be watching her, but he didn't. It was a conversation that could wait for later. Right now what mattered was finding her. "Notify the police. I want a close perimeter and a wide one secured now. Get helicopters up in the air. How long ago was the video taken?"

"Thirty minutes."

"A car can travel outside the city in that time."

"Yes."

"Do we know what they might be driving? If they were driving? Do we fucking know anything besides what you just told me?"

"Not yet, but we will." Phillip radioed the police while Magnus barked orders to the guards in the palace. One was for the royal household to keep all guests in the reception area—no matter what.

His father came to his side. "Magnus, is it true? Has someone taken Rachelle?"

Magnus nodded once.

"Do we know who was involved?"

"Not yet. Go back to the guests, Father. I'll handle this."

King Tadeas put a hand on his son's shoulder. "I am a father first and a king second. My place is with you. This is one fight you won't face alone."

"How can it be faced at all when the enemy is still unknown?"

Delinda joined them. "Has something happened to Rachelle? I have to know."

Magnus and his father exchanged a long look. Would telling her help, or would she impede the search?

To Delinda he said, "Your granddaughter is in great danger. Do you know anyone who would want to harm her?"

"No."

"Someone took her from the property. We don't know what they want yet. If you know anything, you need to tell us now."

The older woman went pale. "I should have said something earlier. I hired a woman, Alethea Narcharios, to follow her. I thought she could keep her safe from anything. I haven't heard from her in two days," Delinda said, clutching at the king's arm as she sagged in shock. "Alethea can be headstrong. I thought she was investigating something she wouldn't want me to know about. But Rachelle might not have been the first they took. Oh my God, what have I done?"

The king murmured something to Delinda that Magnus was beyond caring about. Someone had to have seen something. He would grill every royal guard and their families if that's what it took to find Rachelle.

Just then, two royal guards entered the great hall half carrying, half dragging a man. "Your Majesty. Your Royal Highness. We found this man on the property." They deposited him at Magnus's feet.

The man stood, brushed himself off, and said, "Before you congratulate them on nabbing me, you might want to explain to them the difference between walking toward the house to tell you something and running away."

He reminded Magnus of a man Rachelle had once described. "Reggie?"

The man held out his hand. "Yes. Nice to meet you, Mr. Prince, or whatever people call you."

As insane as it was to hope, Magnus shook his hand and asked, "Did you see something?"

"I saw everything. That's why I'm here."

"You saw Rachelle get kidnapped?" Delinda asked in a high pitch.

"Easy, lady," Reggie said. "I was on a hike with my family, mostly minding our own business. The kids wanted to see how far we could get onto the palace property before someone caught us, but when I saw that the guards had guns, I sent my wife and kids back to the hotel."

"While you did what?" Phillip asked.

Reggie shrugged. "Just checked things out. Eric asked me to watch over Rachelle, and I try be around if she needs me."

"Did you see who took her?" Phillip asked.

"Yes."

"And you did nothing to stop them?" Magnus growled.

Reggie threw both hands up. "Four guys. All armed. I could have tried to fight them myself, but then I wouldn't be alive to tell you what happened."

"No, but she might be. You let someone take her while you did nothing?" Magnus wanted to strangle the man.

His father moved between them. "Magnus, let the man speak."

"He doesn't deserve to live to voice another word. He should have done something. Every moment she's gone is one he could have prevented."

"I tried to call your emergency numbers, but they thought I was pranking. Sorry if you don't have a 1-800-Someone-Stole-Rachelle hotline. I rushed here as fast as I could. And not all of it was pleasant." He glared at the guards who had brought him into the palace. "Now we can stand around all day and discuss what I could have done better, or I can tell you who took her and where they went."

Magnus grabbed Reggie by the shirt collar. "Who took her? Where did they go? What did you hear?"

Reggie pulled himself free and squared his shoulders. "I'll tell you as long as you all keep your damn hands to yourself. I might have some of this wrong, because I couldn't exactly ask any questions, but I stayed and listened to what the men were talking about after one of them left with Rachelle. I guess you have some crazy cousin who thinks you cheated him out of his crown or something. He's waiting with his son at some cabin or lodge or someplace he thinks your father, pardon what I'm about to say about you, Mr. King, sir, stole from him when he took the crown. I would have come to tell you sooner, but those guys were real chatty, and I had to wait for them to leave before I came out from the rock I was hiding behind. I gave myself a real cramp, too."

A cold fury rose within Magnus. He'd faced and won against his cousin in the past, but he should have exiled him or worse. Like a cancer, time had only allowed him to get worse. "I know where he would take Rachelle. I'll need a sniper team, Phillip."

His father straightened to his full height. "Reggie, would you recognize those men if you saw them again?"

"Absolutely."

"Then you're coming with us. Phillip, have the royal guard lined up in the driveway. Reggie, if you see one of those men, point them out to us. We'll deal with this on a larger scale once Rachelle is safely back with us."

"I'm coming with you," Delinda said, straightening.

"No," Magnus started to say, but his father raised a hand to silence him.

"When you go to war, son, bring your allies with you," the king said.

Reggie waved a thumb toward the king. "I'd listen to your father. He seems pretty smart."

Magnus glared at Reggie, but he could not deny that without Reggie, he and his men would still be chasing their tails. By hiding and then delivering information to him, Reggie might just have saved Rachelle. "Okay, we go together. But this happens on my command."

His father nodded. "Not even I would dare stand between a man and the woman he loves."

Magnus took a moment to absorb his father's declaration, then decided it was accurate. No one could have come between him and Rachelle. She was a part of him now.

Reggie spoke to the royal guards who had hauled him in. "Hear that? You guys might have worked here longer, but I bet I end up a knight or something."

Delinda, still clutching the king's arm, said, "I have people I trust, but they'd take too long to arrive. I don't know how to help you. Tell me what I can do that won't put her in more danger."

"Trust my son," the king said. "He will bring her home."

Delinda wiped tears away from beneath her eyes. "I don't have a choice, do I?" She turned her attention to Magnus. "If there is anything you need, any way I can help you, just say the word."

Magnus nodded toward Reggie. "Keep him away from me." Then he turned to Phillip. "We don't have time to drive. Get us and those snipers in a chopper. We have the element of surprise, but not for long."

Chapter Twenty-Three

A short time later, still bound and silenced with duct tape, Rachelle lay on her side on the floor of a large cabin deep in the woods. The royal guards who had carried her in had tossed her to one side, uncaring of how she landed. Rachelle was sure she had bruises, but she'd discovered that adrenaline canceled discomfort. She had never been so afraid in her life.

In the movies it all looked simple. She should be able to wiggle or squirm, release the restraints, and be given some kind of opportunity to escape. The reality she was facing was that duct tape didn't allow for that kind of wiggle, and fear was paralyzing.

Soon after the guards had deposited her as if she were nothing, they'd walked into another room. She had strained to hear what they were saying, hoping to hear something useful. What she'd heard were several shots fired, then the thud of bodies hitting the floor. Had someone killed them? Had they just killed someone else they'd taken? She had no way of knowing, and asking herself those questions didn't help.

Was there time to get away? She rolled away from the wall and knocked into the side of a chair. She attempted to rise up enough to inch forward, but her dress slipped and bunched beneath her, sending her back to the floor each time without successfully moving her ahead.

She heard two male voices coming toward her and froze. There was nothing she could do, no way to escape. All she could do was pray they wanted something that required not killing her.

A man who looked to be in his seventies looked over at her and made a sound of disgust. "I wish we could kill her now. We can't. He may need to hear her voice. Get her out of the middle of the room before she knocks something over."

The younger man, who appeared to be in his forties, walked over to Rachelle and gave her a kick in the side. "You heard him. Get against the wall." He went to kick her again, but Rachelle quickly rolled back against the wall.

Although the situation was horrific, she knew it could have been worse. If they wanted her quiet and out of the way, she would do what she could to draw as little attention to herself as possible.

"Did you have to kill the guards?" the younger man whined. "What if we need them?"

"We won't. No one knows we're here."

"Not even the ones we paid to find her? The ones back at the palace?"

"Think, Erwin. Would I leave them alive?"

Erwin shuddered. "Couldn't we have paid them off?"

"Only the dead keep secrets."

Erwin looked over at Rachelle, and she closed her eyes. She didn't want to connect with him. "Are you sure the royal guard will follow us? What if they don't?"

The older man snarled, "How did I raise such a weak son? They won't have a choice. After Magnus is gone, we sit back and wait for Tadeas to die a natural death. Or help him along, too, if he lingers. After that, I am next in line for the crown. It's my birthright. You will one day be king, son. I'll make sure of it."

"What if Magnus finds out where we are?"

"He won't. In an hour he'll receive a message that his girlfriend is on her way out of the country to be sold off to the highest bidder unless he meets me alone."

"He's smart, Father. He won't go alone."

"He doesn't have to. I have enough people in place to take out whoever shows up."

"It's going to be a bloodbath."

"That's why we're here. And if it's done right, it'll look like he tangled with the wrong country and they took him out."

"What do we do with her afterward? Are we really going to sell her?"

"Erwin, I need you to start using your brain. She knows who we are. She can hear us now. Does she live or does she die?"

"She dies?" Erwin asked like a child, unsure if his teacher would accept his answer.

"Of course she dies. Your mother was one of the dumbest women I ever fucked, but she was beautiful. If I could go back in time, I'd pick an ugly wife with a brain. Maybe then I'd have a son who had half a chance of holding on to the crown."

Oh my God. Rachelle started praying then, for herself, for Magnus, for Vandorra, if these two men came into power.

◆ ◆ ◆

In the early dark of the evening, Magnus left no escape route for his cousin. He landed the helicopters early and drove to the cabin with enough men to form a stealthy, quickly closing perimeter. Every public and private resource available to him was on hand, including a police-force hostage expert.

Snipers were in place, using thermal scopes to sweep the cabin. Two standing bodies. Two prone cooling bodies, potentially dead. One smaller, still-warm body on the floor of the main room. Kill shots could be attempted, but the expert warned that there was too much they didn't know. Weapons might be trained on her—weapons that might be fired instinctively even as someone went down. Or she might be rigged with a device.

A search of the Pavailler Palace grounds had produced the bodies of three dead men in royal guard uniforms. Davot had the blood of several already on his hands—underestimating him would not be wise.

Magnus took Phillip aside. "No matter how it goes down, you save her. If it's between me or her, don't choose me."

Phillip looked away.

Magnus grabbed him by the arm. "She leaves here alive, no matter what it takes. Do you understand? If she dies, everything good in me goes with her."

Phillip put his hand over Magnus's. "We'll get her out of there."

Magnus nodded. "We knew he'd be back. We should have killed him when we had a chance."

"That will be remedied today."

The hostage expert approached. "Your Royal Highness, everyone is in place. It's time to call him."

Magnus took out his phone and dialed his cousin Davot's number. It rang several times before it picked up. "Magnus?" his cousin asked.

"Yes, Davot."

"I wasn't expecting to hear from you so soon."

"Yes, well, today is full of the unexpected, isn't it? Whatever you were planning is over. I'm willing to give you the option to live, though."

"How dare you speak to me in that manner!"

"I dare because the cabin you're in is surrounded by my men, who will shoot to kill on my command. The only chance you or your son have of surviving this is if you send Rachelle out."

His cousin took a moment before answering. "Is Tadeas with you?"

"Yes."

"I want to speak to him."

Magnus looked to the hostage expert for confirmation, then brought the phone over to his father, who was surrounded by a wall of guards.

The king took the phone, put it on speakerphone, and raised his eyes toward the cabin. "It didn't have to come to this, Davot."

"This is exactly what comes when you steal a crown from someone."

"Your father served his role as regent, and he did it with dignity, but I was the heir to the throne. I stole nothing. Come out, Davot. You don't have to die today."

"You think I care about dying? My days are numbered anyway. What I want is for my son to have what you denied me."

King Tadeas shook his head sadly. "You want something that cannot happen. Send out the woman. Send your son with her. They're both innocent of this."

"You think I'm a fool? I send her out and I get nothing I want."

"Your son lives. You might even live. Isn't that what matters most?"

"This morning it might have, but not now. Maybe this is a better way for it to go. Tell your son the only way I send the woman out is if he comes in."

Phillip spoke to the hostage expert, then said to Magnus, "You can't go in. We lose all control if you do."

Magnus asked for a bulletproof vest and conferred with the expert. "Tell him I need to see her. Tell him I don't believe she's alive."

King Tadeas said, "My son will go nowhere near the cabin unless we know she's alive."

Davot snarled, "No, I am not sending you out, Erwin. You will stay and fight like a man, for once in your pathetic life."

A moment later, Rachelle yelled, "Don't send Magnus in. He'll kill us both." She cried out as if someone hurt her, and Magnus fought not to charge in right then. Instead, he secured the vest and motioned to his men that he was heading toward the cabin. Nothing would be achieved by staying where he was.

His father called to him, "Magnus."

Delinda rushed forward, whispering, "Be careful."

Magnus said, "I will."

Phillip stepped closer and spoke softly. "All we need is a clean kill shot, Magnus. Get us one and it's over."

Magnus took the phone from his father. "You want my crown? I'll abdicate. All I want is Rachelle."

Davot said coldly, "He's lying, Erwin. No, it's not worth a risk. You think either of us are getting out of here alive?"

"You still can," Magnus said as he walked closer to the cabin. "I could have killed you the first time, and I didn't. I don't want blood on my hands. Give me Rachelle, and you and your son will be free to leave, as long as you don't return to Vandorra."

"Shut up, Erwin. It's impossible to think when you whine like that. I don't want the woman, Magnus. I want you. Come in and I'll release her."

Magnus stood at the bottom of the porch. "Show her to me now. How do I know you didn't just kill her? I'm not taking another step forward unless I can see her."

The door opened. Davot held Rachelle by her hair in front of the open door, still bound at her feet, hands behind her back. She met Magnus's eyes across the short distance. He had never seen a braver woman. He couldn't tell her what to do, but he motioned quickly with his eyes for her to drop. With that, she threw her head back then forward violently, and fell to the floor when she broke free.

Magnus rushed forward, and a shot whizzed by him, piercing the wall and taking his older cousin out. A wave of movement crested behind Magnus as he reached Rachelle and pulled her off the floor. Erwin grabbed a gun and got off a shot at Magnus before he was also taken down by a sniper.

Hugging Rachelle to his chest, Magnus sheltered her from the sight of his men, ensuring neither cousin would ever be a problem again. He looked her over quickly. Her face was bruised, and she was probably in shock, but otherwise she looked unhurt.

He dropped to his knees and unbound her legs and arms. Once she was freed, he pulled her into his arms again and held her tightly, rocking her back and forth as he blinked back tears of relief. Only now that she was safe did he allow himself to face how close he'd come to losing her.

Delinda appeared beside them, her face wet from her tears. She touched Magnus's arm in a silent request. He stepped back.

"I love you so much, Rachelle," Delinda said as she wrapped her arms around her granddaughter and wept. "I'm so sorry."

Rachelle burst into tears then. "I know, Grandmother. I love you, too."

His father ordered the men to clean up the area while Phillip guided Magnus, Delinda, and Rachelle away from the scene. SUVs pulled up to whisk them away.

Phillip stood beside Magnus. "Do you want me here or at the hospital?"

"Hospital?" Magnus asked, looking over Rachelle again, this time noticing blood on her dress and face—more blood than he remembered.

"You've been shot, Magnus. Your arm." Phillip called to a man to bring a roll of bandage over.

Only when Magnus looked down and saw the blood running down from a hole in his upper arm did it begin to hurt. It also made him unsteady on his feet. He'd never been good with the sight of his own blood.

"Is he okay?" Magnus heard Rachelle ask as if from inside a tunnel. He knew he should look away from his wound, but the world around it became dimmer and dimmer until he saw nothing at all.

Chapter Twenty-Four

The scare of being taken and nearly killed, followed by the frightening sight of Magnus dropping limply to the ground, sent Rachelle into a fog. She dropped and hugged his head to her chest, begging him not to die.

Phillip rushed to assure her that Magnus was suffering from nothing more serious than a small flesh wound and a lifelong inability to deal with the sight of his own blood. She didn't believe him, couldn't believe him, until Magnus shook his head and came to.

"Don't ever do that again," Rachelle scolded. "You scared me."

His answer was to pull her head down and kiss her deeply, passionately—a kiss they both needed and one that held more promise than words ever could.

When the kiss finally ended, Rachelle sat there, cradling his head to her. Someone began wrapping his arm in a bandage, but Rachelle didn't look away from Magnus. "This was my fault," she said. "I walked off by myself."

He winced. "You should have been safe anywhere on our property. I failed to protect you. We all did."

She kissed his lips again softly. "If you failed, why am I still here?"

He sat up, leaning on his good arm. "Because there is no life I want to live that doesn't have you in it."

She kissed him again. "I love you, Magnus."

"I love you, too, my little Rachelle."

She smiled. She was no longer offended by that term because she heard the love behind it.

A helicopter touched down on the grass beside the cabin, and several armed men along with one woman exited it. The royal guards trained their weapons on them.

"She's with me," Delinda called out, approaching them. "She's late, but at least she's alive."

Delinda hugged the woman and looked as if she was lecturing not only her but the man at her side.

"How did you find me?" Rachelle asked, turning her attention back to Magnus.

Magnus rose to his feet, then helped Rachelle to hers. "Reggie was in the woods when you were taken. He came and told us everything he saw and heard."

Rachelle looked around. "Is he here?"

Magnus nodded toward the driveway.

Phillip said, "The car is ready to take you to a private wing at the town hospital. We can fly you back to the city, but I thought you'd rather get patched up first."

"Good thinking, Phillip," Magnus said, and started to guide Rachelle toward the car.

"Wait," Rachelle said. She walked over to Reggie and wrapped her arms around his thin frame. "Thank you, Reggie. Thank you for looking out for me. I'll tell Eric what a good friend he has in you."

Reggie hugged her back awkwardly, then reached into his pocket and pulled out her phone. "Hey, you dropped this in the woods. I figured you might want it. It's not easy to get a new phone, and sometimes you have photos you haven't yet uploaded. It can be a real bitch."

Rachelle laughed even while wiping away tears. "I love you, Reggie."

"Oh, now, don't go saying that. My wife is already asking a lot of questions like, 'Why are we following her around town? Why are we hiding in the woods?' I told her I'm doing it as a favor, but you know how women can be weird about their man stalking another woman."

Magnus put his good arm around Rachelle's waist. "Reggie, I owe you a debt I could never repay. Is there anything you want?"

"Yeah," Reggie said. "Can we come to your wedding? My wife would shit herself if we got invited to something like that."

Magnus exchanged a look with Rachelle, then said, "You will be our honored guests."

"Awesome. Hey, can you also dub me a knight? You know, touch a sword on my shoulders or something."

"That's not—"

Rachelle finished for him, "Possible unless your wife and kids attend the ceremony. Would you like that?"

"They'd love that. I can't wait to tell her she's going to be Mrs. Reggie the Knight of Vandorra Land." He walked off to call his wife.

As she and Magnus made their way to the car, he said, "Knights are a thing of the past in Vandorra."

"He doesn't know that," Rachelle said. She slid into the car and cuddled against Magnus as they made their way to the hospital. The whole day felt unreal, but the man whose arm was protectively holding her to his side did not. Simply because she didn't want to burst into tears, she joked, "And he saved my phone. You know how hard it can be to replace photos."

Magnus kissed the side of her forehead and said dryly, "Yes, thank God, we didn't lose those."

There was so much Rachelle wanted to say, but it could all wait. She was alive. He was alive. "Oh, shit," Rachelle said, and took out her phone. "I need to text Alisha. I told her I was lost in the woods." She paused, deciding she couldn't handle retelling what had happened yet. "I'll just tell her I found my way back."

Magnus hugged her tighter. "We will marry as soon as my arm has healed."

Rachelle melted against him. "Yes."

He raised his head. "No argument?"

"Nope."

"No suggestion on how I could have said it better?"

She arched an eyebrow, glad to see that despite what they'd been through, it hadn't broken either of them. "Well, maybe just one." She put her hand on the back of his neck and pulled his face closer to hers. "You could shut up and kiss me."

"Gladly," he said, and gave her a long, tender kiss that curled her toes and warmed her heart. She was still shaken from what she'd been through, but Magnus had risked his life to save hers. He was her hero, her lover, the home she'd been searching for.

Being with him had taught her to have faith not only in him but in herself as well. Life would throw challenges their way, but she now trusted that they would overcome anything—together.

◆ ◆ ◆

The next morning, in a private hospital suite, Magnus paced, impatient to leave. Rachelle was seated on a couch on the other side of the room, speaking to members of her family on the phone.

Magnus hadn't wanted to stay, but Dr. Stein had insisted on running a full battery of tests on both him and Rachelle. She'd slept beside him in the hospital bed. They were now showered and changed into clothing that the staff had sent over. He would have left, but Phillip informed him that his father was on his way back to the hospital.

Rachelle put her phone aside and walked over to stand next to him. "If I never tell the story again, it'll be too soon."

He wrapped his good arm around her and pulled her to his chest. "Are they really all flying over?"

"Even my father," she said with a smile. "I told them I'm safe now, but they're worried about me. That's a change. I'm usually the one mother-henning them."

"Then we shall marry while they're here."

"I have no problem with that, but doesn't a royal wedding take forever to plan?"

"Something tells me your grandmother and my father could pull one off."

"I bet they could."

Magnus tipped Rachelle's face up toward his. "I am not a man who easily speaks of how he feels."

"I know."

"Yesterday when I saw you in the doorway, I knew I would gladly take a thousand bullets for you. My life belongs to my people and Vandorra, but none of that would have mattered if I had lost you."

Rachelle raised a finger to his lips. "I've never been so afraid, but I felt sorry for your cousin. His father was a sick and twisted man. Your cousin never had a chance."

"He did, though. He would have lived had he fought for you."

"What happened to the men he sent to ambush you?"

"They chose their fate. The royal guard deals with traitors harshly, especially when they're some of their own."

"Why so glum?" a loud male voice boomed from the doorway. Magnus looked up and did a double take. "Eric?"

Fully outfitted in his Water Bear Man spandex superhero suit, Eric was pushing Finn in a wheelchair. "No, it is I, Water Bear Man. Is there a prince in need of cheering up?"

Finn looked Magnus over with eyes wise beyond his years. "I heard you were shot. I bet you were scared. When I'm scared, I find something to laugh about, and it's not so bad."

Eric ruffled Finn's hair. "I could not say no to this kid."

King Tadeas entered the room. "I went to visit Finn this morning, and he'd already heard about you being hurt. He wanted to come to see you. Since his surgery is not for a week still, his parents thought it might be good for him."

Eric flexed his arms and said, "So prepare to laugh, Mr. Fancy Pants Prince. I will tell you a joke."

"You're going to love it, Prince Magnus," Finn said. "I helped him write it."

Eric asked, "Why are princes good at riding horses?"

"I don't know," Magnus said, feeling both amused and a little sorry to be putting Eric through this.

"Because they know how to reign," Eric said heartily, fully in character.

Finn laughed. "Get it? Reign like a king?"

King Tadeas chuckled.

Magnus smiled. "Do you know who I bet would also love that joke? The children downstairs."

Finn looked up at Eric. "Could we go visit them?"

"I am at your command, Finn of Vandorra," Eric said.

Magnus walked over and shook Eric's hand. "Thank you."

Eric fell out of character briefly. "No, thank you. I heard what you did for Rachelle."

Rachelle hugged her brother. "Reggie saved me, too."

Eric hugged her back with warmth. "He told me. Several times. I told him his family is welcome to stay with me as long as they want."

"He cares about you."

"I know that now," Eric said. "And I care about you, Rachelle. Thank you for not giving up on me. I checked myself out today to be here, but I'm going back for a while longer. It's helping. Thank you." He nodded to Magnus, then puffed up his chest again. "Take care of my sister or Water Bear Man will return."

He had turned to wheel Finn out of the room when Rachelle called out, "Eric, have you seen Grandmother—"

"Not yet," Eric answered. "But I will. When I'm ready."

"She loves you," Rachelle said.

"I know," Eric said, then disappeared out the door.

King Tadeas waited until they were out of earshot, then said, "Delinda wanted to go see Eric, but I convinced her to let him come to her."

"She listened to you?" Rachelle asked in surprise.

Magnus chuckled. "He is the king."

Epilogue

Thirty minutes before she was scheduled to walk down the aisle, Rachelle took a moment to stand alone in front of a large mirror in a beautiful suite of rooms in a building next to Vandorra's largest cathedral. Her long-sleeved lace-over-silk bridal gown might have seemed simple except for its long train. She'd never imagined that her wedding would be televised to millions of people around the world, and it added to the normal wedding-day jitters.

Would the flowers be perfect? Aunt Nissa assured they would be.

The photos? Nicolette had wanted to take them, but since she was in the wedding party, she'd settled for choosing photographers for the event.

The guest list? After Rachelle and Magnus drew up an initial list, Delinda and King Tadeas had handled the rest—which had actually been a relief.

Rachelle didn't doubt that the wedding itself would run smoothly or that a life with Magnus was what she wanted. Still, she was making a commitment to more than a man that day—she was also vowing her loyalty to his country. It was an honor but also a responsibility she prayed she was the right woman for. When she looked in the mirror, she saw a first-grade teacher, not a queen.

A movement behind her had her spinning around, her hand flying to her throat. "Reggie. What are you doing in here?"

Despite being dressed in an expensive tuxedo, Reggie still looked a little rough around the edges. "Before you do this, there's someone you need to talk to."

Rachelle tensed, then told herself to relax. Memories from a few weeks earlier came back with sickening speed. She fought to keep them from bringing fear with them. Strange as Reggie was, he'd always had her best interest in mind. She wouldn't doubt him now. "Who?"

"King Tadeas brought some of the children from the hospital. Most of them look happy, but there is one little girl who is close to tears. I'm not going to enjoy this wedding if she sits across from me bawling through the whole thing."

"Who is it?"

"Hey, I'm a knight of Vandorra Land now. I don't have time to go around memorizing everyone's names."

"Bring her to me, please."

"I've got my own kids to worry about. I just thought you should know." He left, shaking his head.

Rachelle opened a side door where the women in her family were gathered. She took a moment to savor the sight of all of them, from her grandmother to her youngest sister and sisters-in-law, all getting along. "I need someone's help," she said.

The room went instantly silent.

"There's a little girl out there from the hospital. I heard she's upset. Could one of you see who it is, and if it's possible, could you bring her to me?"

Delinda and her mother volunteered at the same time. "Why don't you both bring her?" Rachelle requested.

A few minutes later, the two returned with the little girl Magnus had offered a Disney trip to, being carried by her mother. Her mother was flustered and apologetic. Rachelle rushed to reassure her that they'd summoned her out of concern and not because her child had been an issue.

Rachelle went to the beautifully dressed little girl and said, "Thank you for coming to my wedding, Tinsley. I'm so happy to have you here. Why are you so sad?"

Two big blue eyes filled with tears. "I will never be a princess now. You're marrying my prince."

Her mother tried to comfort her daughter while apologizing for her comment.

Rachelle dabbed a tear from her own eye before it had a chance to ruin her makeup. This little girl and her mother were *her* people now. Her heart ached for them as if they were truly her family. She saw now how they could be just as important. "May I speak to your mother for a moment, honey?"

Rachelle's mother took the little girl while Delinda spoke to her.

As soon as she was out of earshot, Rachelle said, "Is she well enough to walk by herself? I would love to have her as part of my bridal party. I don't have a flower girl. Please, don't feel that you must say yes. Think about it. You may walk with her if you wish. I'd like to give her a princess moment."

Tinsley's mother brought a hand to her mouth, and she began to thank Rachelle for her kindness. She said it would be the greatest honor her daughter and her family could ever imagine receiving.

Rachelle motioned for her own mother to bring the little girl back to her. "Tinsley, I have a problem that I'm hoping you can help me with. I don't have a flower girl. Would you like to be a princess for a day? My little princess flower girl?"

Tinsley looked to her mother for confirmation. Her mother nodded and explained what role she would play. "I don't want to walk alone," Tinsely said in a suddenly timid voice.

"Your mother could go with you," Rachelle suggested. When the little girl still looked uncertain, Rachelle added, "Or you could hold my hand and walk with me."

"Really?" The little girl's eyes widened with wonder.

"If it's okay with your mother."

Tinsley looked about to faint. Her mother said, "Thank you. Thank you a million times and a million times more. You will never know how much this means to our family."

With that, the rest of the women in Rachelle's family swooped in and welcomed the little girl, making both her and her mother feel as if they were a natural part of the group. Delinda said softly, "I came to Vandorra for all the wrong reasons, but you are staying for all the right ones."

Rachelle took her grandmother's hand in hers and gave it a squeeze. "I still have a lot to learn about planning social events and formal etiquette. I wonder if you know anyone who could give me some guidance in that department."

"I'll help you with whatever you ask, Rachelle, but you are already who Vandorra needs."

"That sounds like a compliment, Grandmother."

"I'm learning as well, Rachelle."

With a mischievous smile, Rachelle added, "Magnus says his father is quite smitten with you."

It was the first time Rachelle had ever seen her grandmother blush. "I don't have time for such silliness. I have two more grandchildren to marry off."

◆　◆　◆

In all of Magnus's life, he had never seen a more beautiful sight than Rachelle walking slowly down the cathedral aisle holding the hand of a small child, both smiling widely. Rachelle stopped along the way to introduce the little girl as if she were the reason for the event.

Kindness trumped protocol for Rachelle, even during a moment that should have been all about her. She was the perfect woman for him and for Vandorra.

They reached the altar. Magnus bent to thank Tinsley. Her mother came and escorted the little girl to a seat in the front. Breaking tradition, Magnus took Rachelle's hand and held it straight through their vows. Though the formal affair was steeped in tradition, it held meaning for his father and his people. The kiss he gave her was respectfully appropriate.

When he and Rachelle turned to the crowd and were presented as a married couple for the first time, he whispered, "Aunt Nissa wants to give us something before we go to the reception."

"I love that she sat beside Zinnia. What do you think she has for us?"

"My father told me Aunt Nissa got my mother and him tipsy before their reception. They did shots of courage together, which he said were potent."

"I can't do that," Rachelle said.

Magnus chuckled. "You need not imbibe as much as last time."

"I don't want to imbibe at all until I've seen a doctor."

Magnus froze. "You—you think you might be—"

She searched his face. "Yes. I'm very late."

He spun her around, winding her long train around them, then kissed her soundly. Alisha, her matron of honor, warned, "Don't move or you'll trip."

"I've already fallen," Magnus said, hugging Rachelle to him. He didn't care that they should already be walking down the aisle. He was where he wanted to be. Let the world see it.

Rachelle kissed him again briefly and joked, "And you say you're not romantic."

"Only for you, little Rachelle. Only for you," Magnus said. Rachelle had not changed him, but she had brought a balance to him that changed the way he looked at the future. He would always be the warrior his people needed him to be, but with Rachelle at his side, he would also be the loving man his father had hoped he would become.

He looked up and caught Zinnia watching them with a disapproving look. She never did like to be kept waiting. He waved to her. One day, God willing, she would chase his children out of her yard, and they would be better rulers for it.

Acknowledgments

I am so grateful to everyone who was part of the process of creating *Royal Heir*.

Thank you to:

Montlake Romance for letting me explore my royal side. Special thanks to Lauren Plude for rolling with what can sometimes be a wild ride.

My very patient beta readers. You know who you are. Thank you for kicking my butt when I need it.

My editors: Karen Lawson, Janet Hitchcock, Marion Archer, Krista Stroever, and Marlene Engel.

My Roadies for making me smile each day when I log on to my computer. So many of you have become friends. Was there life before the Roadies? I'm sure there was, but it wasn't as much fun.

Thank you to my husband, Tony, who is a saint—simple as that.

About the Author

Ruth Cardello is a *New York Times* bestselling author who loves writing about rich alpha men and the strong women who tame them. She was born the youngest of eleven children in a small city in northern Rhode Island. She lived in Boston, Paris, Orlando, New York, and Rhode Island (again) before moving to Massachusetts, where she now lives with her husband and three children. Before turning her attention to writing, Ruth was an educator for two decades, including eleven years as a kindergarten teacher. *Royal Heir* is the third book in her Westerly Billionaire series. Learn about Ruth's new releases by signing up for her newsletter at www.RuthCardello.com.